NIKOLAI

THE VOLKOV EMPIRE

SANDY ALVAREZ
CRYSTAL DANIELS

1

NIKOLAI

One Year Earlier

I bolt upright in the bed, broke out in a cold sweat, and my heart jackhammering against my chest. It takes me a second to get my bearings and remember where the hell I am as my eyes adjust to the darkness of my surroundings. My blurred gaze fixates on the large window across the room, and I focus on the way the moonlight illuminates the highest peaks of the trees and watch the slight sway of the branches rocking with the breeze. Finally, my breathing levels out.

Tossing the covers aside, I get out of bed. The wood floors beneath my bare feet give me a sense of feeling grounded as I make my way to the en-suite bathroom.

Leaving the lights off, I walk into the open shower, already aglow with the moonbeams filtering in through the floor to ceiling privacy window. I turn the water on, and it falls like rain above my head. The water is cold at first when it hits my bare skin, and I welcome the shock to my system before it turns warmer.

I haven't had that dream in years. Replaying the memory

haunting me, my skin soaks in the heat of the water. I was eight years old—just a damn kid. I never knew my family was much different than any other family. As far as I knew, my life was typical—normal. Men were coming and going all the time—whispers behind closed doors. Everyone respected my grandfather and my father, doing whatever was demanded of them, no questions asked. One day I learned the power and fear behind the Volkov name when a noise woke me from sleep the night before my eighth birthday. I wasn't supposed to leave my room after going to bed, but this time I had. Sneaking out of my bedroom, I crept down the darkened hallway, making my way to the west wing of the house where I had heard the noise coming from one of the rooms. Just as I closed in on my grandfather's closed office door, it swung open, and I was met with a stone-cold stare from a man I had never met before. "Well, what do we have here?" his dark eyes narrowed at me. The man opened the door further, revealing my grandfather with a gun in his hand.

My grandfather's head turned to look, his eyes landing on mine, and I knew I was in trouble. One thing no one did was cross Alexander Volkov, and I was no exception. "Come here, Nikolai." His voice was deep and low with anger. Not wanting to upset him further, I forced my feet to move, stepping into his office. My eyes widened, and my heart began to beat rapidly. I saw a motionless man lying on the floor, face down in a pool of blood. Knelt beside him, a woman, her pretty face streaked with tears. "You think you are man enough not to follow the rules in this house? You get caught spying on things that are none of your concern; then, you will be man enough to stand here and learn what it means to be a Volkov," my grandfather said, his gun trained on the woman in front of me. Her eyes lift to mine. Tears rolled down her face, but she made no sound and no attempt to run. I watched the bullet rip through her head the same time I heard my grandfather's gunfire. When her lifeless body hit the floor, her eyes were still locked on mine. I wanted to turn and look away, but rough hands gripped my chin, and pulled at my hair, keeping me from tearing my eyes away. I watched the woman's eyes glaze over with death. Quickly, I was spun around, my grandfather's hard disapproving stare keeping me rooted in place, and I did my best to hold back tears. "Never cry for our enemies." His grip on my chin tightened to the point his short nails dug into my skin. "And don't ever spy on me again."

It was the first I had ever experienced genuine fear. It was also the last time I would let myself feel that way again.

In between becoming who I was born to be, a soldier, a good son—a Volkov, I started drinking—heavily. Alcohol became my way of coping with the outside world and my own. I hid it well. At first, it was hard. Not that my father wasn't around, he was. But he was trying to take the reins of an Empire while trying to navigate dealing with his father, and a marriage I knew he was unhappy to be in. It wasn't until a few years later, I would learn just how deep his hatred for my grandfather, and my mother was.

Pressing my palms against the stone wall of the shower, I hang my head. Not even my mother knew I was in a downward spiral. Not that she would have cared. The only part she played in my life was giving birth to me. The only things that seem to matter to her are money and power. Closing my eyes, I push the unpleasant thoughts of my past away as the water begins to run cold, and I'm no less tense than I was when I stepped into the shower.

Turning the water off, I walk out, jerk the towel hanging from a nearby hook, and dry myself. Throwing on my gym shorts, I walk out of my room and down the long corridor until I reach the elevator, riding it down to the basement. The door slides open, revealing the gym in the center of the room, and a regulation-sized octagon ring. Strolling across the room, I bypass the weight machine, heading straight for the heavy bag. Grabbing a roll of tape nearby, I start to wrap my knuckles, before sliding on a pair of sparring gloves.

Rolling my shoulders, I take my stance, then land my first blow —the impact of my padded knuckles against the leather cracks. Blow after blow helps the world and what I'm feeling fade away. I lose track of time until I sense someone watching me. Turning around, I find my father sitting at the far end of the room, his stare intense, and worried. "I thought I was alone." I wipe the sweat from my brow with the back of my glove. Striding a few yards, I bend, pulling open the door of the small refrigerator, and grab a cold bottle of water. Flicking the top off, I throw my head back, downing half the contents, rehydrating myself, then crunching the bottle in my hand. "How long have you been watching me?" I ask him.

"Since you walked in here." Silence hangs between us for a short time before my father speaks again. "Trouble sleeping?" I don't answer him, finish what's left of my water, and throw the empty bottle in the trash. "Join me." My father rises from his seat, and I notice he's wearing his sparring gear.

I follow as he climbs inside the octagon, watching him remove his gloves, leaving his knuckles taped, and I do the same. It's been a long time since he and I fought one another. He's helped train me in all that I know, along with Sasha and Victor. When my father noticed my struggles as a teen and ultimately found out I was drinking at such a young age, he intervened. That's when he decided my training should begin. Spetsnaz, which is Russian military hand to hand combat training. Many of his soldiers, the men who work for him, are either ex-military or trained as such, including himself. I was younger than anyone Victor and Sasha had taught before, but nevertheless, my father believed it would reform me, and give me more control and focus. *"Liquor clouds your judgment. I'm not saying you can't have a drink. Control it, don't let it control you. Never lean on it or any other substance to give you peace.*

You need to find that within yourself with meditation and channeling your anger into something more useful."

It turns out he was right. The training was brutal, and they didn't show me mercy just because I was younger and smaller. I didn't let that defeat me. I used it as motivation. In time, I got better, bigger, stronger, and faster. My skills surpassed many of the men around me.

I climb into the ring, where my father waits. "I'll take it easy on you," I smirk.

He laughs. "I promise only to hurt you a little, my son." Our hands raise, and we circle each other.

I quickly throw a left hook, which misses its mark as my father dives for my left leg—bringing my knee up, which connects with his temple, causing him to stagger. He quickly recovers, hitting me with a jab and a right hook to my upper body, knocking the wind from my lungs. Keeping my feet moving, I shake off his blow. "Not bad, old man," I tease.

"You talk too much." He stalks around me.

As soon as my father steps into striking distance, my knuckles connect with his unprotected jaw, his head whipping back. Stumbling backward, my father hits the cage. Recovering quickly, he wipes the blood from where I just split his flesh open. Looking up at me, he grins. "That's more like it."

By the time my father and I are through sparring, we're both left catching our breaths. Every muscle in my body is burning from the workout. Silence hangs between us before I speak. "Thank you."

I ROLL MY SHOULDERS, trying to work the soreness from my muscles. It's been several months since taking a step back from Volkov family affairs, and now, here I am, standing beside my father, Victor, and Sasha as we watch a wrecker pull a submerged car from the water at the east end of our shipping yard. One of our employees went missing a few nights ago, but that's not what brought us back to Russia. Twenty-four hours after one of our men disappeared, we also had a vital shipment of weapons stolen. The two incidents happening so close together hinted at trouble. Not taking any chances and needing to show a united front, I didn't hesitate when my father asked me to accompany him this time.

Shoving my hands into the front pockets of my suit pants, I watch as the cops peer inside the car belonging to our missing employee. By the looks on their faces, there is a body inside.

"I'm gone less than a week, and this shit happens," my father remarks, his tone flat. "Any word on who's behind this?"

"We're looking into it. The security feed is being examined as we speak," Victor is quick to answer my father.

One of our black sedans pulls into view. I can't see through the tinted windows, but as soon as the car stops, the door swings open, and Sergei steps out, my mood turns sour. I don't like Sergei. Never have, and never will. His distaste for me shows on his ugly face the moment he notices me standing with my father, and his face hardens. He clearly wasn't expecting me to be here.

Sergei has been with my father for a long time, but I don't trust him. Everything about the man makes me question his integrity and long-term loyalty to the family.

"I wasn't informed you would be accompanying your father home," Sergei addresses me in a monotone voice.

"What I do or where I go is no concern of yours. You work for me. Best, remember that," I warn, secretly daring him to step out of line one more time. His eyes shift in my father's direction, who says nothing, and I smirk.

"Sergei, I do not need you here," my father tells him. Sergei goes to speak, but my father is quick to shut him up. "I'll be gone from the office most of the day. Reschedule all of my meetings until next week." Unmoving, Sergei's face flushes with anger from being dismissed, before walking away.

Two investigators walk in our direction; both we know well from several encounters over the years. Officer Natalya lets her eyes travel over my body before eye fucking my father as well. I keep my expression neutral, and my cold stare hidden behind dark sunglasses. "Demetri," she addresses my father. "Who the hell did the two of you piss off?" she asks as she takes in my bruised jaw and my father's busted chin.

"We are not on a first-name basis, Officer Mikhailov." My father's tone is a warning to her overstepping with her pleasantries.

The other officer, her partner, Pavlov, takes a step forward and clears his throat. He pulls a small notepad from his pocket, along with a pen. "Recognize the vehicle?" Pavlov keeps his eyes down, his pen to paper ready to take notes.

"Yes," my father answers.

"And the name of the owner?"

"Abram Popov." My father gives him another short answer, and Pavlov raises his head.

"Does he work here?" the officer asks, dragging the questioning out like he's talking to a child. The two have a strong dislike for one another. Not because they are from opposites sides—criminal and cop, but because Pavlov here has a hard on for his partner, but his partner wants to sink her nails into my father.

Before he can fire off another question, officer Mikhailov interrupts. "Ivan, would you please take one of Mr. Volkov's men to identify the body in the car?" Tearing his eyes from my father's stare, Pavlov reluctantly turns on his heels and walks away.

Even though I won't like what we find, I take it upon myself, and head for the car, water still dripping from the bottom of the closed doors, leaving my father to deal with the authorities. A second later, Sasha is at my side. Victor and Sasha have been with us for years. They've become a permanent part of my life—part of the family.

"You okay?" Sasha asks in a low tone.

I'm a little edgy. Been this way since arriving here an hour ago, and it doesn't surprise me Sasha has picked up on it. "It's not like I haven't seen a corpse before." My words are sharp, laced with irritation that isn't directed toward him, but the situation.

"Not what I meant," Sasha responds, unaffected by my rudeness. Saying nothing in return, we continue to make our way toward the car. We stop about a foot from the back end, the trunk is slightly cracked open, and the smell of death pollutes the air we breathe. An older man, wearing a hazard suit lifts the trunk, the metal hinges squeaking along the way. Inside lies Abram, our trusted employee, with his wrists and ankles bound with rope, and a bullet hole in the middle of his forehead. His face is bloated, like the rest of his body, but it's his eyes, void of life that I fixate on. He was a good man—a family man.

"Shit. Bossman won't like this." Sasha motions for the guy to lower the trunk, and officer Poplov catches his partner's attention, waving her over.

"We have a positive ID?" Mikhailov stops in front of me.

"Abram Popov," I confirm.

"Any idea who would have killed him or wanted him dead in the first place?"

"No," I lie, and both officers know it. The truth is, it's a risk anyone takes working for us.

Knowing they won't get details and the information they are searching for, she sighs. "Tell your father I'll be in touch." Not waiting for more questions, Sasha and I walk away. "We'll need security feed from the past 48 hours," Mikhailov yells, but I don't respond. She knows she'll only get what we want her to have, and nothing more.

"Novikoff," Sasha says as we head back toward my father.

"Looks like it. It fits his MO," I agree with him.

Both Victor and my father's eyes lock on mine, and my nod confirms what they already suspected.

As we walk away from the scene, toward the car, my father asks, "How?"

"Hands and ankles bound with rope. Single-shot between the eyes." I don't have to say who, my father says it for me.

"Novikoff." I hear the anger in his voice.

Once inside, I grab a glass tumbler and the bottle of vodka sitting next to my father's whiskey. Pouring one shot worth, I down the clear liquid, welcoming the slight warmth it gives as it slides down my throat, then quickly pour the same amount into the glass again before putting the bottle back in its place. I can put a bullet in a man, ending his life without any regrets, but seeing Abram like that is like a punch to the gut. I've known the man my whole life, and he didn't deserve to die in such a manner. My anger grows. My father slides in, sitting on the other end of the seat, and pours his amber-colored whiskey in a glass before leaning back. Victor and Sasha climb into the front, with Victor behind the wheel. The partition between them and us rises, giving us privacy.

"Novikoff's dealers are getting brazen and craftier than they used to be and increasing their numbers like cockroaches in a crack house." His eyes drop to the liquor he's swirling in his glass as he thinks.

I run my palm down my beard. "How often are incidents like this happening?"

My father lets out a heavy sigh as the car starts moving. "Alek Belinsky was hit roughly four weeks ago. His warehouse took a major hit, and so did his pockets. The theft cost him a few million." He downs half his whiskey.

Staring out the tinted window, watching the industrial side of town disappear into sparse open land, I ask, "Perhaps we meet with Belinsky. With Novikoff being a nuisance to both our operations, he will be willing to give us any intel they have acquired."

Reaching over, my father presses a button, lowering the window between us and the front of the car. Victor peers into the rearview mirror. "Sir?"

"Arrange a meeting between Alek Belinsky and me."

"Yes, sir."

2

LEAH

The first strike of my father's leather belt across my back seeps into my skin, setting my senses on fire, catching me off guard, and I scream. It's my fault for falling asleep instead of lying in wait. Had I been awake, I could've at least prepared myself for the punishment. Being away at school has weakened me, and I have become careless. I have forgotten how important it is to stay alert. I should have known when I came home this afternoon this was going to happen. Dad came back from work, acting his normal self, but mom was more nervous than usual. My mom always knows when dad is about to dole out one of his punishments. She never warns me, because that would warrant her the same beating, but she has certain ticks about her that I've cataloged over the years. Ticks that remind me of what's to come. Only today, I slipped and didn't pay close enough attention—a grave error on my part.

"Ahh!" I scream again as the belt strikes the back of my head. My scalp burns when the strap tangles with a large chunk of my hair, ripping strands from my scalp. "Stop! Dad, please!" I scramble out of my bed, landing on the bedroom floor with a thud. My move only allows me two seconds of reprieve before my dad is standing over me, face red and chest heaving in anger. I get a moment's glimpse at his snarling face before I cover my head with my arms, shielding my face from the next blow.

"You thought you could go away to college and start acting like a little tramp! Move in with a whore and that boy from school! You thought you could get away with going to bars and dressing like a slut! You stepped out into public and allowed men to see you dressed like that!" my father yells, delivering blow after blow, the leather hitting every inch of my body. I hear my mother's sobs from the hallway, but she doesn't intervene.

Part of me hates her for being so weak; for not protecting me. But the last time she tried, she ended up in the hospital.

"Were you stupid enough to think I wouldn't have eyes on you?" Thwack, thwack, thwack.

"I'm sorry," I scream between lashes, every inch of my body feeling my father's wrath.

"You're not sorry. But you will be by the time I'm through with you."

Soon, each strike of my father's belt mixed with my screams, his heaving breathing, and my mother's sobs begin to echo off the walls of the bedroom. The same bedroom I grew up. If these walls could talk, I know the nightmares they would tell.

I don't know how long the punishment lasts. My father won't stop until he's exhausted himself, this much I know. That's usually not for a while. The only thing I can do is pray that the next blow will be the one to knock me out. At seven years old, I stopped praying for God to make my dad stop hitting me and started praying for the strike that would take away the pain.

A second later, my prayer is answered when the metal buckle lands across my head, and I'm swept into darkness.

MY EYES FLUTTER open sometime later to an empty room—a peak of sunlight filters in through the curtains of the window above my head. The immediate pain that washes over my body is crippling. I bite my lip and suck in a sharp breath as I bring myself up to my hands and knees.

I mentally start checking off any symptoms that would warrant a trip to the ER. No nausea or dizziness, that's usually my main concern. Once I make it to a sitting position, I brace my arms on the edge of the bed and hiss when my ribs pinch in protest. I don't think they are broken, but they are sore and most likely bruised. Slowly, I make my way over to the floor-length mirror next to the dresser. Lifting the hem of my t-shirt, I take in the size thirteen boot print my father left behind, proving my suspicion right. Lifting my eyes to my face, I take in my split lip and the significant swelling around my left eye. I touch a finger to my injured flesh along my cheek. My chin wobbles, and I hold back a sob as I stare at my reflection.

My father said he had someone watching me while I've been away at school. I should have known. I knew going to Crossroads with Alba and Sam was a mistake. My father has his ways of finding out everything. My dad, James Winters, is Post Creeks's Chief of Police. He has several resources at his disposal. One of them is being able to keep tabs on me, even if I am nearly four hours away in Bozeman. If it wasn't one of his rookie lackeys doing his bidding for him, then it was the pastor's son. Last I heard Pastor Lawson's son, Aaron, has joined the academy. Aaron is probably my father's number one butt kisser these days. James Winters has everyone in this town fooled. On the outside, he's an upstanding citizen—the respected Chief and all-around wholesome family man who is front row at church every Sunday. Dad grew up in this town alongside Pastor Lawson. You can say the two are good friends. My father preaches the word of God in our house and holds my mother and me to a certain standard.

SANDY ALVAREZ & CRYSTAL DANIELS

Although, I don't think God would agree with him beating them into us.

He's not a man of God—he is the devil in disguise.

HEARING my mom bustling around the kitchen, I head to the bathroom across the hall from my bedroom to clean up. My father will be expecting me at the table for breakfast this morning. That's one of his many rules; meals are eaten together as a family. Family. What a joke. Biting back tears that threaten to spill as the pain wrecks my body, I wash my face and change my bloody t-shirt. I stand rooted in place and take several cleansings breaths to prepare myself mentally and physically for the day ahead before I make my way down the hall and into the kitchen. When I walk into the kitchen, dad is sitting at the table with a coffee mug sitting in front of him. He's dressed in his uniform and ready for the day. He doesn't bother looking up from his phone when I pull out a chair and sit down across from him. My mother abandons her post at the stove, shuffles over to me and kisses the top of my head. "Morning, Leah." Then goes back to scrambling eggs, not even batting an eye at my injuries—something else I'm used to.

"Morning, mom," I murmur.

A minute later, she sets a plate of eggs, sausage, and toast down in front of my dad, followed by setting the same in front of me. But before her hand leaves the edge of the dish, dad stops her. "No. Leah gets oatmeal. Not only has her behavior spiraled while she's been away, but so has her weight."

Shame washes over me, and my cheeks heat. I've struggled with my weight most of my life. One day I had the body of a little girl, and the next, I was wearing a bra to accommodate my large breasts. Also, my hips spill over the sides of the chair when I sit, and I have a bit of a chubby tummy. It didn't take long for my father's side, handed comments over the years to affect how I looked at myself. The bullies in high school didn't help either. My father insisted my peers taunting me would serve as motivation to lose the weight. It didn't. If anything, it made me hate my appearance even more. Being short and chubby, paired with frizzy hair and glasses, made me a target. The same kids that tormented me in school were the same kids who sat next to me at church on Sundays. Life has a way of showing us how sick and twisted it can be for someone like me. No matter how bad things were at school, they were never as bad as my existence at home. It's pretty messed up when you prefer to spend your days with the kids who bully you, rather than go home and face your father.

Finally, looking up from my lap, I push my glasses up my nose and meet my father's eyes. "You'll never find a husband to take you on if you continue to let yourself go. No man wants a fat wife, Leah."

He should know. My father still controls every bite of food that goes into my mother's mouth. I bite my bottom lip as the humiliation of his words washes over me.

Mom sets a bowl of plain oatmeal down in front of me. I sit for several seconds. My eyes once again cast down. The words my dad speak next has my head snapping in his direction and all the air leaving my body.

"I want you to head back to Bozeman today, pack up your belongings, and be back home by the time I get off shift tomorrow. You're done with school. It was a mistake to send you. You have proven too unruly for me to allow you to continue your education away from home."

My protest is on the tip of my tongue, but my father holding my stare reminds me better of it. In this house, his word is the law. There is no negotiating, and there is no arguing. It was a miracle my father let me go to college at all. A woman's job is to stay home and take care of her husband and kids. Not go out into the workforce to support their family alongside her husband. Nope, that would make her an equal. Being equal to any woman is not something my father can fathom. His reasoning for allowing me to go to school is he doesn't believe I will find a man to marry me. He says I need to make myself useful so I can take care of myself. James Winters' beliefs are outdated, and he is misogynistic. Thank God he and my mom never had a son to pass his warped way of thinking down to.

"Do I make myself clear, Leah?" he snaps when I don't answer right away.

I swallow. "Yes, sir."

Satisfied with my response, my dad stands from the table, walks over to my mom, and kisses her cheek. I watch as she closes her eyes and leans into his touch. After almost twenty years with the monster, you can still see the love and devotion she has for him. I want to hate her. I want to hate her as much as I hate him. I want to grab her, shake her and ask, "How can you still love him? Why do you keep letting him do this to us?" Mom always takes his side. Not that she doesn't love me, because she does. I just think she loves him more.

The moment dad walks out of the front door, and his truck can be heard pulling out of the driveway, mom sits down in the chair next to me. Bringing her hand up, she palms my bruised cheek. "Oh, Leah."

I finally let the first tear fall.

"Why must you anger your father? You knew he would have someone checking up on you. I told you not to fall in with the wrong crowd, Leah. Your father told me about the dress and the bar. He says you have been spending a lot of time around a football player and even moved in with him and a pregnant girl. For God's sake, child." Mom shakes her head.

She's referring to my friends Sam and Alba. My only friends. Two people who have been able to look past my outer appearance and how insanely awkward I am to the real me. I've never had true friends like that. And now I am being forced to give them and school up. With no energy to deal with my mom, I brace one hand on the table and the other on the back of the chair and stand. The movement causes my ribs to pinch, and I whimper. Mom looks away with shame marring her face. "I'm going to get ready and head to Bozeman," I tell her then make my way back to my bedroom. I don't bother trying to explain anything to my mom. It doesn't matter that Sam is just a friend. Male friends are against the rules, and I broke the rules. I broke another one by dressing the way I did and going to that bar. It doesn't matter that my actions were harmless. All that matters is I went against the boundaries my father set in place.

"I'm sorry, Leah," she says just before I close the door. I don't bother with a response.

As I'm about to leave and head back to Bozeman, I spot Mrs. Mae sitting on her front porch across the street. I've known Mrs. Mae my entire life. Growing up, I didn't have friends, but when I was five, I was out riding my bike in front of my house when I heard music coming from an open window of Mrs. Mae's house. It didn't take long for my curiosity to get the better of me, so I'd snuck across the street to peer in. That's when I found the source of the music—Mrs. Mae was playing the piano. I was mesmerized.

"Are you just going to stand there, child, or are you going to come in?" she asks.

I smile big and rush up the steps of her porch. Mrs. Mae is already at the door to greet me. "You're the Winters' little girl, aren't you?"

I nod, my curls bouncing over my eyes. "My name is Leah."

"It's nice to meet you, Leah. My name is Mae. How about you come in while I phone your mom, let her know where you are so she won't worry."

"Okay, Mrs. Mae"

I watch as Mrs. Mae calls mommy. They speak for a minute before

Mrs. Mae hangs up. She gives me a warm smile. "Would you like to learn the piano?"

I nod vigorously.

That was the day Mrs. Mae became more than just a neighbor. She became my best friend and my haven. Mrs. Mae taught me how to play the piano, and how to cook. She was my shoulder to cry on when the outside world would chew me up and spit me out. It didn't take long for Mrs. Mae to realize I was starved for some kind of emotional connection to another human. Mrs. Mae lost her husband before they had the chance to have children of their own, and she never remarried. I might have been a kid, but I think I was her best friend too.

Mrs. Mae stands from her seat on her porch and waves me over. I don't want her to see my current state, but I won't ignore her either. It's not like she hasn't witnessed the evidence my father's belt leaves behind. Besides my mother, Mrs. Mae is the only other person who knows what goes on in my house. She thinks I don't know about the time I was ten, and she confronted my father. I had shown up for my piano lesson with a black eye. Mrs. Mae paid gravely for that talk she had with my dad. The very next night, someone attacked her during a home invasion. Mrs. Mae suffered a broken wrist, and her home ransacked. I knew my dad was behind the incident, and I suspect Mrs. Mae knew as well. It only made me love her more for trying to stand up for me.

As I start across the street toward her house, Mrs. Mae gives me a big smile. The closer I get, her smile drops. Her shaky hand covers her mouth. "Dear God. Come here, child." Taking me in her arms, she leads me inside to the kitchen table. "Sit here so I can get a look at you." Her face hardens when she flips the light on, getting a more unobstructed view of the damage. "Something has to be done. Someone needs to put a stop to that man."

My shoulders slump, and I shake my head. "There is no stopping him. My father is the man people go to when they need help. It doesn't work that way when the person who is supposed to protect you is also hurting you."

Mrs. Mae sits in the chair next to me and takes my hand in hers. "You should leave this place, Leah. Leave and don't ever look back."

I swipe the tear that rolls down my cheek but don't say anything. I wish it were that simple—that I could just hop in my car and leave my problems behind. I have no money, no family, and nowhere to go. Several minutes pass before Mrs. Mae stands and gives me the peace I was looking for when I crossed the street. "Come and play something for me before you go."

Sitting down on the familiar bench with Mrs. Mae at my side, I run my fingertips over the familiar keys, and for the first time in twenty-four hours, I smile. From the moment my fingers first touched these piano keys at the age of five, it became my escape— a way of letting go of all the pain. The old piano weeps as I pour my sorrow into the notes. Closing my eyes, the world around me fades away, and I turn my pain into a beautiful melody.

The sun has set by the time I reach the apartment I share with Sam. A few months ago, I met Alba and Sam at the campus library. They approached me one day out of the blue and struck up a conversation. The three of us have been inseparable since. Sam is from Texas and is a football player here at Montana State University on a scholarship. Alba is my age and is in her first year, like me. She came to Bozeman from Polson. Long story short, Alba found out she is pregnant and wanted to live off-campus and take online courses. She and Sam asked me about living in an apartment with them. I stupidly thought my father wouldn't find out. It's been months since he has ridden me about anything. I figured if I gave my weekly updates and came home often, he wouldn't snoop.

Pulling up and parking my old Toyota in front of the apartment, I turn the car off and suck in a deep breath. The four-hour drive was brutal. I wanted to cry with every turn and bump I hit. The pain reliever I took hours ago has done little to ease my discomfort. Grabbing my bag from the passenger seat, I reach inside and find the pill bottle I'm after. Unscrewing the top, I fish out two more pills, pop them into my mouth, and down half a bottle of water. After taking a moment to collect myself, I scan the near-empty parking lot for Sam's truck. I breathe a sigh of relief when I don't see it. As of a few weeks ago, Alba no longer lives here. She ran into some trouble with a stalker and went back home to Polson. The whole situation was scary. Alba, Sam, and I had been out to dinner. And when we returned home to our apartment, it had been ransacked. Not only that, but there had been a skin-crawling message left for Alba. I had taken a terrified Alba home to Polson while Sam stayed behind and dealt with the police. I was shocked when Alba directed me to an MC clubhouse. It turns out her family is The Kings of Retribution. I don't know much about the MC, but I don't live so far under a rock that I haven't heard of them either. You hear about things when you have a cop for a father. Alba has had nothing but good things to say about the club. To be honest, I trust her word over my father's any day.

Shaking those thoughts away, I open the car door and step out, allowing the cold winter breeze to whip at my battered face. Pulling my coat snug around my body, I make my way to the apartment. Luckily, it's not the same apartment that had been broken into. Sam was able to get him and me into a different one. Still, I get creeped out whenever I'm home alone.

Using my key, I unlock the door and step inside. Once I have the lock in place, I flip on the lights. I planned to stay here tonight and get some rest before packing and driving home tomorrow, but Sam texted me on my way here saying he left his father's place early and was catching the first flight out of Texas. I can't risk Sam seeing me in my current state and then explaining to him why I have to move. So, I'm going to get busy packing now and drive back home tonight. What I want to do is crawl inside my bed here, where I feel safe and wait for my friend to come home. Once in my room, I sink to the floor beside the closet just as a sob escapes my mouth. I feel so hopeless.

I don't know how much time passes with me hunched over on the floor and my emotions taking over my body, but the sound of Sam's deep voice calling out my name causes me to startle. Quickly, I pull the hood of my sweatshirt over my head to conceal my face and use the sleeve to wipe the tears away as I do my best to hide my anguish from my friend. But nothing gets by Sam.

"Leah, what's wrong?" he asks his voice filled with concern.

"Nothing," the lie rolls off my tongue as I try to hold back the quiver in my voice.

"Bullshit. Look at me, Leah." The tone of his voice drops. I hear him shuffle further into the room behind me. Crouching down, Sam clutches my elbow, forcing me to face him, and I don't resist. I don't have the strength.

He sucks in a sharp breath just before his feature turns murderous. One thing about Sam is he's very protective of those he cares about. "What the fuck, Leah. Who did this to you? I'm going to fucking kill them." His nostrils flare.

His concern does me in, and I break down. A cry escapes pass my lips, and Sam doesn't hesitate to take me into his arms. I ignore the pain in my side when he squeezes me. Only my flinch doesn't go unnoticed. His body stiffens, and he gently pushes me off his chest. His eyes drop to my torso. "Show me."

Sam's eyes blaze with intensity, and I bravely do as he demands. Lifting my sweatshirt over my ribs, I show him the damage my father left behind.

"Leah," Sam grits. "Who did this to you?"

"My father," I choke on my words with a steady stream of tears running down my face.

"I..." I suck in a deep breath. "He's making me go home and quit school."

"Hold up. Slow down, sweetheart. Your father did this to you?"

I nod. "Yes. My father has been watching me and knows I'm living here—about going to Crossroads. I broke the rules, Sam."

His jaw ticks. "He did this to you because you went out to a bar, and you're living with me?"

I cry harder. "Yes. I screwed up. I wasn't careful enough. I just wanted to have a normal life. I wanted to have friends. I thought I could be happy and hide it from him," I hiccup.

"Shh." Sam pulls me to his chest. "Everything is going to be okay."

"It's never going to be okay, Sam. Never."

A SHUFFLING NOISE startles me from sleep. Opening my eyes, I find myself lying on my bed. I don't even remember falling asleep. Sam must have put me here. Reaching for my glasses on the table beside the bed, I slide them on then look at the time. It's nearly one o'clock in the morning. I spot Sam standing at my closet, stuffing my things into a garbage bag. "Sam, what are you doing?"

He peers at me over his shoulder. "We're leaving. I'm not letting you go back home to that bastard. I'm taking you away from here and away from him."

My heart rate picks up, and a knot forms in my stomach. "I can't do that. My father..." I don't get the words out before Sam cuts me off and fully faces me.

"You are not going back, Leah," he says adamantly.

"My dad will find me and drag me home. I can't hide from him, Sam. He's a cop. He has his ways."

Sam drops the garbage bag to the floor and sits on the bed next to me. "Do you want to go back? Tell me the truth."

I shake my head. "I never want to see him again. But..."

"No buts. You're not going back. All I ask is you trust me. Can you do that? Can you trust me to handle this?"

Sam is my best friend. I don't hesitate to answer. "Yes." My response comes out shaky. I'm terrified. I've thought about running away a million times, but with no money of my own and no place to go, leaving has never been possible. Sam is giving me an out. So, no matter how scared I am, I have to try and escape that monster.

"We'll only take what we need for now. I'll come back for the rest later."

Panic starts seeping in. "Sam, what if my dad has someone watching me now. How am I going to leave here with you without him knowing?"

"I have that covered. After you fell asleep, I left and parked my truck in the parking lot on the backside of the complex and came back through the patio door. We're leaving now. I'll get us a hotel room." Sam shoves the last of my clothes into the bag and ties it. "This is the last of what you'll need for now. Everything else is in the truck. Grab your purse. It's time to go."

My head starts to spin with how fast everything is happening. "Are you sure about all this, Sam?"

"Hell yeah, I'm sure. Now come on. Let's get you up."

Sam helps me stand from the bed. He holds my coat open so that I can slide my arms in, and then I grab my purse. Opening the sliding glass door that leads out to the back patio, Sam tosses the garbage bag over the rail. He then climbs over before helping me do the same "It's a bit of a walk to the truck. Can you make it, or do you want me to carry you?"

"I think I can make it."

Keeping his arm wrapped around me for support, Sam and I make our way through the wooded area behind our apartment until we reach the opposite side of the complex where his truck is parked. Sam tosses the garbage bag into the back, then jogs around to the passenger side to help me climb inside. Once he settles into the driver seat, he cranks the heat up full blast. I turn, reach over and grab hold of his arm, squeezing it. I go to open my mouth to thank him, but the words get stuck in my throat. I cry for what seems like the millionth time in twenty-four hours. Luckily, words aren't needed. Sam gives me a reassuring look just before shifting the truck into gear and pulling out of the parking lot.

3

NIKOLAI

It took some doing, but we finally got Alek Belinsky to agree to a meeting, and the only way he would do it was on his turf, which is why the car is rolling to a stop outside one of the few casinos in the territory he runs, The Gold Star. My father and I both exit the SUV on opposite sides. It's late, just around dinner time, and night has fallen. "Wait here," my father tells Victor, who nods then climbs back inside the vehicle

Belinsky's men greet us before entering the building and give us a thorough pat-down before leading us past red velvet ropes separating the regular club from the VIP lounge.

The room is dimly lit with blue lighting, and the private booths are draped in lush blue crushed velvet, giving the room a relaxing ambiance. We're led to the farthest corner of the room. The booth Belinsky is seated in is twice the size as all the others, with a small private bar to the left.

"Demetri." Belinsky stands and shakes my father's hand. "Welcome. I do not believe you have ever been to my fine establishment."

"Alek. I appreciate you agreeing to this meeting," my father says, eager to get down to business.

"Yes, well, we will see if this meeting is beneficial to us both, but first," Belinsky motions for us to take a seat, "let's drink. Sit." As I lower myself to the plush couch, Belinsky continues with small talk. "Nikolai." He eyes me as he drops his large frame back in his spot on the couch across from me, only a glass table separating us. "There's talk going around that you wish to no longer take over for your father one day." His bold statement causes my father to tense, and his mood changes, though I'm the only one to notice. To Alek Belinsky, my father is unfazed by his attempt to pry.

Cocking my head, I study Belinsky for a moment, watching the beads of sweat roll down his temples. All of this—him meeting us here, flashing his wealth around, and feeling as if he's got the upper hand in this situation is nothing more than a facade. What he doesn't know is we are aware of his financial situation. The bastard spends more than he brings in. Alek Belinsky makes most of his money nowadays running strip clubs, casinos, and smuggling drugs across borders for various associates. "I'm afraid you were misinformed, and it would be in your best interest to not encourage such rumors." My eyes lock with his, and fear dances across his face.

He clears his throat, ridding himself of his nervousness before he throws his hand in the air, waving a young woman over. As she bends forward to sit a tray filled with three glasses and a bottle of top-shelf liquor on the table in front of us, Belinsky gropes her, running his meaty palm between her thighs. The waitress's eyes fall on mine. Her blank stare is a mask but does nothing to hide her feelings of disgust, shame, and anger. I break eye contact with her. When I look back at Belinsky, he's staring at me once more. "You like her? She's one of my best girls," his thick brow raises as he shifts his eyes to her lean body. Not that she isn't a beautiful woman. My eyes travel the length of her frail body as she holds her shoulders back. She's too thin for my taste. I like more to my women, a flare to their hips and heaviness in their breasts. I want something to grab onto when a woman is riding me.

My father lifts the bottle of vodka from the table and pours the clear liquid into the already chilled glasses. Leaning forward, I raise a half-filled tumbler from the table, then press myself into the cushioned sofa and rest my ankle on my knee. "I am not here to get my dick wet. You agreed to this meeting because we share a mutual problem—Miran Novikoff." Belinsky's nostrils flare as he holds his tongue. I look to my father, waiting to see if he wishes to take control of this exchange of words. Lifting his glass, he gives me a tight nod, which is my signal to take the reins. I lift my gaze to the waitress still poised next to Belinsky. "Leave us," I dismiss the woman knowing my slight overstep in his establishment has angered him, but I don't care.

He clears his throat. "What exactly is it you wish to gain from this meeting, Volkov? I'm busy, and you are the ones requesting my time and my help."

"Don't be presumptuous. Let's be clear that you do not hold all the cards. You have obliged us with this meeting, but don't take our hospitality in requesting your time as an attempt to disrespect our positions in the game." Belinsky's face reddens for being put in his place. "Novikoff has been a thorn in our sides long enough. He has hit your business multiple times in the past year, am I correct?" In the center of the table sits a small humidor case. Reaching out, I lift the mahogany lid, retrieving a cigar. I punch a hole in one end, then cut the tip of the other, before striking the tip of a matchstick. The flame flickers as I stoke the cigar.

"That is true." He watches me closely.

"And our resources tell us one of your men has embedded himself within their organization."

"That is also true." Belinsky eyes me over the rim of his glass as he takes a sip of his drink.

"And yet you have done nothing to end or at least cripple his operations." My father and I know why he hasn't made a move, but I want to hear it for myself. We know he can't risk making a solo attempt.

He lets out a heavy sigh. "Don't patronize me. You know I am in no position and do not have the manpower to do much of anything. My guy filtering information has allowed me to stay ahead of who and when they will strike next. However, I'm smart enough to know information is desirable and comes with a price as well."

I grin at him, but it is my father who responds to his snarky attempt at bribery. "What you will get out of this exchange is your life," my father warns him. "You would do well to remember your place."

"You came here asking for my help, and you threaten me?" Belinsky stands, puffing his chest.

"Who would you rather your enemy be? Me or Novikoff?" Belinsky opens his mouth to speak, but my father cuts him off, "Think before words are spoken that you can't take back. You give us all your intel, and we use our manpower to send a message to Novikoff. This benefits us both." My father tips his glass back, downing the remainder of his drink. "Better to have me as an ally."

Silence hangs between the three of us. Finally, Belinsky speaks. "A large cell of Novikoff's operation is operating about an hour north of us, out of a warehouse."

"What about security?" I ask.

Belinsky shakes his head. "My man says the place is a fortress. One way in. One way out through a ten foot steel gate."

"How many men?"

"Last reported? Nearly sixty soldiers, armed with a massive supply of weaponry and ammunition," Belinsky states. The numbers are high but don't surprise me. We may not be able to take out Novikoff's entire operation, but we will damn sure blow a massive hole in it. My father sits his glass on the table, then stands, and I follow suit—Belinsky moves to rise as well.

"Stay seated." My father adjusts his suit. "Thank you for your time." He offers his hand to Belinsky, who shakes it. "My men will be in touch soon. Give them what you have on Novikoff, including locations."

"And you agree to protect me? If word gets back to Miran Novikoff that I had insider information, he'll do his best to kill me." Belinsky's face shows fear as it should.

"You have my word," my father states.

"Everything in place?" I ask Maxim from our current position, just outside the perimeters of Novikoff's central warehouse, located in a town three hours south of my family's controlled territory. The entire area is desolate. The condition has made it a perfect breeding ground for Novikoff and his men to operate without any interference from authorities. The vile things that go on here are largely ignored. It's more or less a dumping ground for the underbelly of society.

"The explosives are in position and ready to be detonated when you give the word," Maxim states.

It took a few days for my men to get in and out undetected to set the charges, due to the increased amount of activity. Novikoff caught wind that our family would not turn a blind eye to his thievery like so many others have. His threats against those who would stand against him or in his way mean nothing to my family. This was his first offense against us since severing ties a few years ago. Destroying his most massive warehouse, which happens to be the base of his operation, will serve as a warning —to back off. He will lose many of his men today, as well. A price he must pay for his disrespect. "Any word on his whereabouts?" I ask as I stand outside the SUV that drove me here.

"He is out of the country, relaxing at his vacation home near Pylos," Maxim confirms.

"Light it up." I give the command, and Maxim speaks into his two-way radio. Within seconds the bombs detonate, causing the earth below our feet to tremble from the blast. Another explosion erupts with a loud clap, and orange flames billow outward. The sounds of steel splintering and windows shattering can be heard as a large section of the building's structure collapses. Even as I stand here, a safe distance away, I can feel waves of heat rolling off the blaze on my exposed skin, watching Novikoff's warehouse burn.

Satisfied, I turn to the vehicle. "Send word to Novikoff. Inform him the next time he disrespects the family again; he will pay with his life."

4

LEAH

A few days after Sam and I left our apartment behind, I am sitting on one of the two full-sized beds in the hotel room, watching TV when he walks in carrying several grocery bags. Climbing to my feet, I shuffle across the room to help as he sets the bags down on the small table in front of the window. "You're only going to be gone one day, Sam. I don't need this much food."

He smiles. "I brought you more than food." Opening one bag, he pulls out a packaged Kindle. "I know how much you've been missing your books and TV is not your thing."

He's right. I usually read from my phone, but Sam made me leave it behind at the apartment when we left. He didn't want my father to trace where I am.

"You shouldn't have spent your money on me. You've done so much already. You're paying for the hotel and all our food."

Sam shakes his head, cutting me off. "Zip it. You're my friend, Leah. I want to help. Just like I want you to accept the gift." He holds the package out to me, his eyes daring me to say no. Finally, I relent and take his offering.

While unloading the groceries and placing some of the items

in the mini-fridge, Sam changes the subject. "You sure you don't want to come with me to Polson? It's only one day, but we can make a weekend out of it."

"I'm sure. Alba has enough on her plate. I don't want her to see me like this and ask questions. It will upset her."

"She's your friend, Leah. She'd want to know what's going on. She'll be pissed at us for hiding it."

"I can't, Sam. Not yet, anyway."

He sighs. "Okay. I get it."

This time I am the one to change the subject. "Did you hear back about the apartment?"

"Yeah, but I'm having second thoughts about it. I think we should move out of Bozeman."

"But your job is here."

"I can drive back and forth or get another job."

"Sam..."

"Not going to hear it, sweetheart. We already talked about this. Stop worrying about me. Making sure you're safe is what's important."

Looking down at my feet, I sigh. I hate feeling like I'm a burden. Sam has completely uprooted his life for me.

"Hey." Sam stops what he's doing, his stern tone catching my attention. "Stop whatever it is you're thinking." He strides toward me and opens his arms. "Come here."

I take his offered hug. "I'm sorry," I croak.

"You have nothing to be sorry for. We're going to figure this shit out together."

LATER THAT NIGHT, I toss and turn in bed. Sam left for Polson hours ago, and I'm starting to regret my decision to stay behind. I don't do well with being alone. Since Sam and I have been staying in the hotel, I lay awake most nights, terrified my dad will find me, even though Sam assures me I'm safe. I left my cell phone and my car behind. I also haven't stepped a single foot outside the hotel room since we checked in. My father knows about Sam. What if he had someone follow him here?

The ringing of the hotel phone brings me out of my wandering thoughts, and I nearly jump out of my skin. Reaching over, I pick it up and answer. "Hello?"

"Somehow, I knew you'd still be awake."

I close my eyes. "You guessed, right."

His soft chuckle vibrates through the line. Over the next hour, Sam helps put my nerves at ease. He's good at that. I wasn't lying when I said he was my best friend. Alba is too, but since she moved back to Polson, Sam and I have become closer. Our friendship is strictly platonic. I think of him as a brother, just like he sees me as a sister. "I'll see you tomorrow afternoon."

"Thanks for calling. Tell Alba I said hi."

"I will. Try to get some sleep."

Ten minutes after hanging up with Sam, I fall asleep.

"WHERE—WHAT?" I stare up at Sam the next day, minutes after he arrived back from Polson. And he's just dropped a bomb on me.

"I said we are moving to Polson. I talked to Alba."

"You told her?" I cut him off.

"I know I said I wouldn't, but she pried it out of me. You know how she is. It's like she can smell a secret a mile away." My shoulders slump because he's right. "The club is going to help. Alba is filling Gabriel in on the situation. Polson is the safest place for you."

"Just like that?" I ask.

"Just like that. It's time for a fresh start—for both of us."

"What about the apartment you said you found and your job?"

Sam shrugs. "I'll find a place in Polson. Also, the club and Logan's brother Nikolai own a construction company. I'm going to try and get a job there."

"How soon are we leaving?"

"When I hashed out the details with Alba, I said I need at least a month to secure us a place to stay and a job. She called me on my way back. The club found us an apartment. We can move in whenever we're ready. So, we leave soon."

Gabriel is Alba's boyfriend and the father to her unborn baby. He is also the Enforcer for The Kings of Retribution. Suddenly, just the mention of the MC has my heart rate picking up. I've been to the clubhouse once, and those men are next level intimidating.

Sensing my onset of panic, Sam comes to stand toe to toe with me. "Leah, I know those guys just as much as you do, which is not a whole hell of a lot, but one thing I do know is they are good people, and they can protect you. Alba wouldn't have suggested the idea if she didn't trust the club. Staying here in Bozeman is risky, Leah. You having any association or living anywhere near The Kings of Retribution is the last thing your father would expect from you, and Polson is probably the last place on earth your dad will think to look."

I nod, swallowing past the lump in my throat. "You're right. My father would never look there. Staying here longer than necessary is a risk."

Sam squeezes my shoulders. "I know this situation is scary, and things are moving fast, but I'll be with you every step of the way."

"I don't know how to thank you for everything, Sam. You're giving up a lot to help me."

"I'm not giving up anything important. Like I said before, your safety is my number one priority. And this move is for me too."

Sighing, I step back and plop down on the bed.

"I'm serious, Leah." Sam sits next to me. "With me quitting school and the shit I'm going through with my dad, I need a fresh start like you. I don't want to go back to Texas, and there is nothing for me in Bozeman. I can't explain it, but something tells me this move will be good for both of us."

Sam wasn't lying when he said his relationship with his dad is rocky. Sam attended the University on a football scholarship, but he was facing suspension from the team when he got into a fight with a teammate. That alone would have put his scholarship in jeopardy. Sam ended up dropping out before the situation came to a head. Alba was sick over what happened since the fight he was in was over her. He was quick to assure her he had no hurt feelings or regret over his decision. Like me, his only reason for going away to school was to escape his home life and put as many miles between him and his dad as possible.

THE NEXT DAY I am hanging up the phone after talking with Alba when Sam comes bursting through the door of the hotel room. It's only a quarter past nine o'clock in the morning, and he's supposed to be at work, so showing up with a frazzled look on his face, sets me on edge. "Sam, what's wrong?"

"Your dad showed up at my job."

I jump from the bed. "What! He found me?" My stomach sinks.

Sam's jaw clenches, and he shakes his head. "I don't know. I didn't speak to him, but he did ask around, trying to find me. My boss, Henry, covered for me. He told your dad I was out on a job site. I think he suspected something was up since I put in my two weeks this morning. He tried grilling me on why I was suddenly quitting since he was going to lose one of his best workers. I didn't tell him the details, only that I had a family emergency and was moving. After your father left, I asked my boss what he wanted. Your dad didn't say much, only that he was looking for me. Henry told me not to worry about finishing out my two weeks. He said he would give my next employer a glowing recommendation and wished me good luck."

"Did you come straight here after leaving work? Do you think my dad followed you?"

Sam shakes his head. "I'm pretty sure no one followed. I watched your dad leave out of the parking lot. He headed in the opposite direction. I also drove around a bit to make sure."

I close my eyes and blow out a relieved breath.

"Your dad has gotten a little too close for comfort. I want us to pack and be ready to go within the hour."

I don't say anything. Sam is right. My dad showing up at his job means he's on our trail. I'm sure by now he's been to the apartment. And if he was there, he saw my cell phone and car were left behind. On that thought, another one comes to mind. "I should call him."

"What?" Sam levels me with a look.

"This is ridiculous, Sam. I'm legally an adult. I shouldn't have to hide from my father. Maybe I just call and tell him I am not coming home. Right? It's not like he can make me."

"Do you honestly think it will be that simple? That your father will simply leave you to live your life in peace?"

"No. My father demands control. Especially over his family. But I have to try." I can tell Sam doesn't like my idea but passes me his phone anyway. Taking it from him, I type in my dad's number and place the phone to my ear. On the third ring, he answers.

"Winters."

Just the sound of my dad's voice has me clamming up. But I manage to keep it together. "Dad."

The other end of the line is silent for a moment. "Leah, where the fuck are you, young lady? Do you know I have been out looking for you? Why the hell are you not home?"

"I'm not coming home, dad."

"Do you need reminding as to what will happen if you disobey me, Leah?" The tone and underline threat my father delivers sends a chill down my spine. Memories I live with every day, and the bruises on my body remind me. "You're with that boy, aren't you? You've gone against my word to slut around, is that it?"

"No, dad, that's not it at all." My voice sounds small.

"We'll discuss this when you get home, which I expect to be by the end of the day," he clips.

I suck in a deep breath and close my eyes. "I am not coming home," I say for the second time, and my father loses it.

"Listen, you ungrateful little bitch. I want you home, now," he roars through the phone. "Do you honestly think that boy is going to put up with you for very long? Don't kid yourself, child. As soon as he's done using you, he'll toss you out like the trash you are. Save yourself and me the trouble and do as you're told. Do I make..."

My father doesn't get the chance to finish his tirade because suddenly, the phone is ripped from my hand, and Sam ends the call. The tick in his jaw tells me he heard what was said. My eyes well up with tears, and my body begins to shake. I don't understand why my father is fighting so hard to make me return home when he hates me so much. You would think he would be relieved not to have to deal with me anymore.

"We're leaving, now," Sam growls, and the two of us begin packing.

WE ROLL into Polson just before nightfall. My nerves start kicking in again when Sam pulls into a small apartment complex and parks next to a motorcycle. I immediately recognize the man as Gabriel. All The Kings men look the same...intimidating.

"Give me a minute," Sam says, hopping out of the truck and making his way over to Gabriel. I take this time to scan my surroundings. Polson is a small town, much like the town where I grew up. The complex that I assume is our new home looks new. I like the fact it's not massive. I only see a dozen or so units. And it's located just on the edge of town. We drove past a garage called Kings Custom on the way here. I remember Alba saying the club owned the garage, and her sister works there. We are also well within walking distance of several stores, a plus for me since I don't have a car. Hopefully, I can get a job soon and start saving for one. I also want to start paying my way. I can't allow Sam to support me for too long. I just need to wait for the dust to settle with my dad. Once I have taken in my new home, I bring my attention back to Sam and Gabriel. The two shake hands, then Gabriel hands something to Sam while pointing to the apartment on the top floor in front of us. They exchange a few more words before Sam makes his way back toward the truck. Gabriel starts up his bike and takes off. How anyone can ride a bike in the cold is beyond me.

"Come on. I have the key to our place," Sam says as he grabs some of our bags from the truck's back seat. Nodding, I climb out of the passenger seat and go to help him with our things. "Leave them. I'll come back for the rest once I get you upstairs."

Holding onto the rail of the stairs, Sam helps support me as we make our way up to apartment eight. For the most part, I have healed from my injuries, though I still have a slight pinch in my ribs, and my face still has a significant amount of bruising that has faded from a colorful shade of purple to more yellowish-green. Using the key Gabriel gave him, Sam lets us into the apartment. The moment we step inside, a man steps out from the hallway, making me jump. Sam is quick to reassure me. "It's okay, Leah. That's Reid. He's a member of the club."

"Sorry for scarin' you like that, sweetheart. I'm here to install the security system. I'm finishin' up now."

"Th...that's okay," I whisper.

Reid doesn't say anything else. He just stands there for a

moment, taking me in, and when his gaze lands on my bruises, his face hardens. Several seconds pass before Reid and Sam share a look then give each other a nod.

"I'll be done in five," he tells us.

"Thanks, man. We appreciate you coming and helping on short notice."

"No problem," Reid says and looks at me again. "You're safe here."

With one final jerk of his chin, Reid strides past Sam and me then disappears out the front door.

5

NIKOLAI

Polson, Montana. I take in what has become my new home for the past year as I drive down the winding road leading to my brother's clubhouse. He's the Vice President for The Kings of Retribution MC. Funny how our lives and ways of living mirror one another, considering it was only last year we finally met. Logan is the product of a whirlwind romance my father had years ago before marrying my mother.

It's mid-evening, and the sun is starting to set on the horizon, turning the sky several shades of blues and purples. It's getting warmer this time of year, but snow still covers the mountain peaks off in the distance. As soon as I landed, I had an unread message from my brother. It seems a bunch of shit went down while I was gone. A man is dead, and Reid is recovering from pretty significant injuries sustained during the situation. On a good note, Alba and Gabriel's sister are okay, and so is their unborn child.

I turn my truck off the main highway onto the dirt road heading for my final destination. As soon as I crest the hilltop, the clubhouse comes into view, and coming home never felt so good. The Kings took me in like I was one of their own, even gave me my own private room at the clubhouse to crash in whenever I like. Looking around, I notice all the men are here, minus Reid's bike. Parking my truck along the side of the building, I climb out and make my way inside. The blast of warm air and the smell of tobacco hit my face the moment I pull the front door open. Inside, I find the guys sitting around a large round table in the center of the dimly lit room.

"Nikolai. Get your ass over here," Jake's boastful voice carries throughout the room. An empty chair is waiting for me as I step to the table. "Good to have you back in town." He slides a glass from the center of the table toward me. A bottle of my favorite vodka is sitting in the middle, along with some bourbon. Reaching out, I tip the bottle, pouring myself a shot worth in my glass.

A short cigarette balances between Jake's fingers as he leans back in his chair. "How were things back home?" raising his hand, he takes a toke off his cigarette.

"Unresolved," I pause, taking a sip of my drink before finishing my statement. "but nothing we can't take care of."

Jake chuckles. "Oh, I do not doubt that."

I look to my brother, who sits across from me, his looks mirror my own, except our hair color. Logan speaks, "Good to have you home." He lifts his drink in the air.

"It's good to be home." When I say those words, I mean them. Polson is a world away from where I grew up and what I called home for so long, but Polson feels like the place I was always meant to be. I want my roots to take hold in these mountains. Pulling a deep breath through my nose, I let out a long exhale. "Aside from enjoying a drink with my brothers, what else is our meeting about?" I ask as I look around the table.

"Gabriel's woman has a friend who is looking for work. The girl needs to lay low for a while," Logan informs me, and I watch Gabriel become a little tense, and I wonder if this has anything to do with what Alba just went through.

"Is this related to your woman's attacker?" my eyes settle on Gabriel.

"No. Never again will a man harm her." Gabriel's tone is low and full of promise.

"Alba's friends Leah and Sam are looking to find work. We figured they could work at Kings Construction. That's if you are cool with it. It's Leah who is in trouble, but both Sam and Leah need a fresh start," Jake adds.

A woman?

"Leah's hiding from her family, her father, to be specific. We don't know every detail, but enough that he beat the shit out of her a couple of weeks ago, and it has happened before. She's scared to death of him." Jake doesn't have to say more.

"Have you dug around to find more about her father?"

"We're looking into who he is," Jake tells me.

"If she's under your protection, she is under mine as well." I look to Gabriel since he can most likely get word to them much faster than anyone else. "Have them at my office first thing tomorrow morning, and I'll get it all sorted." Gabriel nods his response, then pulls his phone from the inside of his cut, his fingers tapping at the screen. My thoughts briefly shift to the problems my father is dealing with, and the fact that I'm back here instead of there helping him with our future shipments.

"How's the old man doin'?" Logan asks.

"He is well."

"You mentioned things overseas are unresolved. Anything the club can help with?" Logan pours a little Jameson into his glass. The rest of the men eye me, waiting to see if I'll indulge their curiosity.

I let out an exhausted breath as jetlag starts to set in. "Unfortunately, there is nothing to be done from here. A shipment of weapons was stolen from its departure point, as well as the unfortunate death of one of our men." Abram's cold dead eyes followed by the memory of his wife's tear-streaked face after we paid our respects to her family comes to mind, and my hand tightens around the glass in my hand.

"Damn, brother. Sorry to hear that. Any clues to who is behind it?" Logan asks, before striking a match across the rough surface of the table, and lighting a cigarette.

"We suspect Miran Novikoff is behind the thefts. There have been similar incidents involving other syndicates in other territories," I tell them.

"Novikoff," Jake repeats. "The name sounds familiar."

"They've been around for some time now. Novikoff was a good friend of my grandfather, and they were in business together. Novikoff used to have dealings here in Montana and still conducts business in Canada. Back in the day, he would accompany my grandfather on his trips here. That's probably why his name is familiar to you. When my grandfather died, my father cut all ties to Novikoff. You can say there is bad blood between the two families. Up until now, he hasn't been an issue. Over the past year, his operations have grown in numbers, though. Smaller groups are popping up all over Russia. They're recruiting by the masses."

"What kind of shit do they dabble in?" Quinn, who has been quiet this entire time, speaks.

"Anything that will bring them money. Drugs, sex, human trafficking," I tell Quinn, and his face hardens.

"Fuckin' despise people who kidnap and use human life like currency." Quinn downs his beer. "All of us here are criminals in our own rights, and have done things in our lives that are better left unsaid, but human trafficking is just about as low as you can get in my book. Selling women and kids." Quinn shakes his head. As long as I've known Quinn, this is the first time I've seen him genuinely passionate about a subject. "Fuckers like that are bottom feeders of crime, and I'd happily rid the world of them if given the opportunity." All the men at this table, including myself, nod in agreement.

My eyes feel heavy, and my head is starting to throb. Leaving what's left of my drink untouched, I push myself from the table and stand. "That long flight has kicked my ass. I think I'll crash here for the night." I fight off a yawn.

"I think the rest of us are ready to call it a night as well. We'll touch base with you tomorrow," Jake announces. "If anyone needs anything, you know where to find me. I'm too fucking exhausted to drive home tonight."

THE FOLLOWING MORNING, I wake before the others in the clubhouse, dress, and head for the office, a small single-story building that sits on the property where we house all our supplies and machinery for the jobs we do. Punching in a security code, the gate slides open, and I pull my truck into my usual spot.

Once inside, I turn on the lights. First things first—I need coffee. Walking into the small breakroom, I set up the coffee maker and wait for the machine to fill my mug. This is how most of my work days start. In roughly two hours, my men will start arriving. Jake has been juggling Kings Construction and the shop while I've been out of town. Plus, Reid is recovering from his ordeal and is unable to take care of the company's emails and potential job bids over the past couple of weeks. With my coffee in hand, I head for my office and get to work.

The next couple of hours pass by quickly as I bury myself in emails, invoices, bank statements, and payroll disbursements. I hear the unmistakable sound of Gary's old pickup truck pulling in outside, and chuckle to myself when the damn thing backfires before he cuts the engine. A few seconds later, he's rapping his knuckles against my open office door, and I raise my head.

"Hey, bossman. When did you get back in town?" he asks, shoving what's left of his breakfast sandwich in his mouth. Gary is one of our job foremen and a damn good one.

"Last night." I lean back in my chair, stretching the kinks from my back.

"Shit. And you're here before the butt crack of dawn?" he shakes his head, and I chuckle at his choice of an American phrase—butt crack of dawn.

"No rest for the wicked, my friend," I tell him.

"I hope you at least took some leisure time while you were gone," he adds. Gary is about as fatherly as a guy can get. He's like that with most of the men that work here. That's another reliable quality of his, giving a shit about his men. In return, they have tremendous respect for the man, and so do I. Gary turns his head when he hears another vehicle pulling into the parking lot, alerting us to the fact the other guys are showing up for the day. "Well, I'll leave you to it. I'm going to head out and get this safety meeting over with, and get these men where they need to be."

Before he leaves, I grab the pile of checks sitting on the corner of my desk. "Give these out for me."

Gary grabs them from my outstretched hand. "Will do. It's a shame that Miss Martinez left us. I'm going to miss her coffee and those coconut pastry things she would bring in from time to time."

"What's wrong with my coffee?" I raise a brow. Gary hangs his head, and his shoulders shake with the laughter he's holding in. Before he has time to answer, I hear someone coming in through the front door. Gary pokes his head into the hallway.

"Hey there, young man, how can I help you," Gary says as he steps out of my office altogether, and at the same time my phone pings, vibrating against my desktop. Turning it over, I swipe the screen, reading a text from Gabriel.

Sam and Leah should be there soon.

I place my phone down. Looking up, I find Gary standing in my doorway. He points his thumb over his shoulder.

"A guy named Sam is out here, with a young woman."

That must be Leah. They showed up early. I like that. It shows eagerness. "Send them in."

Gary nods. "I'll check in with you later, boss," then disappears.

Seconds later, Sam appears at my door. "Mr. Volkov."

"Sam?" I stand.

"Yes, sir." He extends in hand, and gives me a firm short shake.

"I was told you were to arrive with someone else." At my words, Sam looks to his left and holds his hand out. I watch as a young woman appears stepping to his side.

"Yes, sir. This is Leah." Sam introduces his friends and my eyes stay glued to her face for a second before taking in the rest of her appearance. Her oversized clothing does nothing to hide the full curves beneath them.

"I'm assuming Leah can speak for herself." I clear my throat and wait for her to slowly lift her gaze to mine. Amber-colored eyes, framed by dark lashes and a pair of glasses nervously, look into mine, and it feels as if someone sucks the oxygen out of the room.

What the fuck?

I shake off whatever the hell came over me. "Sit," I wave my hand to the two chairs in front of my desk, as I take my seat. "I hear you are looking for work?" I look to Leah as she settles in her chair.

"Yes. Will you require references or work history?" Leah asks nervously. My eyes drop between her and Sam, where she hasn't let go of his hand, and I find it irritating.

"The Kings vouched for you." My attention shifts to focus on Leah. Her bouncing knee shows how uncomfortable and on edge she is, and her deer in headlights look confirms the fear she is living with. I think back to the conversation I had with the guys at the clubhouse yesterday, which is why she is under their

46

protection. My eyes linger on the fading bruises that mar her face. Anger churns in my gut. I study her a bit longer, only for a second —taking in her heart-shaped face, and long unruly curly hair. Biting her lip, Leah lifts her hand and fidgets with her glasses. My mouth twitches when her eyes drop to her lap, and her cheeks flush. "Leah," her name brushes past my lips and prompts her eyes to snap back to mine. And fuck if it doesn't affect me. "Have you ever worked in an office before?"

Leah's lips part and she takes a long breath before she speaks, and I find myself anticipating what her voice will sound like. "No, but I pick up on things quickly and know my way around a computer." Her voice is soft and sweet.

"I have no problem teaching you," I assure her, and a small smile graces her face. Damn. She. Is. Beautiful. I look at Sam. "How soon can you start?"

"Today," he says eagerly.

"Good." Spinning my chair around, I open a file cabinet drawer, thumbing through papers until I come across an application form. Turning back around, I reach across the desk, handing it to him. "Fill this out and find Gary. He is the older gentleman you met earlier. He'll put you on whatever crew he needs you on." After a brief moment of discussing pay, Sam stands, as do I.

"I appreciate the opportunity." And we shake hands again. He then looks at Leah, who is still seated. "You okay with finishing out your interview alone?"

Before Leah can reply, I answer for her, "She's safe with me."

After a moment's hesitation, Leah nods to her friend. "I'll be okay, Sam," she offers him a smile, and I wish it were for me. I briefly wonder if the two are more than friends and find myself not liking the concept.

"I'll be waiting to take you home at the end of the day," he assures her, then walks out of my office.

Silence fills the room, and I can tell Sam's presence was keeping her grounded because now that he is gone, she seems tenser than before. "Would you like some coffee, or maybe water?" I ask.

"Um, water, thank you." Getting up, I exit my office, cross the hall to the breakroom, and grab a bottle of water from the refrigerator, and walk back to my office. I close the door behind me.

Leah's posture stiffens, and she looks frightened. Hell, I don't blame her. What woman would trust any man after being beaten by one? "I promise to learn quickly and not be in the way," she suddenly blurts out.

"You had the job before walking in here, Leah."

"I did?" she questions, cocking her head, causing her loose curls to fall across her face.

"Jake told me you are hiding from your father. Correct?" Instead of sitting in my chair, I sit on the edge of my desk, directly in front of Leah.

She looks away, staring out my office window. "Yes."

I don't know what comes over me. Reaching out, I brush my fingers along her chin, forcing her to look at me. I was expecting her to flinch at my touch, but she doesn't. The sadness in her eyes pulls me in, and I feel like I'm drowning in it. "Do you trust Jake and his club?" Her bottom lip trembles, but she nods. "Good. You should. They are good men, and they are asking you to do the same with me. Do you think you can do that?"

Leah blinks. "Trust you?"

"Yes."

"My father is a cop," she gives a bit of information I wasn't aware of. "He's resourceful, and probably won't give up until he finds me."

My look turns severe and cold. "I'm going to assume you are

aware that the men protecting you will go to any lengths to keep you safe."

I have to hold back a grin when Leah rolls her eyes at me, showing me a hint of another side of herself. "I don't live under a rock. I've heard things." Her arms cross beneath her large breast, making them look fuller.

I want her to understand this next part, so I make sure I have her full attention. "Then know your father never wants to cross paths with me either." I pause for a moment, letting my words sink in. "You'll work here for me. I'll pay you in cash every week. Keeping you off the payroll will help keep you off his radar. You need something, tell me. I'll keep you safe." Like that, I have pledged to do whatever it takes to keep Leah out of harm's way—away from her father.

6

LEAH

"Are you coming to the clubhouse this evening with Sam?" Alba asks over the phone.

"I told you yesterday I'd be there."

"I know, but you flaked the last two times we made plans."

I sigh. Alba is right. It's been a couple of weeks since she gave birth to her and Gabriel's son, Gabe. Not only has Alba been recovering from that, but she has also been getting over the ordeal with her stalker who broke into her home, beat her, and nearly killed Gabriel's sister, Leyna. Luckily, Alba and Leyna are both on the mend.

"I promise I'm coming this time. Now, I need to get off the phone before I get into trouble for taking personal calls at work."

"Fine," Alba huffs. "Just know that if your booty is not here later like promised, I will hunt you down and drag you out of that apartment."

"Okay, okay. I'm hanging up now." Alba's giggle is the last thing I hear before disconnecting the call. I figured that's why she was calling me at work. Here I wouldn't be able to dodge her like I have been when she calls Sam. And I have flaked on going to visit her. I went to see her right after she got home from the hospital, but that was it. Now she wants me to come to the clubhouse this evening for dinner. Just thinking about it makes me uneasy. I'm not good with people, especially large groups of people. And Alba said everyone would be there. On that thought, my mind drifts to a certain someone, and I wonder if he will be in attendance. Nikolai. I can't take being around my new boss more than I already am. God, that man is scary intense. Not that he does anything for me to be afraid of him. It's more about this look he gets. I can't explain it. It's like he has a storm brewing behind his eyes. Eyes that glue to me and demand my attention, yet warn me to stay away at the same time. Over the years, I have perfected the craft of becoming invisible; at staying under the radar. Not that boys ever gave me much thought. Being the awkward, chubby girl doesn't get you noticed by guys. But when I met Nikolai the other day, the intensity in his eyes made me feel he wasn't looking at the shy fat chick. For a fraction of a second, something flashed across his face, and it was like he liked what he saw in front of him. A look that was gone just as quick as it showed. It was a ridiculous notion anyway, a man who looks like that being interested in someone like me. Let's not address the fact I can't bring myself to look directly at his face when he speaks to me. I find myself looking at his shoulder or his chest. Sometimes I pretend to pick at a piece of imaginary lint on my shirt. Nikolai Volkov is gorgeous. He stands at 6 feet 2 inches tall. Has dirty blond hair shaved close on the sides and long on top that compliments his blond beard perfectly. And don't get me started on his unique eyes: one green and one blue.

The ringing of the phone knocks me out of my stupor. Picking it up, I answer, "Kings Construction, can I help you?"

"Hey, Leah."

"Hi, Sam. You need to talk to Nikolai?"

"Naw. I called to see if you wanted some lunch. I'm making a run to the lumber yard but can swing by and drop something off for you on my way through town."

"No. I brought my lunch."

"You sure? You don't have to pack your lunch every day. I don't mind bringing you a burger or something."

"Yeah. I'm good, Sam, but thanks."

"Alright, sweetheart. I'll see you later."

"Bye, Sam."

After hanging up the phone, I note the time. I'm allowed an hour lunch break every day at noon. Reaching under the desk for my bag, I pull out the plastic container I packed away in there this morning. Popping the lid off, I swipe one of the carrot sticks and take a bite. Closing my eyes, I try to imagine it's a juicy hamburger. I huff, taking another bite. Sadly, it doesn't work. The bitter taste of the carrot rolls around on my tongue, making me all too aware that my trying to lose weight is going to be torture. I decided a couple of days ago it was time to go on a diet. I keep trying to tell myself it's not because of how I want my new boss to look at me or because I can't stop hearing my father's voice inside my head telling me no man will ever want me.

"No man wants a fat wife, Leah." My father planted those seeds at an early age, and they took root. And when something like that takes root, it's hard to pull out. It also doesn't help when those roots are watered. It allows them to keep growing.

Squeezing my eyes shut, I try to suppress the monster's voice that continually reminds me I'm not good enough.

"What are you doing?" I'm drawn out of my musings by a familiar husky baritone voice. When I open my eyes, Nikolai is standing over my desk. Eyes laser-focused on my face. Me being my usual awkward self, I become mute. So, when I don't answer his question, he asks again, this time more slowly. "What are you doing?"

I suddenly worry that I have unknowingly done something

wrong. How long was I spaced out? Is my hour up already? Taking a glance down at my watch, I note it's only fifteen minutes past noon. Then I peer back upward at the man standing in front of me. Well, I look at his t-shirt covered chest because, like any other time he speaks to me, I can't look at his devastatingly handsome face. God, I'm so lame. He must think I'm an idiot.

"Eating my lunch."

When Nikolai doesn't respond, I take a quick peek up. His eyes dart from my face to the bowl of carrot sticks and apple slices sitting in front of me. The second I see his jaw tick, I look away.

"Let's go."

At his abrupt command, I snap my head up, settling my gaze on his forehead. "What?"

"Now, Leah." Nikolai turns on his heel and walks out the door. Confused but not wanting to defy my boss, I stand, grab my purse, throw my coat on, and shuffle out. Nikolai is standing at the passenger side of his truck with the door open as he waits for me to get in. "Shouldn't you lock up?" I gesture toward the entrance of Kings Construction.

"Nobody around here is stupid enough to fuck with the place. Let's go."

Shuffling toward his vehicle, I do as he says. Once I climb in, he shuts the door. My pulse races as I watch him move around the hood to the driver's side and climb behind the wheel. Nikolai doesn't say one word as he backs out of the parking space. Less than ten minutes later, we pull up to Polson's local diner. Nikolai barks another command, "Stay."

"What am I, a dog?" I say to an empty cab.

Nikolai opens the passenger door for me. He waits without a word for me to slide out. When I do, my body freezes up at the feel of his palm against the small of my back as he guides us into the diner. I walk stiffly, aware of Nikolai's touch burning into my skin. If Nikolai notices my reaction, he doesn't say a word. A few seconds after we enter, we are shown a booth, and a waitress comes over to greet us as she places our menus down on the table.

"Can I get you two something to drink?"

I peer up at her. "I'll have water, please."

"Coke," Nikolai grunts.

The waitress walks away, and I take the time to look over the menu. There is not much to accommodate my diet, so it seems like I will be ordering a Cobb salad, although the thought of the cheesesteak sandwich or a juicy burger and fries is making my mouth water.

"You decided what you'd like to order?" I take my eyes off the menu to address the waitress once again. "I'll have the Cobb salad with dressing on the side."

"No, she won't," Nikolai cuts in and I snap my head in his direction.

"She'll have the bacon and Swiss burger with fries. I'll have the same but with onion rings. Bring her a Coke too." He hands the menus to the waitress, and she smiles.

"Sure thing. I'll have your order out in a few and be back with that Coke in a second." The waitress walks away, and I speak.

"I wanted a salad."

"Tough. You're getting a burger instead."

"I...that's not what I wanted," I say, not meeting his eyes.

"You eat with me, you eat. And not any of that shit you had back at the office."

I fidget at his terse tone and decide not to argue. Luckily, the waitress returns with our meal, and Nikolai doesn't say anymore. My stomach rumbles when my plate is set down in front of me. I sit and stare at my food while Nikolai picks up the burger on his plate and digs in. The whole time he does this, I can feel his eyes on me. His attention is uncomfortable, and I begin to squirm in my seat.

"Are you going to eat?"

I pick up the glass of soda beside my plate and take a sip. "I'm not hungry," I mumble. My stomach decides at that moment to let out another loud rumble.

"Leah." When Nikolai calls my name, it's done with a softer tone, and I can't help to look at him. Not his forehead or his chest, but his eyes. We stare at each other, neither of us saying anything. I know by the way his unwavering gaze bores into mine, he sees what I was hiding.

"Eat your food." He jerks his chin toward my plate.

Biting my bottom lip, I push my glasses up my nose. After a beat, I nod. Then I pick up the burger and take a big bite. And I swear it is the best tasting hamburger I've ever had.

When we arrive back at Kings Construction, and I take my seat behind the reception desk, Nikolai picks up the container of carrot sticks I left on my desk and tosses it in the trash. He does this without saying a word then disappears down the hall to his office, missing the small smile that appears on my face.

"So, how do you like the new job?" Alba asks from where she sits across from me at the clubhouse. True to my word, I rode out here to have dinner with Alba and her family. Now here I am, sitting on the sofa holding her son, Gabe. The little guy is fast asleep in my arms, and I can't help but be mesmerized at how beautiful he is. With his head full of dark hair, he is the spitting image of his dad. It doesn't take long for him to realize he is no longer in his momma's arms, so when he starts squirming, I pass him back to Alba.

"I like it, okay. I just sit behind a desk and answer the phone all day."

"How are you and Nikolai getting along?" At Alba's next question, Bella and Sam, who were having their own conversation, halt and bring their attention to us.

I shrug. "He's a nice boss, I guess."

"He's a nice boss?" Alba parrots.

"Yeah."

Sam decides to cut in. "You know, I saw the two of you eating lunch at the diner in town today."

"Nikolai took you to lunch?" The question comes from Bella, Alba's sister.

"Yeah."

Alba, Sam, and Bella look as if they are waiting for me to elaborate. Don't know why. There's nothing more to say.

Bella cocks her head to the side. Something across the room catches her attention. Or should I say, someone? When I look over my shoulder, I find Nikolai sitting at the bar with his brother Logan. Logan is talking to him. Only Nikolai's attention is fixed on our little huddle. Bella continues to look back and forth between Nikolai and me. Then a smile spreads across her face. I look to Alba, who is looking at her sister. She shares the same smile.

"What?" I ask.

"Nothing," the sisters say in unison. Alba and Bella seem to have some secret code. They can communicate with just a look. That's something I have noticed since hanging around them more. It's something special, but annoying at times.

I look to Sam silently, asking if he knows what their deal is. He just smiles and shrugs. But he too has a strange look in his eyes, like he is in on some big secret I know nothing about. *Strange.*

"You guys are acting weird."

Bella waves her hand in front of us and changes the subject. "So how are you liking Polson? You get settled into the apartment okay?"

"The apartment is great. I've been meaning to thank the club for all they've done."

"You're family now, "Alba says. "The guys were happy to help."

At the mention of family, I let my mind drift and start thinking about my own. It is not lost on me that The Kings have done more for me in just a matter of weeks than my mother and father have in eighteen years. People who hardly know me have shown me what it is to be a family—like Sam, who dropped everything to move because I needed to escape to someplace safe. Family is people who help you find a safe place to lay your head at night and give you a job with no questions asked. They are the people who accept you just the way you are. I'm blessed enough to have found two of the best friends anyone could ask for.

"You okay, Leah?" Alba's voice fills with concern. "You looked miles away just now."

Shaking my thoughts away, I decide I need a moment to collect myself before letting my emotions get the better of me. "I'm fine," I give my friend a small smile. "I do need to use the restroom, though. Can you point me in the direction?"

"Sure." Alba points to her left. "Down the hall, last door on your right."

"Thanks. I'll be back in a minute."

Standing, I make my way through the common room and past the bar. And though I don't look up from watching each step my feet carry me, I feel a familiar set of eyes watching my every move. It's unnerving yet makes my tummy flutter. Once I reach the bathroom and rush to lock the door, I lean my back against the wall in front of the mirror and take a deep breath. This is why I don't have friends and why I don't like crowds. I'm not good at making small talk or inserting myself into the conversations going on around me. I don't understand when the people around me give each other cryptic looks spoken in secret code. Regardless of those things, I have to admit; it feels good being around my friend again and seeing how happy she is. If anyone deserves to be happy, it's Alba.

Deciding I've hidden in the bathroom long enough, I exit and head back down the hall. I don't make it far when I hear my name called. "Leah?" Jake Delane, the club President, stands in the doorway to his office. Jake is just as big as the rest of the men in the club. Only his presence holds more authority. He has a bushy beard, tattoo-covered arms, a broad chest, and kind eyes. "I'd like a word with you, darlin'."

Not waiting for my response, Jake turns, walks further into his office, and plants himself behind a desk. I follow behind and take a seat in front of him.

Settling in, Jake picks up a pack of cigarettes from his desk, sticks one in his mouth, lights it, and takes a long drag. Out of nervous habit, I stare down at my hands, resting on my lap while waiting for him to speak. "Darlin'," Jake grabs my attention, and I look up. "You got nothin' and no one to be scared of here. You get me?"

"Yes, Sir."

Jake nods. "I only wanted to see how you were settlin' in. See how you're likin' the job."

"I'm settling in okay. I like my job, and everyone has been nice."

"That's good, sweetheart." Jake's face goes soft at his next question. "Now, about your dad. Have you tried talking to him again?"

I shake my head. "No, Sir. Not since before Sam and I moved to Polson." Curious about Jake's line of questioning, I ask, "Do you think he knows I'm here? Have you heard anything?"

Jake takes another drag from his cigarette. "The club is handlin' your dad. We're keepin' tabs, and he hasn't been sniffin' anywhere near my town. If he does, I'll know about it."

I let out a relieved breath.

Jake leans forward, resting his arms on the desk. "The club's got your back, darlin'. Don't you worry. I'll also add, Sam told me what went down with you and your old man. I assure you that the things he told my men and me won't go beyond these walls. You can trust me, and you can trust my club. I want you to know you can come to us for anything. You got me?"

"I got you. Thank you, Mr. Delane. I know you don't know me, but your help means a lot."

"No thanks necessary, sweetheart. Alba vouches for ya and considers you family. If you're Alba's family, you're Kings' family. That's all there is to it. We take care of our own."

7

NIKOLAI

P resent

ANOTHER NIGHT OF RESTLESS SLEEP, although this time, my insomnia has nothing to do with my past. No, I can't seem to get a particular curvy brunette with amber eyes off my mind. I close my eyes, and she's there. Awake, I want nothing but to lay eyes on her. That is a problem. I shouldn't want her the way I do. For starters, she's barely legal, and Leah is not ready for a man like me. I pull a pair of gym shorts from the dresser drawer and slide them on. Needing a distraction, I walk out of my room. It's a few hours before dawn, so I head toward the other side of the house and enter the gym. The one here at my father's estate in Polson is smaller than the one in Russia but offers a much better view during a workout. I step up to the heavy bag and begin pounding my bare knuckles into the black leather. When thoughts of Leah continue to plague me, my strikes become harder and faster until my flesh is raw, and my body is drenched in sweat.

Breathing slowly and frustrated that my workout proved useless in my efforts to concentrate on more than a beautiful young woman, I make my way back to my room. Stripping out of my shorts, I stride into the bathroom and turn the shower on. As I wait for the water to warm, I pause, looking at my nude reflection in the mirror. Twisting, I take in the three large scars on my back. They're hidden—blended almost flawlessly with my tattoos. No matter how I disguise them, they are reminders of my past, and of the man my grandfather was.

My fists tighten at my sides as the memory surfaces. The second time in my life that I defied my grandfather. By this time in my life, there wasn't too much I didn't know about my mafia family. However, I still wasn't privy to all the inner workings. I wasn't killing people or committing crimes, but I was accompanying people here and there to places like restaurants, bars, and strip clubs. No one ever questioned why I always tagged along or was invited to go. At fifteen, I was as tall as I am now, besides, why would they refuse to let me enter? I'm Nikolai Volkov. Cocky to say, but true. There was this one fucker, a real piece of shit by the name of Zavier Minsky, the son of a prominent business associate to the family. The entire meeting went smoothly until I caught the asshole raping an unconscious woman in the men's bathroom at the topless bar, where we were conducting business. Long story short, I beat the shit out of him.

Rolling my shoulders, I take one last look in the mirror before stepping into the shower. Unfortunately for me, Zavier felt disrespected, and my grandfather thought I needed another lesson in respect. I had to endure whatever punishment the Minsky family saw fit, as long as it didn't result in the loss of my life. It turns out; they have strange barbaric customs for such things in their family. I was horsewhipped several times. Some of those strikes left open lacerations across my back. Needless to say, my father wasn't pleased to hear about the incident upon his return. I don't know what transpired between my grandfather and my dad, but I know nothing like what I was put through ever happened again.

Pushing dark memories away, I shower and get ready for the workday ahead.

Before heading to the office, I swing by the bakery owned by Jake's woman. "Good morning, Nikolai," Grace greets me with a smile like always as I walk through the door. "What would you like today?" She places a fresh tray of blueberry muffins into the display case.

"Four of your warmest croissants." I pull my wallet from the back pocket of my jeans, then notice a small pyramid stack of miniature jars filled with various jam flavors sitting beside the cash register. "And a jar of jam."

"Which flavor?" Grace asks as she places my order of pastries into a small pink box.

I stare at the selections available, wondering which one Leah would like best. "Fig."

Grace nestles the small jar in the center of the croissants. "Good choice. Our neighbor's wife makes them, and they are so good. Oh," she looks around, retrieving a wrapped plastic knife with a few napkins, and sits them on top of the closed box. Handing her my credit card, I pay for my order. "How's Leah?" she asks as she rings up my purchase.

"Good."

"She's a sweet girl." Grace hands over my credit card along with my order.

I nod but decide not to reply. Instead, I tell her, "Thank you, Grace." I turn and walk toward the door.

"Be gentle with her, Nikolai." Grace's words cause me to pause as my hand hovers above the door handle. "I suspect she's suffered for a long time." There's a brief pause, followed by a soft sigh. "I see so much of myself in her. She probably feels like her life is beyond repair right now, but I've noticed the way you look at her."

I keep my eyes forward, staring out the glass door. "I would never hurt her."

"I know. You are a good man. Just..." Grace leaves the rest of her thoughts unsaid before adding, "with time, she'll learn to spread her wings. I have a feeling there is much more to Leah than she allows to show," Grace expresses, and I agree with her observation.

I look over my shoulder. "Have a good day, Grace."

"You do the same," she waves to me as I walk out the door.

The rest of the drive to work, I think about Grace's words and wonder if others have been just as observant of my feelings for Leah. As the office building comes into view, I notice her car parked in its usual spot and look at the time above the truck radio. She's almost forty minutes early. I park my truck beside it, cut the engine, and grab the bag sitting in the passenger seat, then climb out. The front door is unlocked, and the thought of Leah being so careless angers me. Anyone could walk in and harm her. I fling the door open, only to find her desk chair empty. Sitting the bag in my hand on her desk, I stride down the hallway, spotting the backdoor open. My pace quickens. The closer I get to the door, I hear the rumble of a man's voice and my pulse races. And the words he speaks as I close in on him makes my blood boil.

"Come on. A big girl like you should take what she can get, and I'll give it to you good too. You know you want it."

Clearing the opened door, I catch sight of Leah, pressed against the side of the building. The man who currently has his hands on my woman, John, one of two crewmen we hired three weeks ago. I'm on him in two seconds flat. Grabbing a fist full of his hair, I pull him off Leah, and slam him, face-first into the wall.

"What the hell?" The bastard falls to his knees, holding his face. "My nose. You broke my goddamn nose."

Leah blinks. The tears rolling down her cheeks, fill me with more rage than I've ever felt before. This piece of shit hurt her. Leah brings her eyes to mine. "Go inside," I order, but she makes no attempt to move. "Leah. Inside. Now," I raise my voice, which causes her to flinch. I hate to use such a harsh tone with her, but she needs to listen. Leah has seen enough violence in her life; I will not add to it by allowing her to witness what I am about to do. Without further prompting, she steps away. Once she's safely inside, I lift the guy off the ground. "On your feet, motherfucker."

"Shit, man." John grunts from the force of me, shoving his back against the brick wall. His eyes land on my face, finally noticing who the fuck he just pissed off. "Shit." He throws his hands up. "Look, dude, I'm sorry. I didn't realize..."

"Didn't realize what you worthless piece of shit." My accent is thick as I wrap my hand around his throat. "Didn't realize a man doesn't put his hands on a woman uninvited?" My grip tightens, causing his face to redden from lack of oxygen.

"I didn't know she was yours, man." He pries at my fingers, trying to remove them from his neck as I constrict them more. But before he passes out, I release my hold on him.

He coughs as he takes air into his lungs. "It won't happen again," John sputters.

"Damn right, it won't." My knuckles connect with his ribcage, making him double over in pain. The second he comes up swinging, something else inside me takes over as I land blow after blow to his face.

"Boss, Boss." A muffled voice begins to drag me from my rage-filled haze. "Nikolai. Stop before you kill him." Finally, I recognize Gary's voice.

Heaving, I take in the sight of John's face as I release the collar of his shirt, and he slumps to the ground at my feet, his face swollen and bloodied by my hands.

"Get yourself cleaned up," Gary tells me, and I look down at my hands covered in another man's blood.

"He touched her," are the only words I manage to say.

"I put two and two together once I took in Leah's appearance inside, then found you out here beating John half to death." Gary sighs. "I got daughters and a wife of my own. I get it." He pulls his phone from his back pocket. "I'm assuming I need to call someone to handle this?"

Walking to the hose laying on the ground at the corner of the building, I turn the water on and rinse the blood from my hands. "You have Jake's number?"

"I do."

"Call him." Turning the water off, I dry my hands on my pant legs, then check myself before walking inside.

I find Leah in the breakroom, sitting at the table, staring at her hands folded in her lap. The moment I hear her wheezing, I realize she's in the middle of an asthma attack. Rushing to her desk, I search for her inhaler. When I find it, I hurry back, and drop to my knees beside her, placing the medicine in her hand. "Here."

Leah gives her inhaler a shake, then brings it to her lips and inhales.

After a few deep breaths, her breathing levels out.

Adrenaline still coursing through my veins I ask her, "What were you thinking? You shouldn't be here alone." She flinches. The moment my harsh words are spoken, I regret saying them. Reining in my anger, I spin her chair to face me. "I apologize. None of this is your fault." I lift her chin, needing her to look at me. "Give me your eyes." Her lids flutter open, her lashes wet from tears. "Are you okay?"

She nods. "Yeah."

"He touched you." I keep my voice calm, even though my insides are far from it.

"His words hurt a lot worse than his touch."

The pain in Leah's voice guts me. "Those things he said are not true. You're beautiful, Malyshka."

Leah shakes her head, not believing a word. Dropping her head, she whispers, "I wish that were true."

"Look at me, Leah." She lifts her eyes to mine once more. "I would never lie to you. You. Are. Beautiful." Her chest rises and falls, and her pupils dilate. When her lips part, I find myself aching to taste them.

A knock turns both our heads toward the door. "Hey, boss. Jake is here to see you." Gary looks between Leah and me.

"I'll be right there," I tell him.

"I'll let him know." Gary disappears down the hall, leaving me alone with Leah once again.

I stand, and Leah follows suit. "Um. What happened to John?" she asks.

"I taught him a lesson he won't soon forget," I admit since I just told her I would never lie to her.

"You hurt him?"

"Yes."

"Bad?"

"Yes," I admit freely again, then effectively end the discussion. "Come. You should eat. I left breakfast on your desk." Waiting for Leah to lead the way, I follow close behind her as we walk out front. Jake is waiting at the door when we step out.

Putting a smile on her face, Leah greets him. "Good morning, Jake."

"Mornin', sweetheart." Jake then turns his attention to me. "Let's talk outside." With a final look at Leah, I follow him. Once outside, I notice Quinn, and Sam, loading John's limp body into the back of a van. "He's breathin'," Jake pauses a beat. "You worked him over pretty good."

"He deserved more than what he got."

Jake runs his fingers through his beard. "From what Gary told us, I believe you. I've done far worse to defend Grace."

"I appreciate the clean-up. I owe you."

"You don't owe me shit. All I ask is you be careful with that girl in there."

I've known Jake long enough to realize the meaning of his words. "Grace had something similar to say to me this morning."

Jake laughs. "She did, huh?" Then crosses his arms across his chest, and we watch the guys drive the van off the property. Jake turns, clasping his hand down on my shoulder. "Well, then. Nothing more to be said." He lets his hand fall to his side, walks over to his bike, and throws his leg over it. "I'll have the guys dump the asshole near the hospital. Catch ya later."

I watch Jake ride off before returning inside. Leah has the phone to her ear, so I leave her to her work and head for my office. Sitting on my desk is a steaming cup of coffee, a croissant, and a small yellow sticky note stuck to my computer screen.

Thank you.

8

LEAH

A noise wakes me from sleep. It takes me a second to realize that the sound I hear is voices coming from outside my bedroom window. And one of them is my dad's. Then there is another voice, and that one sounds angry. Me being curious, I climb out of my bed, put my glasses on, and pad over to the bedroom window. My bedroom is at the back of the house facing the backyard, and standing in the backyard in the dark is my dad and three other men. Two of the men are standing over next to the big oak tree I liked to climb. The other man: the one with the scary voice, is standing with my dad by his work shed. The man takes two steps and puts his face close to my dad's. His voice gets louder. My heart starts pumping fast because dad doesn't like it when people raise their voices to him. When I raise my voice to daddy, I get punished. Daddy doesn't punish this man, though. Daddy doesn't do anything. A minute later, the scary guy says something to the two men by the tree. Then my daddy turns toward his shed and unlocks it. The shed is where daddy keeps his tools for when he fixes stuff around the house. Maybe the scary man is here to help daddy fix something. But why would they do that in the middle of the night?

Clutching my teddy to my chest, I watch as the scary man and *daddy step inside the shed. Daddy turns the light on, and I gasp. There's a girl in there. She's sitting on the floor with her arms hugging her knees. She has long blonde hair. I can't see her face because it's buried in her knees. I watch as daddy crouches down next to the girl. When he does, the girl looks up. She looks sad. Her face is wet like she's been crying too, and that makes me sad. Maybe she's lost and misses her family. I bet that's what it is. Not feeling sad anymore, I smile. The man isn't so scary. Like the girl, he was worried too. He must be her daddy. That's why daddy and the man are in the backyard. Daddy must have found the lost girl and is giving her back to her family. That's his job because he's a cop. Daddy helps people. With a big smile on my face, I step away from the window and climb back into bed.*

The next morning, I'm sitting at the table eating a bowl of cereal while daddy sits across from me, drinking his coffee and reading the paper. The TV in the living room is on when the local news starts to play. A picture of the girl from daddy's shed flashes across the screen. The newsman says she's missing. I sit up straight in my seat and point to the TV. "Look, daddy! It's the girl from last night. The one you gave back to her family."

Mom gasps and daddy suddenly looks at me with surprise. His surprise quickly turns to anger. I don't like daddy's angry face. His angry face means I'm going to be punished. Only I don't know what I did wrong.

WAKING FROM MY NIGHTMARE, I fight against the tightening in my chest as my throat starts to close. I reach over to the table beside my bed for my inhaler. Shaking it, I place it to my mouth and breathe in the best I can and wait for the medicine to take effect. That dream is just one of many that play on repeat at night when I go to sleep. I was seven when that incident took place. At seven, I didn't fully understand what I had witnessed that night. My father also made sure I never opened my mouth about it again too. That day, at seven years old, was the day I earned my first broken bone. My father made sure I kept my mouth shut by breaking my jaw. Though officially, I had fallen from the tree in my backyard. It wasn't until weeks later when mom was watching the news and that same girl I saw in dad's shed, flashed across the TV again. She was still missing. I didn't get a chance to hear more before mom quickly cut the TV off. She stood up from the sofa and went into the kitchen to prepare dinner. I could tell by her strange behavior she knew something terrible had happened and that dad was involved. Another lesson I learned at seven years old was that my dad was no hero. He was a monster. Deep down in my bones, I believe my father did something to that missing girl.

What's worse, is to this day, I've kept my mouth shut about what I saw that night. I haven't told a soul about the truths I know; the truth about the man who raised me, not even Sam or Alba. My friends and The Kings think my dad is just an abuser, a man who wants to control his daughter. What they don't know is James Winters doesn't care about having some power trip over me. He cares about my silence. I'm the only person who knows what he has done and what he is capable of. Maybe it's time I tell someone. I want to stop being afraid. I want to stop looking over my shoulder whenever I go out. I want my father to pay for the things he has done. He's made me the scared and weak person I am today. I don't like who I am, who he has made me. Maybe it's time I take my life back.

LATER THAT MORNING, I'm sitting in the kitchen with a cup of coffee when Sam comes in, dressed for the day, his hair still wet from his shower. "Hey, darlin'."

"Morning," I smile.

Sam pours himself a cup of coffee then faces me. He eyes me over the rim of the mug. Last night Sam talked to me about moving out. The Kings have offered him a place in the club. He is officially a Prospect. Or will be later when they have a party welcoming him into their fold. I put on a brave face and assured him I was okay to live on my own. I'm not good at hiding my feelings, so I suspect Sam didn't believe me when I said I would be fine.

"Would you quit looking at me like that," I fuss. "I'll be fine, Sam. Quit treating me like I'm some fragile broken girl who can't take care of herself."

"I don't think of you like that, Leah." Sam sets his cup down. "You are one of the strongest people I know. But you are also one of my friends, and I will always look out for you. You're like a sister to me, Leah."

My face softens at Sam's declaration. "I know. And you're like a brother to me, which is why I am happy for you. I'm happy you're moving on. Now go on and finish packing," I shoo him away. "Stop worrying about me. I'll be fine."

Sam kisses the top of my head. "Okay. If at any time you need anything, you call. The clubhouse is only five minutes away. Understand?" Sam studies me, and I nod.

An hour later, Sam finishes packing his clothes and is gone. I stand alone in an apartment that suddenly feels too big. I lied through my teeth when I said I would be fine. But no way was I going to let my fears and problems hold Sam back from moving on with his life. When he told me his big news last night, I knew I had to put on my bravest face and convince him I was good at being on my own. I'm over the moon for my friend. The connection he has built over the last year with the club has been a true testament that Sam has found his place, his family. And there is no way I can stand in the way of that.

Deciding I need to get out for a while, I go to my bedroom, throw on a pair of jeans, a t-shirt, and a pair of tennis shoes. Next, I go to the bathroom and pull my hair up into a ponytail at the top of my head. As I head out, I make the mistake of catching a glimpse of my reflection in the mirror. I usually go out of my way to avoid them. I suck in a deep breath and sigh at the girl staring back at me. Nothing has changed. Same dull eyes framed by black-rimmed glasses. Same unmanageable curly brown hair, and pouty lips that would look killer on a supermodel but paired with my round face just looks odd. And same pudgy tummy and full hips. Over the last year, I have started and stopped countless diets, but every time Nikolai catches me starting one, he practically force-feeds me. When I go into work in the mornings, there will be pastries or donuts from The Cookie Jar on my desk, and at lunchtime, he drags me to the diner. If he's out on a job and can't take me, lunch is promptly delivered to the office at noon.

Thoughts of Nikolai bring me back to what he said to me the other day, and my tummy flutters. "Those things he said are not true. You're beautiful, Malyshka."

My thoughts drift from Nikolai to what happened with John, the flutters disappear, and a chill runs down my spine. I don't want to think about what would have happened had Nikolai not shown up. When that guy approached me, I froze. I clammed up and felt helpless. His words play on repeat inside my head. *"A big girl like you takes what she can get."* That night when I phoned Alba and told her what happened, she mentioned the gym in town offers self-defense classes. So, that's what I am going to do today. I'm going to see what those classes are about. This morning when I woke up and vowed to get my life back, I meant it. And it starts today.

PULLING up in front of the local gym, I grab my purse and climb out of my car. A car I'm proud to say I saved up for and bought myself. It was Jake who came to me six months ago with it. He bought it off some old guy and fixed it up at the garage. He tried to give it to me. I refused to accept it unless I made a monthly payment to him. Jake didn't like it, but he understood it was vital for me to pay my way. The car is a 2005 Nissan. Not fancy by any means, but thanks to the club, it runs excellent, and it's mine. The registration, of course, is not in my name, and I didn't ask any questions about the Montana driver's license Jake gave me, but I assume it's a fake. The club is smart. They wouldn't do anything that would trace my dad back to me. I've learned to go with the flow and trust the club.

The bell over the gym door chimes, alerting the woman behind the reception desk to my arrival. The woman is tall, at least six inches taller than me, has her long blonde hair pulled back into a high ponytail. She is wearing a shirt with the gym's name and logo on it and a pair of black and yellow yoga pants. When she turns away from the counter behind her, she gives me a beaming smile. "Hi. Can I help you?"

"I think so. I heard you offer self-defense classes."

"You heard, right. Why don't you come on over here and I'll tell you more about the class?"

I step closer to the counter, and when I do, the woman reaches her arm across. "My name is Samantha."

I shake her hand. "I'm Leah."

"It's nice to meet you, Leah."

"You too."

Samantha pulls out a sheet of paper and places it in front of me. "This is a listing of all the gym has to offer. As you can see here," she points, "we teach self-defense classes every Monday, Wednesday, and Saturday. The Monday and Wednesday classes are at 4:00 pm, and our Saturday class is at 1:00 pm. You can sign up for all three days or just one. That's up to you."

"Are you the one who teaches the class?" I ask.

"Oh, no. I teach the senior class and yoga and sometimes work the front like today. Rhett teaches the self-defense class."

"Did somebody say my name?"

At the sound of a deep masculine voice, I look to my left to see a man approaching. The guy is tall, has short blond hair, and an easy-going smile.

"Hi, Rhett. Leah here was asking about your self-defense class. I was just filling her in on the details," Samantha informs the man.

The guy turns away from Samantha and brings his attention to me. He smiles and offers his hand. "Hi, Leah, I'm Rhett, the owner."

Like with Samantha, I take his hand. "Hi."

Rhett gives me a warm smile, and his kindness instantly puts me at ease.

"There is a class starting in ten minutes. How about you sit in and watch, then you can decide from there if it's something you are interested in."

I nod. "Okay."

Rhett jerks his chin. "You can follow me."

Walking side by side, Rhett leads me to the back of the gym, where he has several large mats set up. "The classes aren't huge. We have eight ladies coming in this afternoon."

As soon as the words leave his mouth, three women make their way toward us—all three dressed in spandex shorts. Short so short, the material barely covers their butts and tops that look more like bras. The women are also sporting full face makeup and perfectly styled hair, which makes absolutely no sense to me. One of the women, a redhead, proceeds to size me up. Her lips turn up in a sneer. She looks me up and down before looking to my right where Rhett is standing, then back to me. Her sneer quickly morphs into a smirk. I know what she's thinking. It's what all women think when they see me. Under her watchful, judgmental eye, I begin to fidget. I want to tell her she has nothing to worry about. Unlike her, I'm here to learn something, not land a man. Not that Rhett isn't cute, I'm just not interested. He's not him.

An hour later, the class has ended, and as the women clear out, Rhett makes his way over toward me, ignoring the redhead. "So, what did you think?" He wipes away the sweat on his forehead with a towel."

I push my glasses up my nose. "I haven't decided yet."

"I can't stress how important it is for a woman to learn how to take control of any given situation. It's sad, but far too often, women are hurt or worse because they didn't have the tools to protect themselves," Rhett tells me, and I can hear the passion in his voice.

"I get it. Something happened to me a couple of days ago. I was scared."

Rhett's back goes straight. "Are you okay?"

"Yeah. Luckily, my boss showed up and stopped a guy from harassing me. A friend told me about the classes here, and I figured it was a good idea to come check it out. So, I can prepare for next time."

"I'm glad your friend told you about us. I hope you consider signing up, Leah."

"I think I will. Thanks for letting me watch the class today. I think what you do is important."

Rhett gives me a warm smile, then reaches down to the duffle bag at his side and pulls something out. It looks like a business card. Using a pen, he scribbles something on it and hands it over. "Take my card. I put my cell number on the back. If my current classes don't jive with your schedule and you want me to train you one on one, then that is what we'll do."

I take the card from him and put it in my purse. "Thank you."

"Come on. I'll walk you out."

Accepting his offer, I let Rhett walk me out to my car. "Thanks for everything, and I'll be sure to think about your offer."

"You're welcome, Leah. I hope to hear from you soon."

. . .

LATER THAT DAY, I'm chatting with Alba and telling her about my day when she screeches through the phone. "Oh, my God, Leah! The guy is totally into you."

I roll my eyes. "You're crazy. He was only being nice to a potential client."

"You are oblivious."

"What is that supposed to mean?"

"It means you are a knockout but don't know it. You don't see what everyone else sees."

"I look in the mirror every day. I know what people see."

"Oh, Leah." Alba's voice goes soft. "You are so unbelievably gorgeous. And one day, you're going to open those eyes of yours and realize it."

Uncomfortable with where this conversation is heading, I change the subject. "Hey, did you land that book cover you were telling me about last week?"

Lucky for me, my friend goes along with it.

"Did you ever have a doubt I wouldn't," she teases, and I laugh.

"No."

9
———

NIKOLAI

I spot Logan standing outside as I pull up to the clubhouse. Beside him is the custom Harley he's been working on for the past two months. Climbing from the truck, I stride across the front yard. Logan tosses me the keys. "She's primed and ready for the road, brother," Logan stands to look at his handy work with pride.

Stepping up to the bike, I comb over every detail. The straight chrome pipes have a mirrored sheen—a deep color of crimson coats the gas tank and fender, accented with perfectly airbrushed ghost flames. I run my palm over the luxurious black leather seats and custom saddlebags. I'd ridden a few times growing up, but didn't truly find a love for it and the open roads until moving to Polson. Like fighting, riding has become therapeutic. Throwing my leg over, I straddle my bike. "Thank you, brother."

"Try her out." Logan grins.

"We ride together?" I place the key into the ignition.

"Shit. You don't have to ask me twice," Logan strides a couple of yards away, and mounts his bike.

The loud guttural rumble only a Harley makes seems to beat in sync with my heartbeat, only louder. The engine roars, giving the throttle a few twists, and the smell of gasoline fumes mixed with heat invigorate the senses, as I pull away from the clubhouse with my brother at my side. Once we pull out onto the open road, I open her up. I settle back in the low-slung seat, as we cruise down the highway, feeling the rush of the wind as it hits my face. A calm settles over me, letting the bike become an extension of myself. She's in control now.

By the time Logan and I return to the clubhouse, almost an hour has passed, and the heaviness I was feeling left somewhere on the road. "I needed that," I tell my brother as we make our way into the dimly lit clubhouse.

"Good ride." Logan clasps my shoulder. "I'll hit the road with you anytime, just say the word." Jake and Gabriel are sitting at the bar. "Prez, Gabriel," Logan greets them.

"I was wondering where the hell you two disappeared," Jake grunts, lifting a mug of coffee to his lips.

"Nikolai took his new ride for a spin this morning, and I rode with him." Logan pulls a stool from the bar beside Jake and sits.

Jake looks at me as I settle into the stool on the other side of Gabriel. "My brothers did a stellar fuckin' job on that custom Harley. How'd she ride?"

"Smooth," I tell him, and he nods.

"You should ride with us next weekend. We're going to show support for a young girl who is confronting her abuser in court and hoping for emancipation from her family," Jake mentions, and my mind automatically thinks of Leah.

"Alba took Leah shopping today. I'm sure my woman will be draggin' that girl here tonight," Gabriel tells Jake, something I was already aware of. Sam strides into the room, joining us at the bar as Jake responds to Gabriel.

"I don't know why Alba forces that girl to come here. The poor thing is afraid of her own damn shadow. Being around all us men makes her unease even worse," Jake replies.

"Yeah, but it's not without good cause." Sam drops down on a stool at the end of the bar.

Jake sighs. "No, I guess not."

"Since we are on the subject of Leah," Sam adds, "I wanted to bring up a concern I have about her." His statement catches my attention.

"What is it, son?" Jake asks.

"I'm not feeling right about her staying alone. I know the apartment has top-notch security, and she has assured me she's fine with living by herself, but my gut says she's not ready. I promised my friend I'd take care of her. So, I'm coming to the club in hopes you all can help me figure out a solution to not only keep Leah safe but to make her feel safe."

The moment Sam mentioned he is moving out of the apartment, he and Leah share, I'm all ears. I knew he was interested in prospecting for The Kings, but I wasn't aware that it would be leaving my woman alone and vulnerable.

Aware that this conversation doesn't include my opinion, I interrupt anyway. "I'll take care of Leah." Everyone eyes me as I abruptly stand, my chair screeching as the legs drag along the floor. No one says a word as I turn my back on them and walk out of the clubhouse with only one thing on my mind. Protecting what is mine. Glancing between my truck and my bike, I choose the Harley. The engine roars as I peel down the dirt road, a cloud of dust trailing behind me as I leave The Kings' compound.

Thirty minutes later, I'm pulling up to the lake house. Inside, I head straight for the office, pulling my phone from my pocket along the way. Tapping the screen, I call my father.

"Son. It is good to hear from you." His relaxed tone hints I woke him from sleep.

"Shit. I apologize for waking you. In my rush, I wasn't thinking of the time difference."

"What's wrong?" My father's voice is now alert, and I hear movement from the other end.

"Everything is fine. If possible, I'd like Maxim to join me here in the States," I ask.

"Done," he replies. "Does this have something to with a particular little brunette?" he asks the one question I sensed would be his next.

"It does," I freely admit. My father may not be here full time like he had hoped, but he is here enough to know about Leah. And it's not like I have tried to hide my attraction for her, I just haven't acted on those feelings. "As of today, Sam has moved from the apartment they share. He is now living at The Kings' clubhouse, as their newest prospect."

My father sighs. "It's been a year. Do you believe her father is still looking for her?"

"The Kings have been keeping tabs on him. However, I don't believe he will stop looking for her. I'd like Maxim to be my eyes and ears when I can't."

"Understandable." My father falls silent for a second, then adds, "You see your future with this girl?"

I think about his words, but not for long. "Yes."

"Then use whatever resources you need to secure that future. Maxim has been informed and will be on a flight to Polson in a couple of hours."

Me and my father's relationship hasn't always been as strong as it is now, but over the past few years, the bond between us has grown, and now, it is unbreakable. "Thank you." That's where our call ends.

Next, I call Reid. He's the one The Kings rely on to handle security measures and who installed the current system at Leah's apartment. Reid answers on the third ring. "I was expecting your call," he informs me.

"Word travels fast."

Reid laughs. "Yeah, brother, but you should be used to that by now. I've emailed all the information you need to log into the security system for Leah's place. Currently, the cameras are positioned outside the complex to capture every angle possible."

"And inside?"

Reid clears his throat. "No."

"Thanks."

"Catch you later, brother." Reid ends the call, and I log into my email, open the one Reid sent, then click the link he provided. After entering the password, I begin live streaming video outside Leah's apartment. I scan the parking lot, not finding her car, then remember she's out shopping with her friend. Knowing she isn't alone, slightly eases my mind.

Through the rest of the morning and into the afternoon, I sit watching the security feed. I also decided to order a new phone for Leah. One I know is untraceable and can track down her whereabouts should the need arise. Keeping the video on the desktop, I retrieve my laptop from another room and open the files we have on Leah's father. Unfortunately, we don't have much to go on. He's been on the Post Creek Police force for years, married to Mary Winters. He and his wife attend church regularly. His status within the community there appears to be untarnished. He's clean —too clean. Like someone has tried too hard to paint him as the picture of perfection. That alone sends red flags. I'm not buying into the illusion. My instincts are telling me I need to dig deeper, and I'll need help doing it. Only one name comes to mind. Luka. He has worked with my family before. You need someone found; he'll find them. We need to know every detail about someone's life; he can do that as well. Opening my father's desk drawer, I retrieve the burner phone used to contact him.

James Winters.

624 Sycamore Ln. Post Creek, MT

Cop

I wait for his reply.

Message received.

I slip the phone back into the drawer. Out the corner of my eyes, I catch a car pulling into the complex's parking lot. I zone in, watching Leah park. She waits a few minutes before stepping out of her vehicle, then scans her surroundings.

Good girl.

My eyes stay glued to the screen as she makes her way to her front door, the sway of her hips putting me into a trance-like state. She looks behind her before unlocking her door, then steps inside. She doesn't leave for the remainder of her day.

THE FOLLOWING MORNING, I leave for work later than usual. Reid will be working in the office today and will be there before Leah arrives. Needing the blueprints that should have been delivered by now, I head toward town. After making my routine stop for breakfast, I finally pull up to the front of Kings Construction.

Leah is sitting behind her desk, typing on her keyboard as I step through the front door. Her eyes briefly leave her computer screen to look at me before dropping to the white bag in my hand. Then, she looks away just as fast, red staining her cheeks. She's so fucking adorable. Rounding the corner of her desk, I step behind her. Bending, my arm brushes past her as I sit the bag from the bakery in front of her. Her hair is pulled back in a braid today, giving me full access to lean down and whisper in her ear. "Good morning, Malyshka." She sucks in a breath, and I watch her skin prickle from the warmth of my breath. She swallows.

"Good morning, Nikolai." Her sweet voice makes my cock twitch.

"I cannot join you this morning for breakfast, but I will pick you up for lunch."

"Umm," Leah hesitates.

That's when I notice a blue card sitting beside the bag I just placed in front of her—a business card from the local gym. I snatch it from her desk.

"Hey," her hand darts out, trying to take it from me.

What the fuck? Hell no.

I grow angry as I stare at the card. "Who is Rhett?" I demand.

Leah folds her arms under her breast. "He runs the gym in town."

"I've told you before. There is nothing wrong with you."

Her heavy sighs let me know she is becoming frustrated with me. "I'm considering taking self-defense classes, okay."

"You want to learn self-defense?" I ask her, my tone softening a bit.

Instead of making eye contact with me, Leah bores a hole through my chest. "I need to be able to take care of myself." Then her voice becomes smaller, and she draws into herself. "I felt so helpless the other day."

"Look at me." Quickly her face turns up, her eyes connecting with mine. "I'll teach you."

Her eyes widen. "You?"

"Yes."

"But, why?" she questions.

Does she not realize the hold she has on me? The thought of another man touching her—teaching her infuriates me to the core. The words spill from my mouth before I think twice about it. "I don't want another man touching you." Leah's eyes dilate with the truth in my confession.

"Okay," she says after a long pause.

"Good. Your first lesson will be this evening." Instead of returning the business card to her desk, I place it in my pocket. Walking off, I enter my office, retrieving the materials I need for the workday ahead. I pause before walking out the front door. "I'll bring lunch."

The day seemed to never end after enjoying lunch with Leah. Through several meetings, piles of paperwork, and a formal groundbreaking ceremony, for the massive mountain resort project outside of town, all I could think about was Leah. I've been waiting for her for more than an hour now. Going against my natural tendency to pick her up from work and haul her sweet ass home with me, I opted to text her the address instead. I wanted to see if she would follow through on training instead of risking the chance of making her feel like I was forcing her. Finished moving a few pieces of equipment to make space on the floor to teach Leah, I start to lay multiple floor mats.

Maxim walks into the gym as I place another mat on the floor. "Your girl is on her way."

I catch his use of the term my girl. The mat slaps against the floor. "Thank you, Maxim. You look tired from your long flight. Go, rest," I tell him as I continue my task. Looking up, I find him still standing in the doorway. "Speak freely." I throw the last mat down.

"She means something to you," Maxim states, and it doesn't surprise that he is asking. I've known Maxim most of my life. Damn near as long as I have known Sasha and Victor. Like them, I consider him family.

"She does," I answer him, and glance at the clock on the wall for the hundredth time.

"This is a good thing," Maxim proclaims then walks away.

Ten minutes later, Leah appears. Alone. Wearing black leggings, sneakers, her wild, curly hair up in a ponytail, and a loose t-shirt, she peers around the gym as she crosses the room. "Wow. Your home is amazing, Nikolai. At least, from the glimpses that I caught as I was being ushered in by a large, angry-looking man, who doesn't appear to speak English."

I chuckle at her description of Maxim, although accurate,

except for one detail. "He speaks English very well." Leah shuffles from foot to foot, her eyes glued to my bare chest. "I was starting to believe you had changed your mind," I remark because she's late.

"I almost did," she admits.

"Are you ready to begin?" Leah still won't make eye contact.

"Look at me." Her eyes snap to mine. "Are you ready?"

"Um. Could you put a shirt on first?" she asks, trying her best not to take in my naked torso, and I don't bother hiding my grin.

"Follow me," I jerk my head in the direction I'm moving toward, grab my shirt draped over one of the weight benches nearby, and slip it over my head the same time Leah takes her glasses off, tosses them in her bag and drops the bag to the floor beside the bench. "I'm going to touch you and invade your personal space. Before we begin, I need you to be okay with that, and permit me to do so." I come to stand in front of her, leaving about three feet between us. Leah fails to hide the many emotions she feels as she weighs my words.

She finally nods, followed by a sigh. "I need to do this," her words sound a little unsure as she says them. I say nothing and make no moves, waiting for her to give me the okay. Leah straightens her back, showing a bit more confidence. "I give you permission."

I step a bit closer to her. Reaching down, I lift the hem of her shirt.

"Wait. What are you doing?" her hands cover mine.

I proceed to tie the extra material of her shirt into a knot level with the waistband of her leggings. "Your loose clothing will get in the way," I inform her as my knuckles purposely brush against her skin, and she blushes.

"Oh."

I take a few steps back, and look at her for a moment. Making a twirling motion with my finger, I say, "Turn around", but she hesitates. "A predator will look for someone unsuspecting.

Coming up behind a woman makes them easy prey. Turn your back to me." Moving at the pace of a snail, I wait for Leah to get in position. I take in her backside, and the way her leggings hug her luscious curves. Advancing on her, I put her in a headlock type hold, her ass pressing against my upper thigh, dangerously close to brushing against my cock. I feel her breaths pick up when I pull her tight against my chest. "If your attacker gets you in this position, there are four moves to help you free yourself. Grab my arm." Without hesitating, Leah wraps her fingers over my forearm. "Pull down on my arm, turn your head to the side, and squat."

"Like this?" Leah does exactly as I instruct.

"Good. This will help prevent your attacker from suppressing your airway. Dropping low will give you leverage for your next move."

"Okay."

"Now, step back with your left foot, placing it behind my leg."

"Like this?" she asks.

"Yes. Now shift your weight back and twist." When Leah does this, she frees herself from my hold. "Good."

"Oh my god. That seemed so easy."

I shake my head. "I'm teaching you, not attacking you. In a real threat, your attacker will do his best to overpower you."

"Then let's do it again." Leah pulls her ponytail a little tighter, and her determination inspires me.

We perform the move several times until she feels confident enough to move on to a few more. I show her several ways to break loose and flee an attacker for an hour before moving on to more vulnerable situations. After a brief water break, I instruct Leah to lay down on the ground.

"What does laying on the floor have to do with defending myself?" she says nervously.

"An attacker might try to do more than kidnap you. They may try to force themselves on you. You need to know how to fight off a rapist who has you pinned to the ground." I don't sugar coat my words.

Slowly, Leah lowers herself to the mat, sitting on her ass, before pressing her back against the floor, her legs bent at the knees. I'm the devil for the thoughts that flood my mind as I look down at her, with her eyes glued to the ceiling, and chest rapidly rising and falling with every breath she takes. I shouldn't be standing here picturing my face between her thighs, tasting of her innocence. But I am. I think that and so much more. Gaining control of myself, I push those thoughts aside. Leah trusts me, and I would never do anything to threaten that trust.

Kneeling, I grab her attention. "Eyes." It takes her a moment, but Leah finally looks at me. "Ready?"

"Ready."

Placing my hands on top of her knees, I part her legs, positioning myself between them. "As I lean over you, I want you to put your hands out, palms side up. Push against my chest." Leah does as she is told while I hover above her. "He will try to choke you," I tell her, and gently place my hands around her neck, not applying pressure. "Bring your right hand over to my left, and your left hand over to my right. Remember—over and over."

"Got it."

"Bring your elbows down, on my arms. Hard." She does, then waits for further instructions. "If that doesn't break his grip, raise your hips off the ground, repeat the process, and bring your elbows down while you bring your ass down. This will give you more leverage and force." Leah performs the actions flawlessly, but I want to challenge her further.

"But what if that doesn't work. My upper body strength isn't the best." I can see she is starting to doubt herself, and I won't have it.

"Let's go through the moves again. This time bring your ass down and thrust your hips to the side. I want you to bring this foot up," I tap her left leg. "Place your foot on my pelvic bone. It may be difficult at first but try. Don't stop. Do it again with your other foot on the opposite side. Keep fighting until you can push me away, and break my hold on you." Leah stares up at me, with fear in her eyes. Even though I don't like seeing her terrified of being in such a vulnerable situation, she needs to fight her way through her fear. "I know you are afraid and don't think you have it in you, but you do. You are stronger than you think you got this, Malyshka." I position myself once more and place my hands around her neck. "Show me, Leah. Fight."

This time around, I become more aggressive in the way I'm handling her. I want her to feel what is going on. For a second, she struggles, forgetting everything I just taught her. Suddenly her fight kicks in. She executes one move after the other. A guttural scream leaves her body as she aggressively pushes me away from her, then with added measures, kicks me in the face. I fall back on my ass.

"Oh my God! Nikolai, I am so sorry." Leah scrambles across the floor until she's right in front of me. "I don't know where that came from. Are you okay?" I rub the side of my face. "Let me look," Leah brushes my hand away, and her fingertips gently press against my cheek, her face marred with worry. "I'm sorry. You have a small scratch there too. I'll find something to clean it up." Leah goes to stand, but I grab her wrist, pulling her back to the floor.

"You've done nothing to be sorry." I brush loose strands of hair from her face and fight the overwhelming urge to kiss her. Leah turns her head, hiding her blush.

"It's getting late. I should go."

Desperate for her to stay, I blurt the first thing to come to mind. "Stay. Have dinner with me." It's not a question, but I won't make her stay if she chooses to go.

She hesitates for a moment, biting her bottom lip like she's going to say no, but she doesn't. "Okay."

I get to my feet, pulling her up with me and tug at the hem of her shirt. "You should wear clothes that fit you. I don't like the way you hide your body."

Leah drops her head and tugs at her shirt. I sense her insecurity, and it pisses me off. Not wanting to make her uncomfortable, I lead her into the kitchen, dropping the subject.

"Sit. I'll fix dinner."

"You cook too?" Leah slides onto a stool at the kitchen island. "What can't you do?" she mumbles, and I chuckle.

"There are many things I can't do. But I can cook a decent Beef Stroganov." I tell her as I rummage through the pantry and the fridge for all the ingredients I need. For the next hour, we engage in small talk. Nothing heavy. It's the most we've talked to each other casually since we first met. Leah's guard is down, and she's relaxed.

"Can I ask you a personal question?" Leah sits in her seat, resting her chin in her palms as she watches me prepare our meal on our plates.

"I'll make you a deal. I'll answer a question if you answer one of mine." I place a glass in front of her.

"Personal?" She draws figure eights on the countertop.

"Yes. I'd like to get to know you better." With both plates in my hands, I jerk my chin, "Let's sit in the living room and watch a movie while we eat." Leah stands, following me. I wait for her to take a seat on the sofa.

"Is it true the Volkov's are a mafia family?"

"Yes." I pass a plate and take my seat next to her. Grabbing the remote, I turn on the TV, settling on a random movie channel, and wait for her reaction.

"Ooh. Fools Rush In. One of my favorites." Leah smiles, then lifts her fork, taking a bite. She moans as she finishes her bite then gets her fork ready for another. "The man can cook," she moans around her fork again after taking another taste of food, and the sound goes straight to my cock.

"My turn," I tell her then take a bite of my food. "Will you have dinner with me again?" My question is not what she was expecting, and her fork freezes mid-air as she goes to take another bite. Leah turns her head, looking at me.

"That's it? You're wasting your one question to ask me out?"

I continue to eat my meal.

"Like a date?" she questions as if she might have misunderstood me.

"Yes. A date," I clarify. What she doesn't know is the date will be a first for me. I've had women—plenty of them. But I didn't date until now. Leah makes me crave things in life I've never wanted before.

"I'd like that." She finally puts me out of my misery, and the smile that follows seals the deal.

Finished with our dinner, we sit and watch the remainder of the movie. It was your typical boy meets girl; they fall in love and live happily ever after. I never watch shit like this. I don't cook women dinner, and I sure as hell don't watch sappy ass movies with them. I fuck. That's it.

But Leah is different. Fuck, what is this woman doing to me? I steal glances at Leah, her eyes glued to the TV screen, and wonder, does shit like that exists? She's in danger already. Am I selfish by pursuing her? My family has enemies. Being the son of Demetri Volkov has put a mark on my life more than I can count. If I cross the wrong person, they will kill her just to watch me suffer. Am I willing to risk all of that by loving someone?

By the time the movie has ended, Leah has snuggled into the corner of the plush cushion and is fast asleep. I glance at the time. It's late. Instead of waking her, I stand. Tucking my arms beneath her, I lift Leah from the sofa, pulling her close to my chest, as she buries her face in the crook of my neck. Carrying her upstairs to my room, I lay her down, gently on my bed, remove her glasses, and set them on the nightstand. Then I pull the comforter from the foot of the bed and cover her.

Moving to the chair in front of the window, I sit in the dark, watching her sleep.

10

LEAH

Before I open my eyes, I am aware I'm not in my own bed. The smell lingering on the pillow is what tips me off. I'd know Nikolai's scent anywhere.

Opening my eyes, I blink a few times and rub my palms over my face as I sit up. To my right, I spot my glasses on the table beside the bed and slide them on. The once blurry bedroom comes into focus, and I take in every detail. Nikolai's room is like the rest of his house—framed in dark, rich wood with dark gray walls. I can tell by the view coming from the floor to ceiling window, I'm on the second floor. Nikolai's four-poster bed is larger than the average king and is the same dark finish as the rest of the house. It also sits at least three feet off the floor. My gaze lands on the space beside me, still neatly made, and I realize I slept alone. I don't miss the loose change, wallet, and empty glass sitting on the table with the smallest amount of brown liquid resting in the bottom. Nikolai didn't sleep in the bed with me, but he was in here at some point. I should probably be freaking out because I just woke up in his bed, but I'm not. The only thing I feel is safe. It dawns on me last night was the first night in a long time the monster that haunts my dreams at night was silenced.

Smiling, I blow out a breath and throw myself back on the pillow. Being in Nikolai's home feels like a dream. I know he was just being a good guy by taking care of me yesterday and letting me crash here since I must have fallen asleep during the movie. But what's the harm in taking a few minutes to pretend I'm in his bed for a different reason. A girl can dream, right? Only in my dreams could a man like Nikolai be interested in a girl like me. Nikolai Volkov, next in line to the Volkov Empire, brother to the Vice President of The Kings of Retribution, owner of Kings Construction and the hottest most beautiful man to walk this earth is not in the same league as me. Heck, I'm still trying to figure out why he's insisting on helping me out and dragging me here to his house yesterday. At that thought, something ugly settles in my gut. Is he doing all this because he feels sorry for me? Is that why he asked me on a date last night? Suddenly, I start questioning his motives. I'm aware the people in my life, my friends, want to help and protect me, but most of the time, the way I'm treated makes me feel like a charity case like they see me as weak. I know that's not their intent. Mostly it's me conjuring negative thoughts up inside my head. It's not lost on me; I haven't gotten a handle on my insecurities. Not wanting to start my day off in a bad place, I file those thoughts away so I can stew on them later in the privacy of my own home. If I'm going to have a pity party, I'd rather it be a party of one.

Deciding it's time to get up, I climb out of bed but stop when something grabs my attention, and I catch the squeal that nearly escapes my mouth. That something is my reflection, directly above me, is a mirror. Holy crap!

As my mind starts drifting as to why Nikolai has a mirror strategically placed there, I toss the sheet back and jump out of bed. I don't want to think about the women he's brought home;

the women he has shared his bed with and watched do things that someone like me can only dream about. I might be naïve in some ways, but I'm not so naïve. I don't know why he has that mirror.

Still, in yesterday's clothes, I pad over to the en-suite bathroom. Flicking the light on, I see a spare toothbrush sitting next to the sink. Once I finish taking care of business, washing my face, and brushing my teeth, I decide to go search for Nikolai before I head home. The first place I look is downstairs in the living room. When I don't see him there or the kitchen, I head to the gym. When I hear metal hitting metal, I know I have found him. Nikolai is lying with his back against the weight bench, his legs straddling each side as he presses the weights. I can't help taking in the way his shorts sit low on his hips and the way his muscles flex with each press. My eyes take the time to travel over his broad chest, glistening with sweat, then follow the path of the light dusting of chest hair leading down between his six-pack abs and disappearing into the waistband of his shorts. Even the grunt that comes from his mouth as he lifts the weights is sexy. Not wanting to bother him or get caught perving, I head back to the kitchen. Since Nikolai cooked for me last night, it's only right I make him a quick breakfast before I go. Plus, I need my morning caffeine fix.

Twenty minutes later, I've sucked back a cup of coffee and made Nikolai some cream cheese stuffed French toast with an omelet covered in onions, red peppers, and mushrooms. Nikolai's kitchen is a dream. I could spend hours here. It has a country cottage feel with a down to earth style, making the space homey, comfortable and inviting. The kitchen is painted in glazed cabinets, a farmhouse sink, and open shelving. It also has two gas stoves, two ovens, and two microwaves. Once I have finished admiring my dream kitchen, I get back to work on breakfast.

I've just wrapped the plate for Nikolai in foil and in the process of slinging my purse over my shoulder when Nikolai's deep, velvety voice rings out from behind me, making me jump. "Going somewhere?"

I push my glasses up my nose. "Uh... I'm going to head out. I made you breakfast. Just a little thank you for yesterday," I stammer, sounding like an idiot as I try not to look at the beads of sweat dripping down his bare torso but fail. I also can't help taking in the colorful tattoos covering his chest and arms. Or the piercings he's sporting in both his nipples. Good lord!

When my gaze flicks back to Nikolai's face, his smirk is a good indication he caught me ogling. My face heats with embarrassment, and cast my eyes down to my feet and mumble. "I'll... I'll just get out of your hair."

As I shuffle past Nikolai, his hand clamps down on my elbow, halting my retreat. "Stay. Eat breakfast with me."

"I need to go. I only made enough for you," I'm quick to say, my flight mode kicking in. I'm desperate to scram before I embarrass myself further.

"I'm sure there is enough. We can share."

Not giving me a choice, Nikolai keeps his hold on my arm and walks me over to the kitchen island, pulls out a stool, takes my purse from me by sliding off my shoulder, setting it on the counter effectively puts me where he wants me. He then takes the seat next to me. He's so close. His scent assaults my senses. Who smells good even when they sweat?

No words are spoken. I watch as Nikolai vacates his stool, and rounds the island. Reaching above the counter, he pulls down two glasses, then retrieves the orange juice from the refrigerator, filling both. After he slides both glasses toward me, Nikolai grabs two forks from the drawer. Once he sits back down, he hands me a fork and removes the foil from the plate. "Eat, Malyshka."

There it is again—him calling me that name. Just the sound of his thick Russian accent makes my insides melt.

"This is fucking good. Where'd you learn to cook like this?" he asks around a mouth full of food.

"My neighbor, who lives across the street from my parents, Mrs. Mae, taught me."

"What about your mother? Didn't you cook with her growing up?"

I take a small bite of eggs and shrug. "Not really. My mom didn't have a lot of patience when it came to stuff like that. I didn't have many friends, so I spent all my free time with Mrs. Mae. She loved to cook and bake, and she loved teaching me."

"This woman, Mrs. Mae, means a lot to you?"

"Yes. I don't know what I would have done without her growing up. I know it sounds stupid that a sixty-seven-year-old woman was a little girl's best friend, but she was. She still is."

"That doesn't sound stupid at all, Leah," Nikolai says with sincerity, and I smile.

"Anyway, it turns out I have a knack for it. At first, it was small stuff like cookies. Soon, I was cooking all kinds of things. I make a mean Bolognese."

"Sounds good. You can make it for me tonight."

"What?" I nearly choke on the eggs in my mouth.

"I'm looking forward to it, Malyshka."

"I can't cook for you tonight, Nikolai."

"Sure, you can." He goes about eating as if he didn't just hear me.

"I... I have things to do today," I lie. "Maybe I can cook for you some other time."

Nikolai turns his head toward me. "What are your plans?"

Shit. Think, Leah. "Well, my car is due for an oil change, so I was going to take it to Jake. After that, I need to do my shopping for the week." That's another lie. My car is not due for an oil change for another month.

"No problem. I'll have Maxim take your car in, and I'll drive you to the store. We can pick up what you need to make dinner tonight."

"But... I."

"Finish eating, Leah, so that we can go."

I sit with my mouth hanging open while Nikolai goes back to eating. Several seconds pass with no other excuses coming to mind. Finally, I relent. It looks like I'm making Nikolai dinner tonight. I'll admit, the idea of spending another day with him has me giddy.

After we finish eating, Nikolai excuses himself to take a shower. Once he comes back downstairs, I follow him out through the side door in the kitchen, which leads to the garage. As soon as we step through, motion sensors activate, lighting the room. In the garage sits Nikolai's motorcycle, a black truck, a Mercedes, and a Jaguar. Nikolai leads me over to the Jag, where he hits the button on the key fob in his hand and opens the passenger door for me.

"Can we stop by my apartment so I can change into some fresh clothes?" I ask when Nikolai slides into the driver seat beside me a second later.

Nikolai hits a button on the visor, activating the garage door. "No problem."

As soon as we back out, Nikolai spots Maxim exiting the front door of the house. He stops, rolls the window down, and waits for Maxim to approach the car. He turns to me. "Give me the keys to your car."

Fishing the keys from my purse, I hand them over to Nikolai, who then hands them to Maxim. "Take Leah's car to get the oil changed and whatever else it might need."

Maxim jerks his chin. "Yes, sir."

On the ride to my place, I remain quiet. I think back to a moment ago when Nikolai ordered Maxim to handle my car. I think about his home, the garage full of luxury cars, and I think about my knowledge of the man sitting next to me. Though I have not come out and asked Alba or any of The Kings, it's no secret who the Volkov's are. Nikolai was rather forthcoming last night when I asked him if his family is mafia. And the more time I spend around him, the more questions I have. What is his role in the family? What kinds of businesses do they have? Why does he choose to stay primarily in Polson? Does he miss his home country? Will he ever go back?

"What are you thinking about so hard over there?" Nikolai asks, snapping me out of my wandering thoughts.

"Do you miss your home?"

Nikolai's eyes flick toward me then back to the road. "Russia?"

I nod. "Yeah. Do you miss it?"

"Not really, no. Polson is my home now. Everyone and everything I care about is here."

I watch as something flashes across Nikolai's face as he answers my question, and I decide not to pry any further on the topic of his home country. Instead, I stick to what makes him happy, his family.

"You have an amazing family. Logan and Bella are great. So are Bree and little Jake."

At the mention of his niece and nephew, Nikolai grins. "They are, aren't they? I'm truly fortunate to have found my brother and been able to watch him grow his family. Family is everything."

I give Nikolai a small smile. "Yeah. It's fortunate when you have a family as great as yours."

Nikolai doesn't say anything in response, but by the soft look he gives me, he knows my comment has deep meaning.

THIRTY MINUTES LATER, Nikolai and I are scouring the produce section of the grocery store when an odd feeling creeps up my spine. A sense of awareness washes over me like I'm being watched. Only when I look over my shoulder, I don't see anyone except for the older couple standing next to the peaches. I try to shake the weird feeling away, but a hint of something continues to linger. Still feeling uneasy, I seek out Nikolai, who has made his way over to the deli about thirty feet away. He has his phone to his ear and is scanning the area like he's looking for someone. When his eyes lock on mine, he wastes no time eating up the distance between us. The moment he is at my side once again, my shoulders slump, and my body relaxes—something that doesn't go unnoticed by him as he places his palm on the small of my back. Maybe he senses that being around him puts me at ease.

"Get back to me," he barks into his phone before hanging up, his full attention now on me. "You good?"

"Yeah, I'm good. I only need a few more things then we can go."

Nikolai gives me a tight nod, and I wonder what has made his mood flip. Has he changed his mind about my cooking him dinner?

"Is everything alright? You can take me to my car, and I can come back and finish my shopping later."

Nikolai's face softens, and he winks. "Not a chance, Malyshka."

I smile. That's five times he's called me Malyshka which is the Russian word for baby. Everytime he says it, my knees go weak. And yes, I'm counting.

Just as Nikolai goes to speak again, he's interrupted by someone calling out my name. "Leah?"

Turning, I see Rhett, the guy who owns the gym and teaches the self-defense classes I inquired about, striding toward me. He has a big smile on his face but loses it when his focus lands on the man beside me. Suddenly there is a shift in the air around us, and Nikolai stiffens. Rhett stops two feet in front of me.

"Hi Rhett," I give him a little wave.

"I thought that was you I saw from across the way. You haven't been back by the gym, and you never called. I wanted to see if you had given any more thought to the class or my offer?"

I go to answer Rhett only to have Nikolai jump in and answer for me. "Leah will not require your services," he clips, bringing his arm up from behind me and gently but firmly grips my neck. I shiver when his thumb strokes the spot behind my ear. The move doesn't go unnoticed by Rhett, whose eyes lock on Nikolai's hand.

"No disrespect, man, but I was talking to Leah. It's my understanding she had an incident that made her feel unsafe, so she came to my gym for help. I teach self-defense," Rhett informs Nikolai. And as soon as the words leave his mouth, the atmosphere in our little circle changes, and I swear Nikolai grows a foot taller. His entire demeanor morphs and his accent became more pronounced with his next statement.

"Well, now, you are speaking to me. I am informing you, Leah does not require your services, professional or personal. I will see to her safety and her needs."

"And who is it I'm speaking to?"

"Nikolai Volkov."

Recognition flashes across Rhett's face, and he doesn't do an excellent job at hiding his shock. My guess would be he has heard of the Volkov name. The Volkov's have made a name for themselves in Polson as much as The Kings. The two men engage in an intense stare off for several seconds. Along with the words that just came out of Nikolai's mouth, has me reeling.

Once Rhett tears his eyes away from Nikolai, he brings his attention back to me. He looks like he wants to say something but doesn't. When he regards Nikolai for the last time, he gives him a chin lift. "Understood."

Understood? What does he understand?

Nikolai nods. "Good."

Now I'm confused. What does Rhett understand? What the heck just happened. Why would Rhett and Nikolai hold some sort of macho man stand-off in the middle of the grocery store? Was Alba, right? Does Rhett like me?

. . .

ON THE WAY back to my apartment, I muster up the guts to ask him the question that's been plaguing me since his showdown with Rhett. "Nikolai?"

"Yeah?"

I rub my palms up and down my pant legs. "What was the deal between you and Rhett back at the store? You were kind of mean to him, and he was only being nice to me."

Nikolai's grip on the steering wheel tightens as he answers. "I put him in his place."

Still confused, I ask, "What's his place?"

Nikolai takes his eyes off the road, leveling me with a look. Suddenly it feels like all the oxygen is sucked from the car. "Anywhere you're not."

Holy crap! What do I say to that?

11

NIKOLAI

The remainder of the short ride to Leah's apartment is filled with silence. My mood sour, after the call I received. I keep stealing glances her way only to find her staring out the window. She seems to be unsure of my brief interaction with Rhett. My intentions of taking my time with Leah will remain the same as before, but I have no problem making sure every man in this town knows she is mine. Rhett appears to be a good man. I don't know him personally, but I am aware of his contribution to our town. By the look of recognition when I gave my name, he's heard of me as well. Turning onto the road leading to the apartment complex, I circle the building, looking for anything suspicious before parking my car. Unbuckling, Leah swings her door open.

"Um. I'll be back in a few minutes." She slides her purse over her shoulder.

"I'm coming with you." I cut the engine and pocket the keys. Before she can protest, I'm out of the car and at her side. "Keys," I hold out my hand. Leah sighs as she digs in her bag, then hands them over. Using this opportunity to show her a small but important lesson, I tell her, "Always have your keys in your hand before exiting your vehicle." Flipping the key, I place the narrow, jagged end between my fingers so that it juts out like a knife's blade, and make a fist. "Holding your key like this provides you with a weapon. If someone attempts to grab you, swing, and aim for their face." Not moving, I open my fist. "Show me."

Leah does as I ask, exactly how I demonstrated. "Like this?"

"Good," I tell her. My hand settles on her lower back as we climb the stairs. Once inside, I linger by the door. Tossing her bag on a chair nearby, Leah throws me a quick look over her shoulder.

"Be right back."

While waiting, my mind drifts back to the call from Maxim. Pulling my phone from my pocket, I call Jake. He picks up on the third ring.

"Nikolai. How's it going?"

"Jake." The tone in my voice alerts him.

"Talk to me."

"Word is there's someone in town asking questions about Leah Winters."

"Fuck. I'll get the men on it," Jake says, and I have no doubts. That man knows almost everyone in this town. The club will find the fucker who's nosing around.

"When you find the son of a bitch..."

"You'll be the first to know, brother." Jake ends the call at the exact moment, Leah steps into the living room, wearing a knee length summer dress. "Everything okay?"

"It will be." I'm honest with her without divulging anything. She hesitates for a moment like she wants to ask more but doesn't. "Ready?" I ask.

"Ready."

Twenty minutes later, we're back at my place unpacking the items Leah needed for dinner. Crossing the kitchen, she peers out of the large window at the trees bending from the strong winds outside. "Looks like a nasty summer storm is moving in."

The storm threatening to move in hours ago has finally made its appearance with a vengeance. "I should get home before the weather gets worse." Leah tosses the couch pillow she's holding on her lap to the side and stands. No way in hell she's driving anywhere tonight.

"You'll stay here."

Her eyes widen. "Nikolai. I'm not taking your bed from you again. I need to go home."

I stand. "I'm not letting you drive in that." I point outside just as lightning lights the night sky, thunder follows, rattling the glass window panes.

"I'll drive slow and take my time." Leah looks anywhere but at my face while fidgeting with her glasses. She is so fucking adorable.

"Do I make you uncomfortable?" I take a step forward, looking down at her.

"A little."

At least she's honest.

I run my finger along the side of her cheek, tracing her jawline, then lift her face, bringing her eyes to meet mine. The sweet scent of the strawberry ice cream she just finished still lingers on her breath. "I have no issues with you sleeping in my bed, Malyshka." The way she nervously chews on her bottom lip has the act going straight to my cock. Damn. I want her so bad it hurts.

"Nikolai, I..." Leah's words are breathy from the effect I'm having on her. The woman has no idea she is my undoing. Reining in my desire to claim every inch of Leah's body, I take a step back, giving us both the space we need. "You can stay in the guestroom down the hall from mine if it puts you at ease, but you will be staying."

"If you don't mind, I think I'll turn in for the night."

Grabbing the remote from the coffee table, I turn off the TV. "I'll show you to your room." I take her hand, lacing her fingers with mine. Once upstairs, I lead her past my bedroom. Opening the door, I guide her inside the guest room, which looks much like mine but smaller. "You have a bathroom to yourself," I tell her, and she glances around the space. "Wait here."

Leaving Leah, I stride to my room, go into my closet, and snag a clean t-shirt, and sweat pants from one of the shelves. When I get back to her room, I find Leah staring out of the window overlooking the lake. She peers back at me over her shoulder. "There's something peaceful about stormy nights."

"I agree." I cross the room toward her, spellbound as I listen.

Leah hugs herself as she continues to watch the rainfall. "Wild winds and heavy rain. It feels like a reflection of myself and the chaos I feel inside. But, it's the wrinkle in time after lightning strikes. Just before the thunder?" Leah sighs, sounding a bit emotional. "I wait for those moments of peace. Not the calm before the storm, but the calm within it." Suddenly, Leah stops talking and faces me. "I'm sorry," she apologizes, and I don't understand why.

"Sorry for what?"

"I don't know." Her eyes fall to the floor.

"Don't do that again."

Leah's head jerks up. "Do what?" her eyes widen.

"Don't ever apologize for being who you are. You just shared something beautiful about yourself and how you feel. That is never something you are to be sorry for, Malyshka."

I place the clothes I'm holding in her hands, and she looks at them. "For you to change into."

"These won't fit." She tries to hand them back.

"They will fit." My eyes stay locked on hers, and all I can think is how much I want to kiss her. The worst part—I could tell she wanted it too. I fight my urges and take a deep breath. I need to put space between us before acting on my thoughts. "Goodnight, Malyshka."

"Goodnight, Nikolai."

Instead of returning to my room, I head downstairs to the office, where I lock myself away for hours, thumbing through all the information gathered on Leah's father as I might come across something I or someone else may have missed, but knowing I won't. I throw the papers onto the desk.

Crossing the room, I pour myself a drink. Leah is never going to feel safe until she's free of him for good. Cop or not, I want to kill the bastard. I'd like to make him suffer and pay for all the hell he ever put my woman through. Turning off the lights, I sink into the leather chair and stare out the window. I try to clear my head of everything, only for all my thought to lead back to one person. Leah Winters.

Hours later, I wake to the fact I'd fallen asleep, my drink still in my hand resting on the arm of the chair. Suddenly the silence is interrupted by soft piano music, and I'm on my feet. What the fuck? I pull my gun from the desk drawer, gripping it firmly in my hand as I open the door and make my way through the house's shadows. My steps slow when I notice Leah sitting at the baby grand piano. Transfixed on every note she plays, I watch her fingers dancing along the ivory keys. I watch her body come alive as she continues to play. Slow yet mesmerizing, the music seeps into my soul. Quietly, I put my gun away—my heart beating with each tap of the keys as I quietly move toward her. The beautiful melody pours from her body as her fingertips move with the grace of a well-seasoned pianist. Her haunted eyes open to meet mine as I gaze upon her. To my surprise, she keeps playing. She's so fucking beautiful. It's like nothing I've ever heard before. Leah is telling me her story of pain, sorrow, and fear. I stand watching her until she hits the last beautiful note.

Once more, she avoids my eyes and stands from the bench. "Why do you feel obligated to take care of me—to protect me?"

The pain in her voice causes my chest to tighten. "I'm not worth it." Her eyes stayed fixed on the floor.

Reaching for her, I grab her wrist, pulling her to me, and place her between me and the piano. "I do it because I want to—because I need to." Leah turns her head. "Look at me." Slowly, she brings her stunning eyes to meet mine. "You have worth, Leah." Unable to hold back, I grasp her face in my hands and press my lips against hers. Just like I knew it would be, her kiss is so damn sweet. She's shocked and hesitant at first but soon melts against my touch. With every ounce of willpower, I pull away from her before it goes any further—before lifting her sweet ass onto this piano, spreading her legs and making her come screaming my name.

"We should get some rest." Her big eyes look up at me, stunned, but she doesn't say a word, so I lead her back up the stairs. Before passing my room, Leah slows.

"I can't sleep."

I look at her waiting for her to explain further.

"Bad dreams. It's why I wandered downstairs in the first place," she admits.

Instead of leading her to the guest room, we step into mine and I lead her to my bed. I begin removing my shirt and notice the deer in headlights look on her face. "Get in, beautiful." Leah hesitates. Leaving my pants on, I slide into bed and lift the covers. "We're just sleeping. Nothing more." She removes her glasses from her face, placing them on the nightstand, then slips in beside me. Keeping a small space between us, Leah rolls to her side, staring at me.

Silence hangs between us.

Not one word is spoken.

My eyes grow heavy and start to drag shut as I watch Leah finally fall over. It doesn't take long until I slip off to sleep myself.

JUST BEFORE SUNRISE the following morning, I wake to Leah draped over half of my body, with one of her legs between mine, pressed firmly against my hard cock. Her light snoring causes me to chuckle, which wakes her from sleep. The moment she realizes her body is pressed against mine, she stiffens.

"Oh my God," she whispers, and I try to suppress more laughter. Leah slowly raises her head. At the same time, she works at extracting her leg from between mine. I can't hold back my grin when her eyes meet mine.

"Good morning."

"Hi," she says shyly, her face reddening from embarrassment.

I snake my arm around her, keeping her in place, and take her in as she hovers above me, her wild curls framing her beautiful face. "A man could get spoiled waking to such beauty," I confess, and her face flushes a pretty shade of pink. I'm just about to claim her lips like I did the night before when the moment is interrupted by a knock on my bedroom door.

"Nikolai," Maxim calls out from the other side.

"It better be good, Maxim," I warn, not taking my eyes off my woman.

"Your father is home."

My father is home sooner than expected. That can't be good. Letting Leah pull away, I watch her disappear into the bathroom as I climb out of bed. Snatching my shirt from where I tossed it last night, I pull it on over my head and cross the room. I open the bedroom door to find Maxim waiting. "It's early, Maxim." I run my hand down my face.

"There is a pressing matter that cannot wait." The urgency in his voice sets me on edge. "Does this have anything to do with Leah?"

"No," Maxim is quick to assure.

"Make sure Leah gets home."

"Yes, sir," Maxim walks away.

Closing the door, I turn around and find Leah standing outside the bathroom with a worried look on her face, letting me know she heard part of my brief conversation. Meeting her across the room, I brush the hair from her face and kiss her forehead. "I need to take care of an urgent matter. Maxim will follow you home as soon as you're ready."

"Is it my father?" her voice shakes, and I hate that the mere thought of him frightens her this way.

"No," I tell her truthfully, but I can tell by her body language that my admission doesn't put her at ease. "I may be indisposed for a day or two. If you need anything, promise me you won't hesitate to call." Leah doesn't answer right away, so I tilt her head back, bringing her eyes to mine. "Promise me."

Leah swallows. "I promise."

"Good." I run the pad of my thumb across her lower lip, and her eyes flutter. Lowering my head, my lips brush hers for a second time.

Moments later, I'm fully dressed and have retrieved the weapon that I left downstairs. Slipping my gun into my side holster, I meet my father outside in the SUV, where he is waiting. I hate leaving Leah so abruptly, but knowing Maxim will make sure she gets home safely puts my mind at ease. The instant I climb inside, Victor pulls away. "Where are we going?"

"The Kings' compound. Jake asked for our assistance in getting rid of a problem they are having with Savage Outlaws," my father says, looking tired.

The ride is short, and minutes later, we are pulling up to The Kings clubhouse. Upon entering the building, we find the men hanging around the bar. "I heard some trash rolled into town, so I came to offer my assistance." My father greets them as we stride across the room, with Victor following.

Logan steps up, pulling our father in for a hug, and does the same to me. "Thanks for coming down."

Just as Jake announces he's waiting on a few more men to show, he sets his beer down, then pulls his phone from his pocket. "Our guests have arrived," he grins.

The unmistakable rumble of Harley engines grabs every man's attention. One by one, we file outside. Several men pull their bikes alongside the others parked in the front yard. Each man dismounting their bikes wears The Kings of Retribution insignia. The one wearing the President's patch brushes dust from his cut, then extends his hand to Jake. "I hope we're not late for the party," he grins.

"Just on fuckin' time, brother." Jake turns to face my father and me. "Demetri, Nikolai, this here is Riggs, Fender, and Kiwi. They're members of our Louisiana chapter. Men," he looks to his club members, "meet Demetri and Nikolai Volkov." There's a round of handshakes exchanged amongst us.

"I've heard of you, Volkov's. It's good to meet ya," Riggs says as Jake leads everyone indoors where we sidle up to the bar for drinks. Several of the women venture out of the kitchen to see who has arrived. While nursing a cold beer, I watch and listen to Jake introduce Sam's woman to Riggs, and fill her in on the club's decision to send another woman they've been helping with Riggs back to Louisiana. Luna has a past that is trying to catch up with her. It damn sure doesn't make it any easier the fact that she doesn't speak. "Bring her out," I hear Riggs exclaim.

A few minutes later, Sofia walks downstairs with a frightened Luna at her side. The way she shrinks beneath Riggs' hard stare and avoids making eye contact with him reminds me of Leah. The poor girl becomes frantic after being told she'll be leaving her new home for another with a man she just met. I think I can safely say that just about every man in the room is shocked as shit when Riggs stands from his stool and starts to sign as he speaks to Luna, and speaks loudly as he assures her she will be safe with him and his men. He promises to protect her and keep her safe. As with most women, Luna doesn't take to being told what to do very well, and her hands move feverishly telling Riggs just what she thinks about it.

Riggs chuckles at her defiance. "Looks like I just did, sweetheart."

Luna goes to protest further, but Jake steps in. "Alright. That's enough."

Quinn being himself, opens his mouth. "Come on now, Prez. Where's the popcorn. This shit was gettin' interesting. I want to see what happens."

The rest of us chuckle. Quinn is one of a kind and always finds a way to lighten a tense situation. Riggs' eyes follow Luna as she retreats upstairs. Before long, we're all back to drinking as Jake lays out his plan of attack against the Savage Outlaw.

HOURS LATER, the clubhouse erupts into chaos. Grabbing our weapons, my father and I rush downstairs to see what the hell is going on. It turns out Luna and Sofia were taken. All the men huddle around the security feed Reid pulls up on his computer. Luna had slipped out the back door, walking away from the clubhouse. But what she wasn't aware of was Sofia followed her. Before she could convince Luna to return, a couple of men stepped out from the fog beyond the treeline, taking them by gunpoint.

As we gear up for war against the men who took them, I can't help but worry about Leah. The current situation doesn't put her in any immediate danger, but it reminds me that she is hiding from a threat of her own.

After being asked to canvas the streets, looking for any indication of which way they would have gone, my father, along with Victor and I, load up in the SUV and take off down the road. The streets are dark as we search for clues. It's not long before I spot activity down the road near the old paper mill. "Stop here," I tell Victor, and he turns the headlights off, then pulls on to the side of the road. I point through the window. "You see what I see?"

"Bikers," my father states and retrieves his phone from his pocket. "We have eyes on the place—the old paper mill. From here, we count at least thirteen Savage Outlaw. We will stay in place until you arrive," my father ends the call.

Keeping watch, we wait.

Jake and his men surge past us, rolling in hot on Savage Outlaws, and we fall in behind them. Gunfire erupts, and bullets pepper the side of our SUV. "Looks like we have a runner," Victor yells above the noise. Peering out the windshield, we watch the biker who held a gun to The Kings' women, mount a bike, and speed away from the carnage.

"Follow him," my father orders, and Victor takes off after him.

The biker guns it when he realizes he's being followed. Taking a sharp turn onto a dirt road, he loses control of his bike, laying it on its side. He skids several yards before coming to a stop. Victor brings the vehicle to a halt, and I swing the back door open. The fucker struggles to get his leg from beneath the weight of the motorcycle.

I pull my gun and point it at his head.

"Pull the trigger, motherfucker!" the asshole spits.

"You're not mine to kill," I tell him before knocking him out with a boot to the head.

"Load him up," my father says. Victor and I lift his dead weight from the ground, then toss him in the back, and haul ass back to the clubhouse with a little gift.

12

LEAH

It's been two days since Nikolai, and I shared a kiss. He didn't come into work yesterday either because some stuff went down with the club involving Sam and his girlfriend, Sofia. Sam and Sofia are new, but he's been in love with her forever. Long story short, Sofia and another woman connected to The Kings were kidnapped. I have noticed a pattern over the last year when it comes to The Kings' women. Trouble seems to follow them everywhere. Lucky for them, they all have men who will go to the ends of the earth to keep them safe.

"What's running through your head, Leah?" Alba asks. "You look a million miles away."

It's Saturday, and yesterday Alba stopped by my work, insisting I go shopping with her and Bella today. For once, I didn't fight her on the invitation. Surprisingly, I have wanted to buy new clothes. I don't know if it's how Nikolai makes me feel when he looks at me or how he makes it a point to tell me how beautiful I am, but I find myself more confident and comfortable in my skin.

Snapping out of my musings, I look over the top of the

clothing rack at Alba. "I was just thinking about Sam and Sofia. I'm relieved her, and that the other woman are okay."

"Me too. Thank God she has Sam."

"Yeah. I'm happy for him. They're perfect together," I add.

Alba smiles. "They are."

"Hey." Bella comes to stand next to Alba. "You two want to hit up Grace's for some coffee?"

"I'm in. Just let me pay for this dress, and we can go." I hold up the white vintage floral summer dress.

"Oh, Leah. That's a gorgeous dress," Bella boasts.

"Yeah, Leah. That dress will look hot on you," Alba agrees. Then her lip tips up in a smirk. "You wouldn't be buying that for anyone in particular, would you? Say a certain hot Russian?"

I bite the inside of my cheek. Alba hit the mark. She takes my silence as a yes to her question, and her smirk turns into a full-blown smile. "Okay. I'm going to need you to hurry up and pay so that we can get to Grace's. This conversation needs to happen over coffee and whatever mouthwatering goodness Grace has for us today."

"I second that." Bella ushers me to the register. "I need details."

"Guys, there's nothing to tell."

"We'll be the judge of that," Bella says, and I roll my eyes.

Twenty minutes later, the three of us are sitting inside The Cookie Jar with coffee and fresh-baked cinnamon buns. I pick at my food and take a sip of my coffee while trying to ignore the sisters sitting in front of me. Alba is not having any of that, though.

"Okay, spill."

"I already told you, there is nothing to spill." The moment the words tumble out of my mouth, my thoughts drift back to mine, and Nikolai's kiss and my cheeks heat.

"Liar. You're blushing," Alba calls me out.

I sigh. "Fine. Nikolai kissed me."

I nearly jump out of my seat at the sound of the squeals

coming from Alba and Bella. The sound of metal crashing to the floor from behind the counter where Grace just dropped a pan, because she too was startled. Alba gives Grace a sheepish look. "Sorry, Grace."

She turns back to me. "When did this happen?"

I shrug. "A couple of days ago."

"What! And I'm just now hearing about it?"

I sigh. "It's not a big deal. It was one kiss."

Bella smiles. "Oh, I think it's a huge deal. Nikolai has been waiting a long time to make his move on you. No way will he stop at one kiss." She shakes her head. "That man is just getting started."

"What do you mean he's been waiting a long time?"

Bella's face goes soft. "Leah, that man cares about you. Everyone can see it. As for his reasons, he has waited so long to make it known, are his own."

Alba doesn't hesitate to add her two cents, either. "I'm willing to bet Nikolai is giving you signals that he wants you. I know you, Leah. You're twisting all those things inside your head to make it seem like what's going on between you two is nothing."

I don't bother arguing with Alba's theory. Part of me knows she's telling the truth. It's easier for me to think that way, though. If I don't, I won't set myself up for disappointment.

"Has Nikolai ever given you reason not to believe his intentions are genuine?" This question is coming from Bella.

I shake my head.

Bella reaches across the table and squeezes my arm. "My advice, Leah, is to go with it. Trust in his words and trust in his actions. Try not to get inside your head and turn what you and Nikolai are building into something it's not."

"Do you think something is there between us?"

"Yes," Alba and Bella say in unison.

A second later, my cell phone vibrates against the table with an incoming call. I look down to see it's Nikolai calling. I answer.

"Hello."

"Malyshka," Nikolai rumbles into the phone, and I shiver.

"Hi, Nikolai." I can't stop my voice from sounding breathless. My conversation has also caught Alba and Bella's attention. The sisters look on with interest. They don't bother trying to hide the fact either.

"Where are you?"

"I'm at the bakery with Bella and Alba. We went shopping and then decided to stop by Grace's for a coffee."

Nikolai goes to say something else, but the chime of his doorbell in the background cuts him off.

"Let me call you back."

"Oh, okay."

I hang up and see Bella and Alba looking at me expectantly. "What?"

"He calls you, Malyshka?" Alba swoons.

"You heard that?"

"Oh, yeah. I didn't make out everything he said, but I heard. What did he want?"

I take another sip of coffee. "I don't know. He didn't get a chance to say. There was someone at his door. He said he'd call back."

"Why don't you take him some fresh baked cookies or something," Bella suggests.

"Nikolai likes the blueberry muffins," Grace calls out from somewhere in the back. She's heard our entire conversation and is on board with Bella and Alba's idea. A second later, she appears behind the counter then proceeds to bag two muffins and fixes two coffees to go. "Here you go, sweetheart." Grace sets the bag and beverages on the table in front of me.

"I can't just show up at his house uninvited."

"Sure, you can," Bella urges.

I nibble on my bottom lip, contemplating the idea. Finally, I decide what the heck. Standing, I swipe the bag of muffins from the table.

"That's what I'm talking about." Alba throws her fist in the air. "Go see your man."

I roll my eyes but can't stop the giggle that escapes my mouth as I leave the bakery. Once in my car, I spy the bag sitting on the passenger seat containing my new dress and decide to make a quick detour to my apartment.

Fifteen minutes later, I'm standing in front of the mirror, staring at myself wearing my latest purchase. The white floral vintage dress has a V-neck that shows a decent amount of cleavage but not so much I'd consider it inappropriate. And the hem ends just above the knees. I decided to let my curls flow free by letting my hair down and running my fingers through it. Next, I pair the dress with a simple pair of sandals. Not wanting to overdo it with makeup, I opt for my favorite red berry lip gloss. Besides, my glasses tend to hide any effort I put toward wearing eye makeup. Maybe I should consider contacts.

Somewhat satisfied with my look, I take a deep breath. "You can do this, Leah. Just go over there and act casual. How hard can it be?" I mutter to myself as I turn away from the mirror and make my way out to the living room. Grabbing my things, I step out of the apartment, take in my surroundings, then turn and lock the door. Jiggling the knob, I double-check to make sure it's secure. When I twist back around and start heading down the steps and toward my car, the sudden overwhelming sense of being watched washes over me, it's the same feeling that came over me in the grocery store the other day. Peering around the parking lot, I spot the woman who lives two units down from me, unbuckling her kid from the backseat of her car. Turning, she notices me looking in her direction and waves. I smile and wave back. Shaking off my previous thoughts, I climb into my car and drive to Nikolai's.

When I clear the long winding road that leads to his house, I curiously eye the white SUV parked out front. From the looks of it, he has company. Parking my car next to the SUV, I cut the engine and second-guess my showing up at Nikolai's house uninvited. After being a chicken for five minutes, I elect to follow through with my original plan. Snatching my purse, I sling it over my shoulder, then grab the bag of muffins and the now cold coffee that I'll have to warm up in the microwave. With my hands full, I bump the car door with my hip, closing it. When I reach the front door, I hit the doorbell with my elbow. I don't have to wait long before the door swings open. But the sight that greets me knocks all the air from my lungs. A tall, slim beautiful woman with long, straight black hair and perfect porcelain skin, wearing an expensive-looking, emerald green wrap dress with five-inch heels, greets me. "Can I help you?" she asks in a distinct Russian accent.

I go to open my mouth, but no words come out. The woman speaks again.

"Are you deaf, or are you mute? I asked, can I help you?" This time her tone goes from sugary sweet to nasty.

"I...Is Nikolai here?"

The woman stands taller and narrows her eyes down at me. "Are you the cleaning lady or something? The cook?" The woman smiles, but it's not warm. And I start to feel self-conscious about the way she appraises me. "The cook. You look like a woman who likes food."

Her comment burns, and I try desperately not to let her see just how much.

"We won't require your services today. We'll be dining out."

"Wh..what?"

"We don't need you to cook today. My Nikolai is taking me out.

It's been weeks since I've seen him, and he likes to spoil me, so he'll be taking me out to dinner."

Suddenly my mouth goes dry, and my heart breaks into a million pieces.

"Are you...are you, his girlfriend?" I choke out.

"Girlfriend?" the woman giggles. "No. Niki is my fiancé."

As the word fiancé leaves her mouth, the world around me tips on an axis, and I struggle to swallow the bile that rises in my throat. Turning, I stumble down the steps in front of the door, falling to my knees. I cry out a sob when the gravel digs into my flesh. The coffee and muffins I was carrying spill out onto the ground in front of me. I ignore the burning pain coming from my scraped knees and the voice of the woman behind me, demanding I clean the mess as I climb to my feet and run to my car. Once inside, I fumble with the keys as I try to control my breathing. Please, God. Now is not the time for an asthma attack. I have to get out of here. Finally, the key slips into the ignition, I put the car in drive and peel away from Nikolai's house. Once I hit the main road, I get the inhaler I keep in the console, place it to my mouth, and administer the desperately needed medicine, taking three deep breaths.

"You're an idiot, Leah. How could you be so stupid," I chastise myself. What was I thinking of buying this ridiculous dress and showing up at his house? Of course, he wouldn't look at me twice when he has a woman like that. I just made a fool of myself. How am I supposed to face him after this? I bet him, and his fiancé is having a good laugh at my expense too. My father was right. No man wants a woman who looks like me.

A choking cry escapes my mouth as I swipe at the tears rolling down my face. What's confusing is Nikolai's recent behavior. I mean, why the kiss? Why the late-night dinners and the sleeping over because he's worried about me? Is it because he feels sorry for me? Poor, shy, damaged Leah needs a man to take pity on her.

Make her feel special; make her feel important. Maybe Nikolai thinks he can have his cake and eat it too. Well, screw him.

I shake my head.

No.

The problem is me.

Bella and Alba were wrong. I should have been listening to that little voice inside my head. Had I been, I wouldn't have gone to his house today, putting myself in that humiliating position.

Stopping at a red light, I dig some tissue from my purse and wipe my eyes. The car behind me honks, indicating the light has turned green. Tossing the tissue to the seat beside me, I slide my glasses back on and accelerate through the intersection. The next thing I know, my ears are assaulted by the sound of screeching tires and metal hitting metal as my car is suddenly jerked to the left, causing my seat belt to lock up tight across my chest. The airbag deploys, and a scream escapes my lips just before everything goes black.

13

NIKOLAI

It's been a couple of days since I've seen Leah. Between helping The Kings and tying up some loose ends my father needed me to handle via video meeting with one of our suppliers, I haven't left the house. Then I find out my mother arrived in town late last night. What fucking business does she have here in the States? Furthermore, what made her think her presence in Polson would be welcomed. The only reason I've invited her to the house this morning is to find out why and inform her she is to go back home to Russia. Good thing my father left for Chicago a couple of nights ago. He's warned her numerous times never to show her face. Turning off the water, I step from the shower. My sour mood turns to rage when my eyes find Katya, a woman from my past, sitting on the foot of my bed, leaning back on her elbows.

"What the fuck are you doing here?"

"Come now. Is that how you greet a lover?" Her blue eyes looked me up and down.

"Stop looking at my dick." I snatch the towel off the hook nearby and wrap it around my waist. "Why are you here?"

Katya rises from the bed. "Your mother invited me." She

saunters across the floor in her short dress and five-inch heels. I roll my eyes. She always did try too hard. "I miss you. You never called the last time you came home." Katya pouts. "I have a hunger only you can feed, my love," she tries removing my towel, and I grab her by the wrist, stopping her from making a mistake.

"I have no need for you, Katya."

Ever persistent, and turned on by my aggression, Katya's nipples harden. She presses her body against mine. "I like it when you play rough," she whispers.

Grabbing a handful of her hair, I jerk her head back, her eyes instantly glazing with lust. "Do not cross me, Katya. Now. Leave." The warning tone of my voices takes her by surprise, and her eyes widen in fear.

"You would never hurt me." Katya searches my eyes.

"You are nothing to me." Releasing her, I turn my back, head for the closet and get dressed. When I walk back out, Katya is standing where I left her. She says nothing as her eyes follow me around the room while I collect my weapon, placing it in the holster on my side.

"A woman showed up on your doorstep this morning. She didn't say her name, but I believe she was the cleaning lady or your cook."

Turning, I give her my attention. The vengeful look on her face gives me cause for concern. Katya is a spiteful, jealous woman. "What did you do?" I demand to know.

Shrugging, she says, "I told her the truth. That you are mine."

Her words enrage me, and I'm in her face before she has time to draw another breath. "I belong to only one woman, and it isn't you. It. Will. Never. Be. You." I look down at her.

Katya juts her chin in defiance. "You would choose that cow over me?"

"You are not half the woman she is." My nostrils flare.

Katya gasps. "You love her?" she questions, but I do not answer.

There's a knock on the door, and it swings open. "Sir," Maxim's eyes dart from me to Katya. "Leah was involved in an accident. She's been taken to the hospital."

My eyes land on Katya's face for what will be the last time. "You are to leave my home. If you ever show disrespect by speaking to my family or me again, I will not hesitate to have you killed," I warn her, then rush out of the room and sprint down the stairs. I notice my mother through the open door of my father's office, sitting on the leather sofa. She calls out to me, but I ignore her. "I want them gone by the time I return," I yell to Maxim as he tosses me my bike keys.

"Yes, sir."

I'm not sure how long it took me to get to the hospital, but I gunned it the entire way. Several bikes belonging to men I know sit parked near the emergency room entrance as I bring my bike to a jolting stop. I run through the doors, where Jake and Logan meet me. To my right, the waiting room is filled with some of their women, along with Quinn and Sam. The only men missing are Gabriel and Reid. My speed slows a bit, but I keep moving forward, my eyes set on the doors ahead.

"Shit," Logan mumbles as he and Jake fall in behind me.

"Sir. Sir," a nurse calls to me as I ignore the do not enter signs and barge through the double doors to find my woman.

A male doctor steps in front of me, holding up his hand. "Sir, I'm going to have to ask you to leave."

My feet never stop moving as my hand grips the collar of his shirt, making him backpedal until his back hits the wall. "Stay out of my way."

"Let him go, brother." Logan steps to my side. "Come on. We've all been there. Control yourself."

"Shit. What is it with you men? Nikolai, please let go of Dr. Holland." The use of my name snaps my head in the direction the voice came from. I see Emerson, Quinn's woman, standing at the nurse's station. My fingers go lax, and I release my hold on the doctor, then step away.

I turn my attention to Emerson. "Where is she?"

Emerson's face softens. "Leah is resting."

My patience is wearing thin, and I'm barely hanging on by a thread. I repeat myself. "Where is she?"

"Let's step out into the waiting room for a moment." Emerson looks around, and I take in the fact we have an audience. When I don't make a motion to move, Emerson sighs. "She's in a room getting cleaned up. Leah has a few bumps and bruises. Other than that, I promise she is going to be okay."

"Then take me to her," I demand.

"She doesn't want to see you," Emerson tells me, and I lose my shit.

"The fuck?" Emerson's words feel like a slap to my face, and my brother clamps his hand on my shoulder. I shrug off the hold he has on me. "I want to hear this from her myself." The cords in my neck tighten as I attempt to keep my anger in check.

"I'm sorry, Nikolai. Leah was adamant. I have to ask you to leave." Emerson gives me a final look before turning and walking away.

Every fiber of my being wants to tear this hospital apart until I find my woman. My hands clench at my sides.

"Let's get some air. We need to talk," Jake says.

Unwilling, I follow Jake outside, along with my brother, leaving their women sitting in the waiting room. "I need answers." I roar, then begin to pace to keep myself from losing my mind and barging back inside.

"From what we have learned, the accident was intentional." Logan's words stop me in my tracks. "Eyewitnesses confirm the SUV that plowed into Leah's car was at a complete stop just before gunning for her. He managed to take off on foot before the cops got to the scene."

"Some sorry motherfucker purposefully tried to hurt my woman." The new information pushes me past the boiling point, and the first person that comes to mind is her father. "I want him found." I go to pull my phone from my pocket to make a call.

"Gabriel is out huntin' down the son of a bitch now," Jake says. "With any luck, he'll find him before the cops do."

I level Jake with a hard stare. "He's mine." No sooner do the words leave my mouth, Jake's phone rings, and he pulls it from the inside of his cut.

"What ya got for me, brother?" Jake speaks into the phone. His eyes remain on my face, and judging by his expression, I won't be waiting long to get my hands on the man we're after. "We'll meet you there." Jake slips his phone away, then looks between Logan and me. "Logan, go tell the others we're heading back to the clubhouse." Once Logan walks through the doors, Jake turns his attention back on me. "You claimin' her, son?"

Jake is a good man, and I have a lot of respect for him, so I don't hesitate to confirm something he already knows. "She's mine." None of this would have happened if my mother and Katya hadn't come to Polson. Words of doubt were planted in Leah's head, and now I must try to undo them. If she doesn't want to see me, I will give her the space she needs for now. "Leah needs protection. If she is unwilling to let me provide that, I will ask that you and your men do it for me. She shouldn't be alone."

"Agreed," Jake nods.

I run my palm down my face, letting out a heavy breath of frustration. "I'd prefer she stay at the clubhouse."

"Done," Jake agrees as Quinn and Sam walk out with Logan. "Prospect." Jake grabs Sam's attention. "Stay here. As soon as they discharge Leah, take her to the clubhouse. She's to remain there until further notice." Sam's eyes fall on me for a beat before nodding and walking back inside. "Alright," Jake announces. "Let's ride."

Twenty minutes later, we all arrive at the clubhouse. Instead of parking out front, then heading inside to the basement, Jake leads us to the backside of the property, a reasonable distance from the main building, to a rundown barn. There, I notice a van parked nearby. Dismounting our bikes, we go to enter the old structure. Quinn pulls open the barn doors causing the rusty metal hinges to screech. "Now, there's a sound I haven't heard in some time."

Inside we find Gabriel standing by a dark-haired man, his hands bound at his wrist by thick rope, strung up above his head, his feet barely touching the dirt floor. He's already bleeding from his busted nose. I look to Gabriel, who shrugs. "He needed a little convincing to join the party."

Walking up to our guest of honor, I bury my fist in his gut, causing him to sway. Fuck. Hitting him feels good, so I do it again. "Who are you?" my accent comes out thick.

"Man, fuck you." The man spits at my feet.

"Wrong answer." I land a few more blows, this time to his ribs until he's coughing for air. "Who do you work for?"

The asshole is still coughing, laughing maniacally. "You may as well kill me because I'm not sayin' shit."

If pain is what he is after, I'm happy to deliver. For the next thirty minutes, I beat him, only stopping after I've broken every rib in his body, and blood gurgles from his mouth. His body hangs limp, but he still breathes. I give the poor bastard one more chance, even though it will not spare him his life. "Who sent you?"

Struggling to breathe, the man forces his words out on shallow breaths. "I'm ready to die."

I look over my shoulder, where Jake and the others stand by watching. Without asking if he or his men would like to have a go at him, I pull my gun, face the motherfucker who dares to harm my woman and press the end of the barrel into his eye socket. "Then I'm your executioner."

I pull the trigger.

14

LEAH

Hearing Nikola's raised voice from behind the closed curtain, causes me to jump. I recognize several other voices, two being Sam and Jake. I close my eyes, and my heart rate begins to slow. I told Emerson I didn't want to see him. She came to me moments ago, saying he insisted on coming back. I'm not sure why he's even here or why he cares.

"Hey." I open my eyes and squint to see Sam pull back the drape. He steps up beside the hospital bed I'm currently laying in.

"Where are your glasses, darlin'? Sam asks.

"They broke when the airbag hit my face."

He winces. I haven't seen my face yet, but I'm relatively sure I have some bruising from the way it feels. Luckily, that's the extent of my injuries. No broken bones. Just some scrapes and bruises from the airbag.

"Thank fuckin', God, you were wearing a seatbelt." Sam kisses the top of my head.

"Yeah, lucky me," I say with a sigh. "Pretty sure my car is not as fortunate, though."

"Who the hell cares about a car, Leah. What matters is that you're okay. You scared the shit out of everyone."

"I'm fine, Sam. It's not a big deal. I must not have been paying attention. I thought the light was green. And as you can see, I'll live. Just a few scrapes and bruises."

"What's the deal with you not letting Nikolai come back?"

Crap. I should have known he was going to ask that question. Especially with the scene, Nikolai was making out in the waiting room earlier.

"There is no deal, Sam."

"I'm guessin' there is," he counters, holding my stare.

"Nikolai, for whatever reason, thinks he has a right to be here, and he doesn't."

"You sure about that, sweetheart?"

I give Sam a sharp look. "Yes."

I can tell he's holding back from wanting to say more but smartly keeps his words to himself. He, instead, changes the subject.

"Doc says she's lettin' you go home soon. It's decided you are to stay at the clubhouse for now."

I sit up straight in the bed. "Why do I need to stay at the clubhouse? There is nothing wrong with me. I'd rather go home."

Sam shakes his head. "Sorry, darlin'. The decision was made."

"By whom? Don't I have a say?"

"Everyone would feel a lot better if you came to the clubhouse for a couple of days to recuperate."

"I already told you I was fine, Sam. I don't..."

Sam cuts me off. "Please, Leah. For peace of mind. At least do it for me."

My shoulders slump, and I give in. Sam wouldn't insist unless it were important to him. "Fine. I'll stay at the clubhouse. But only for a day or two."

He kisses the top of my head again. "Thanks, sweetheart."

"Yeah, yeah. Now can you go find out when I'll be getting out of here."

Twenty minutes later, Sam comes back, pushing a wheelchair with Emerson trailing behind. "Good news," she smiles. "I'm letting you out of here. All your tests came back clear. My only recommendation is to take an over the counter pain reliever every few hours and get some rest. You might feel fine now, but you'll probably wake up sore tomorrow. The abrasion across your chest, caused by the seat belt, will be the worst."

I nod. "Thanks, Dr. Beckett." With Sam's help, I climb out of the hospital bed and into the wheelchair. Not wanting to run into Nikolai in the hall, I look up at Sam and ask, "Has everyone left?"

"He's not out there," he assures.

"Who?" I ask, playing dumb. My friend doesn't let me, though.

"Nikolai." Sam wheels me through the hospital entrance to where his truck is idling just beyond the revolving doors.

"I wasn't asking about him," I snip.

Sam sets the breaks on the chair, walks in front of me, and opens the passenger door to his truck. He raises a brow. "Yes, you were."

I ignore the way he silently calls me out as I climb into the truck.

We're almost to the clubhouse when Sam tells me, "Alba and Sofia went to your place to get some of your things. They should be at the clubhouse by now."

"Hmm," I hum my response while leaning my head back on the headrest and gazing out the window.

"You know you can talk to me about anything, Leah. I know I've had a lot going on with the club and with Sofia, but I'll always make time for you."

"I know, Sam. But I promise I'm okay." The lie rolls off my tongue effortlessly. The truth is, I'm not okay. My heart feels like it's been shattered into a million pieces. I stupidly let my brain conjure up crazy notions about Nikolai. I led myself to believe it was possible he felt the same way about me as I do about him. I had been a fool, and now I am paying the price. Nikolai only sees me as a friend, and I twisted it into something it wasn't. Sure, we had kissed, but anyone can slip in the heat of the moment. That just goes to show how inexperienced I am when it comes to men. I've never had a boyfriend and never been kissed until Nikolai. I cannot believe the first time a man shows me a hint of attention, I immediately make it into something it's not. How am I going to face him at work after this?

IT'S BEEN an hour since Sam dropped me here at the clubhouse. When I arrived, Ember and Raine didn't waste any time showing me to my room. Or should I say Nikolai's room? I know it's his because the sheets smell like him. I'd know that scent anywhere. It's ingrained in me. I may have gone rummaging through the dresser drawers and closet, spotting his clothes and a familiar pair of work boots next to the bed. Being in his space is like rubbing salt into the wound.

Sighing, I sit down on the edge of the bed and look down at my dress. The one I wore specifically for Nikolai, and now it's ruined with not only the memory of what happened when I showed up at his house but also my blood from the bloody nose I received as a result of the car accident. A second later there is a knock at the door, followed by Alba poking her head in. "Hi."

I give her a small smile. "Hi."

"You feel like company?"

"Sure."

Alba steps fully into the room, closing the door behind her. She does a full-body scan, her eyes stopping on my ruined dress. "Did you need help with anything? Were the clothes I brought you okay?"

"Yeah. I just haven't had a chance to take a shower."

Alba sits on the end of the bed next to me, biting her lip. Something she does when she is contemplating saying what's on her mind.

"Do you want to talk about what happened?"

"It was just a little accident, Alba. Nothing to worry about, and I'm fine."

I swear if I say the word "fine" one more time, I'm going to scream.

"That's not really what I was asking. I'm talking about what happened after the accident when Nikolai showed up at the hospital ready to crack heads to get to you, and then telling Emerson you didn't want to see him."

Closing my eyes, I take a deep breath. "I made a mistake."

"What do you mean?"

"I mean, I made a mistake by showing up to Nikolai's house."

Alba waits for me to elaborate, and when I don't, she asks, "How was that a mistake?"

I look down at my feet when I reply, so Alba can't see the hurt written all over my face, though she can hear the pain in my voice when I speak. "Nikolai's fiancé answered the door when I went."

Alba gasps at my confession. "Leah, that can't be right. Nikolai doesn't have a girlfriend, let alone a fiancé."

I snap my head toward her. "I'm pretty sure I didn't misinterpret the woman's words. She stated in clear English, she is Nikolai's fiancé."

Alba begins shaking her head, clearly not believing me. "No. No way. You have to talk to him, Leah."

"I'm not talking to Nikolai. There is nothing to say. His personal life is not my business. I shouldn't have thought otherwise. Clearly, he sees me as a friend and an employee. The kiss was a fluke."

"Leah..."

I cut her off. "No. What's done is done, and I'm not talking to him about it. I want to forget this day ever happened." I look at Alba with pleading eyes. "Can we please drop it."

Alba wants to argue, but she doesn't. "Okay, Leah."

"Thank you." I rub my hands over my face, suddenly feeling tired.

"I'm going to go so you can shower and rest." Alba stands and gives me a gentle hug. "I'll come and check on you in a bit."

"Thanks, Alba."

Once Alba leaves, I go through the bag she brought containing my clothes, finding a clean t-shirt and a pair of sweatpants. What I wish I had are my glasses. First thing tomorrow, I need to call an optometrist and set up an appointment to get a new pair. I'm blind without them.

With my clothes in hand, I pad into the en-suite bathroom. Flicking on the light, I come face to face with more reminders of the man I need to forget about. A bottle of his cologne sits next to the sink, along with his toothbrush. Shaking thoughts of him away, I strip out of my dress and toss it in the trash bin beside the toilet. After I remove my bra and underwear, I pull the shower curtain back and turn it on. While it heats, I appraise myself in the mirror. The bruising to my face is minimal—nothing a little makeup can't cover. But the long diagonal red and purple mark across my chest where the seat belt locked me in, is sore and angry looking. Hopefully, the hot water will help.

After spending longer than usual in the shower, I finish drying my body and pull on my sweatpants and tee. I was right. The shower went a long way in making me feel better. As I exit the bathroom, I stifle a yawn and toss the wet towel in the hamper sitting next to the dresser. The room is dark now that the sun has begun to set, so I turn on the TV. I can't see a thing on the screen, but the glow lights up the room, and I like having background noise to drown out my thoughts.

The moment the TV comes on, something sitting on the table beside the bed catches my eye. There is a black rectangular case that wasn't there before. I cut my eyes over to the door to see it's still closed. Walking over to the table, I pick up the box and sit on the edge of the bed. The box is not mine, but it is familiar. I've had one like it my whole life. I open the top and laying inside the case is a brand new pair of glasses. They are a deep purple color and more beautiful than any pair I've had before. The name on the case tells me they cost more than what I could afford too. With the glasses is a small folded piece of paper. With shaky hands, I unfold it, already knowing who they are from.

I thought you might need these, Malyshka.
~Nikolai

15

NIKOLAI

Shortly after my mother left town, I got word that Glory was threatened. I didn't hesitate to call my father, who insisted I remain in Polson. He also informed me the man who is now dead had a Russian accent. With strict orders, our men have the estate on lockdown, and The Kings have done the same at their compound, which makes the entire situation between Leah and me more complicated.

Not being able to sleep, I head for the gym to work out my frustrations. After a few hours of hitting the heavy bag, and running several miles on the treadmill, I'm no less tense than I was when I started. My concentration sucks. No matter what I do, thoughts of Leah plague me. I've tried to get her to listen to reason numerous times, calling and texting her to give me a chance to explain. All her doubts are the direct results of a spiteful woman. The bitch doesn't mean shit to me. Katya knew the terms of our interludes, and I thought I had made it clear more than a year ago that our little arrangement was over.

A short time later, I'm sitting in my office, going over contracts, and building permits when I receive a call from Jake. Already on edge with everything that is going on, my first thought is of Leah. "Jake."

"How's it going', brother?" Jake asks, and from the relaxed tone of his voice, I know his calling isn't an emergency.

"Work is keeping me occupied," I give a short pause before asking, "How is Leah?"

"Your woman is doing fine. Rest assured, she is safe." Jake clears his throat. "But that is not why I have called. I've gotten my hands on some information about Leah's father." The moment Jake makes mention of James Winters, I close the folder in front of me.

"You have my full attention."

"Seems our clean-cut, God-fearing, officer of the law likes to frequent a strip club a couple of towns over twice a month."

Leaning back in my chair, I run my hand through my hair. "You have the address to this club?" I ask.

"I do, and I'm texting the information as we speak," Jakes says, and my phone pings. "He's a creature of habit. Never misses an appointment. He'll be there tonight."

"I believe it's finally time I introduce myself." My body starts humming at the thought of coming face to face with Leah's abuser.

"Why don't you take one of my men with you," Jake offers. "You never know what kind of trouble you'll run into. The Kings have your back—always."

"Thanks," I tell Jake, knowing who I want at my side. "For everything," I add.

"No thanks needed. We're family."

After ending the phone call with Jake, I receive an email from my guy doing his own investigative work. Opening the email, I find what I'm looking at is Leah's medical records. Leaning closer to the computer screen, I scroll through page after page of her painful past. My woman suffered more than any child should ever have. Broken bones. A couple of concussions. Bruises. Why weren't these ever reported? An ache forms in my chest. Having seen enough, I turn off the computer and stand.

The monster inside of me seeks retribution for my woman, and I intend to give into its hunger.

Later that night, my brother and I sit in the smoke-filled strip club, the walls vibrating from the music as heavy bass passes through the speakers overhead. The room itself darkens, as one of the dancers finishes her routine on the stage. While we wait for our guest of honor to arrive, Logan flags a waitress to our table, located in the back of the room. "I don't believe I've seen you two here before," she hooks her thumb in the loop of her leather shorts. "You're not from around here, are you? What can I get for you?" she asks.

"A beer," Logan orders, not answering her first question.

"Sure thing," the young woman nods then looks at me, waiting for my reply.

"I'll have the same." She smiles and heads for the bar. When she returns, she sits the bottles on the table. "Which one is Trina?" I ask the waitress as my eyes travel around the room. Her eyes grow big for a moment before responding.

"Look, if you're here to start trouble, I'll get Robert over there," her head jerks in the direction of the bar, where a large man wearing a shirt with security written across the front stands, "to escort you out of the building." I study her face for a second. She's afraid.

"We are not here to harm her. She knows someone we would like to have a chat with."

She eyes my brother and me. "You're looking at her." The waitress straightens her back. Just as I suspected. I look at my brother then back to her.

"James Winters." The moment I speak his name, her body tenses, and she visibly swallows. When she doesn't talk, I continue. "You're afraid of him." It's not a question but a statement. "Which room?" I ask.

She blinks a few times. "What?"

"He asked you which room in the back will we find him in later tonight?"

"If he finds out I had anything to do with..."

I interrupt her. "He won't harm you. This, I swear."

Another set of music begins to play as a woman takes the stage. "My set is next," she turns to walk away but pauses. "Room 6, at the end of the hall. I'll leave the door unlocked." Not looking back, she retreats.

"Think we can trust her?" Logan lifts his beer and takes a drink.

"She's afraid of him."

Logan nods. "I noticed that too. The moment you mentioned the fucker's name, she turned white as a ghost."

"Leah's father is hiding his true self."

"Look," Logan jerks his head in the direction of the entrance, and my eyes fall on the sorry bastard making his way across the room. He's so close I can smell his cheap cologne as he passes by on his way to an empty seat beside the catwalk. My stare never leaves the back of his head. The music changes once more, and Trina takes the stage, but my focus is solely on Leah's father. After Trina exits the stage, James gets up from his seat. He crosses the room, where he talks to a bald man, then slips him a large wad of cash. He then walks down the hall, where he disappears into a room.

"How do we get past the jughead there?" Logan questions

"We pay," I shrug, gripping the bottle in my hand that I have yet to touch.

"Shit." Logan downs the rest of his beer. "I figured you'd say that."

I stand, and Logan falls in behind me as I stride across the room. We stop in front of the bald guy, and his eyes narrow.

"What the fuck do you want?"

"We're lookin' for a private party," Logan answers.

The guy's eyes dart between my brother and me. "Five hundred for one hour." he stares us down. Movement at the end of the hall behind him catches my attention. Looking past his shoulder, I watch Trina enter the same room Leah's father did. Just as she closes the door, her eyes connect with mine, and I know I will have my vengeance tonight. Pulling a wad of rolled-up cash from the front pocket of my jeans, thumb through the large bills, counting out the price the guy quotes. "Five hundred per customer," he adds. Without hesitating, I count out the rest of the money and hand it to him. He snatches it from my hand. "Room five." He recounts the money. "By the way. If you break it, you buy it," he calls over his shoulder as we walk down the hall.

"This place isn't your ordinary strip club," Logan states. Judging by the bald guy's comment, I would have to agree.

We pause a beat outside room five, and I take a glance down the hall. The guy who took my money stands with his back to us as he watches the girls on the stage. With his attention diverted, we move to room six and twist the doorknob. It's unlocked just as Trina said. My brother and I slip inside.

Once in the room, we find Trina grinding against a blindfolded James, his pants around his ankles. I look around us, taking in the space. There are items used for bondage play attached to every wall. I pull my gun from the concealed holster beneath my shirt. Trina nods, knowing it's time for her to exit the room.

Leaning forward, she whispers seductively in James's ear. "Are you ready for me?"

"Fuck yeah. Give it to me," James says, rubbing his dick through his boxers, as Trina grabs her robe nearby and leaves the room. Logan stands at the door, locking it.

As I press the barrel end of my gun to the middle of James's forehead, he releases his dick. "What the fuck?" his back pushes further into the sofa he's sitting on, and he holds his hands up in the air. I pull the blindfold from his eyes, wanting him to see my face. "Who the fuck are you?" he spits, not showing any fear, then his eyes find Logan standing behind me. "What the hell is going on? You have no idea who you are fucking with right now," he says through clenched teeth.

Wrapping my fingers around his neck, I haul his sorry ass off the sofa. He struggles under my hold, which only has me squeezing tighter, cutting off his oxygen flow. His eyes bulge from the pressure, and he pries at my fingers, seeking relief. I throw him against the wall where a cross with leather straps is mounted. Logan quickly aids me in binding his wrists. Logan then hands me a large ballgag, which I forcefully shove into the bastard's mouth then fasten it as tight as I can. James gags and coughs around the contraption in his mouth, desperately trying to pull air in through his nose.

"Now that I have your undivided attention." I let my hand holding my gun hang at my side while I speak. "My name is Nikolai Volkov." Recognition flashes across his face at the mention of my name. "I see you have heard of me. Good. Then you may also know why I am here." James's eyes follow me as I pace in front of him. "You see, I don't have proof yet, but I suspect that you were behind your daughter's accident the other day." I stop in front of him and look him in the eyes. "You've taken from my woman for the last time." James pulls against his restraints as he tries to kick me. "I'm here to warn you never again to speak her name. You are dead to her. If you ever come near Leah again, I will end your worthless existence. Nothing will bring me greater pleasure than to take your life with my bare hands."

I hand Logan my weapon. "But first, you're going to know what life has been like for your daughter." I backhand him across his face, leaving an imprint on his cheek of my family crest from the ring on my finger. Not stopping, I grind my knuckles into his torso like I would a heavy bag. James foams at the mouth as he tries not to choke on his spit. With every blow, I think of the medical reports I read earlier today, and every broken bone that was brushed off as a childhood mishap. I think about the mental abuse this motherfucker put her through daily, wearing her down until she no longer believed in herself.

Once I've exhausted myself, I stop. I won't take his life today. I want him to live in fear for the rest of his life. I want him to know what it feels like to always look over his shoulder, wondering if that day will be his last. I want him to fear me as Leah fears him. Stepping close to his defeated body, barely able to stand on his own two feet, I whisper. "Who's the monster now?" I seethe. "I'll be waiting for the day you fuck up, and I finally put a bullet in your head."

Turning my back on Leah's father, I approach the locked door. Logan hands back my gun, which I slip beneath my shirt. "Ready?" I give him a nod. Cracking the door open, Logan peeks out. "Coast is clear." As we're closing the door, Trina suddenly appears, motioning for us to follow her. She leads us through the women's dressing room, which leads to an exit door that reads employees only. The warm night air hits us the moment we step outside.

"Is he dead?" she asks, trying to keep up with me and my brother jogging toward the street.

Digging into my pocket, I pull out what's left of the cash I have and toss it to her. "Take this and get out of town," I say, leaving her standing in the club's parking lot.

Throwing my leg over my bike, I look to my brother. "Up for one more stop on the way home?"

"Where are we going, brother?"

"To pay Leah's mother a visit," I tell him.

Forty minutes later, we're rolling our bikes to a stop outside Leah's childhood home in a small quiet subdivision in Post Creek. "I'll wait for you here," Logan says as I'm walking up the sidewalk.

The porch light comes on the moment my foot hits the first step. A light inside comes on, and I see a shadowy figure moving across the window. The locks on the door make clicking sounds before the door opens, and Leah's mother greets me. Her tired eyes widen as she looks up at me. "May I help you?" her voice comes out weak and small, no doubt the direct results of all the years of hard living with a man like James Winters. Part of me feels sympathy for what she has been through, but it is shadowed by the years of abuse my woman suffered. What I feel for Leah, and the retribution I look to dish out toward those who inflicted the pain, or who stood by and did nothing outweighs any compassion I should have.

"How could you stand by for so long and allow your husband to torment your daughter? You're a pathetic excuse for a mother."

Her shaking hand clenches her chest. "Leah," she says as a whisper as her eyes fall to her feet. "How do you know my daughter?" she brings her attention back to my face.

"Leah is my woman." I watch as Mary Winters' demeanor changes slightly, and the unsureness she exuded before, gone.

"I see," she says, giving a look of disdain, judging me.

"You are a God-fearing woman, yes?" I ask, and she doesn't reply. "You stand there, judging someone you do not know, yet you have allowed your husband to break the spirit of a beautiful woman. You brought her into this world, and you should have protected her from filth like him." Mary crosses her arms. For a moment, I thought I saw a flicker of remorse in her eyes.

"My husband is a good man," her chin lifts in defiance as she defends the bastard. "If the only reason you came here tonight was to speak ill of my husband while you live in sin with my daughter, then I will have to ask you to leave." My disgust and anger grow stronger with each word she speaks.

"I paid your husband a little visit tonight, Mrs. Winters. We had ourselves a nice chat over at the strip club in the next town over from Post Creek." She turns her head, diverting her eyes from mine. "Ah, I see you are aware of your good husband's extracurricular activities. Yet, you still stand by him." Mary jerks her head, her eyes meeting mine once more.

"He is my husband," she retorts.

"Your daughter deserves better." I look down at Leah's mother. "I intend to give it to her. Her friends and I are her family now." Turning my back on the woman, I start to walk away.

"She is our daughter. You cannot keep her from us."

Spinning, I lock eyes with her. "I protect those I care for, Mrs. Winters. Anyone who dares to stand in the way of Leah's happiness or tries to harm her in any way will die," I threaten.

I make my way back to where my bike is parked beside my brother. "Mothers like that make me appreciate the short time I had with mine even more," he comments as I settle onto my leather seat.

"You were lucky to have the love of a mother like yours."

Logan glances my way. "Shit. I'm sorry, brother." His apology is not needed. He knows as well as I that my mother is nothing more than the woman who gave me life. Logan, for a short time, got to experience something I never had growing up. A mother's love. "So, where to next?" Logan asks, and I only have one answer.

"To get my woman."

The long stretch of road back to Polson felt like it would never end. All I could think about was Leah. I've had my fill of the distance she has put between us. It's past time I finally claim what is mine once and for all. When we arrive at the compound, Austin lets us through the gate. It appears that everyone is gathered here tonight as we park our bikes next to the others. Leaving my bike running, I swing open the clubhouse door and stride inside. On a mission, my eyes scan the room, not finding Leah amongst those hanging out in the common room, so I head for the stairs. Not one person says a word as I march by.

At the end of the upstairs hall, I zero in on the door to the bedroom, Leah occupies, which happens to be mine. Without knocking, I swing it open, finding her sitting on the bed beside her friend Alba. "Nikolai," her mouth falls open.

"We're leaving." I advance on her.

"I'm not talking to you." Leah crosses her arms beneath her breast, pushing them up.

"This ends tonight." Reaching down, I lift her from her seated position and throw her over my shoulder.

"Nikolai put me down," Leah yells in protest as I carry her ass down the stairs, where we are met by cheers and laughter from family and friends. With a smile on his face, Logan holds open the door as I exit the building.

16

LEAH

"Nikolai! What are you doing? Put me down." I ball up my fist and pound on his back, connecting with solid muscle, my blows having no effect whatsoever. "Have you lost your mind?"

"No, but you have," he growls. "Now, zip it."

My body goes solid. "You did not just tell me to shut up," I seethe.

Stopping next to his bike, Nikolai plants me on my feet. "Twenty-four hours," he grits, getting in my face. "I gave you twenty-four hours to work through the shit in your head and come to me. You didn't. Instead, you spent those twenty-four hours sitting here, stewing on bullshit instead of letting me explain what went down the other day at my house."

"Nikolai, I..." I go to say, but he cuts me off when his body pushes up against mine, backing me against his bike.

"Nope. You had your chance, Leah. You're so far inside your head you can't see what's been in front of you for an entire year."

All the air leaves my body at Nikolai's assessment, and I swallow.

"He fucked with your head your whole life, Leah," Nikolai says, ignoring the way my body jerks, and continues. I know he's referring to my father.

"That son of a bitch made you think so low of yourself that you can't even see what I have been laying out for you. But know this, after today, there will be not one ounce of doubt inside that gorgeous head of yours."

On that note, Nikolai straddles his bike then looks at me expectantly. "You can get your ass on the back of my bike on your own, or I'll put you there myself."

I don't think twice. I get on.

PULLING up in front of his house, Nikolai cuts the engine to his motorcycle and waits for me to climb off. When I do, I stand beside his bike and try to avoid the way his eyes are boring into mine. He doesn't speak, and neither do I. I can't help but wring my hands together in front of me as I think about what he said. There is some truth to his words. I also can't ignore the other facts that were front and center yesterday.

"Stop that, baby." Nikolai reaches over, covering my hands with his. The tone in his voice has gone from clipped to gentle. "No matter how pissed I get, I would never hurt you."

I swallow past the lump in my throat. "I... I know you wouldn't. I'm not scared of you, Nikolai. I just..." I sigh.

"You what? Tell me." He climbs off his bike.

"You're confusing me is all. I don't know what to make of what just happened back at the clubhouse. And whatever this is," I splay my hands out in front of me, "is overkill."

"What went down at the clubhouse was me showing my ass because my woman was showing her ass, and I'd had enough."

My heart skips a beat. "Your woman?" I whisper hiss.

"You sleep in my bed the other night?"

"Yes, but..."

"You let me taste your sweet lips that same night?"

My face heats. "Yes, but that..."

"That makes you mine."

Having enough of Nikolai cutting me off, I narrow my eyes and snap. "Your what, Nikolai? Your dirty secret you have on the side? What would your fiancé have to say about that?"

"Seeing that I do not have a fiancé, there is nothing to say." Nikolai's jaw ticks. "And had you let me explain that shit yesterday, you would know what that bitch said to you was a lie."

My next retort vanishes as Nikolai lays the truth out in black and white. I open and close my mouth, unable to string two words together.

"I see you're getting it now."

Shocked, I stay rooted in place. Nikolai takes a step in the direction of his house then stops as if he's waiting on me to follow.

"What, I get to walk this time?" The snarky comment rolls out of my mouth, shocking myself.

Nikolai's lip twitches. I squint and peer up at the amused look on his face. I don't like it. "I don't see anything funny about this situation, Nikolai. The past twenty-four hours have not been pleasant. I went from feeling happy for the first time in my life because I thought the man I had feelings for felt the same way, and in the blink of an eye, I had my heart ripped from my chest then stomped on by a pair of five-inch heels. I have been crushed, humiliated, and to top it off, I end up in a car accident to where I then spend an afternoon in the emergency room. Now, please tell me what part of all I just told you, do you find amusing?" By the time my mini-rant is over, Nikolai has dropped his smirk, and his body has gone rigid. He folds his body forward, getting in my space, one hand gripping the back of my neck, and the eyes I love so much pin me in place.

"Don't for one second think I get joy out of anything that causes you pain, Malyshka."

"Nikolai," I breathe, closing my eyes.

The grip on my neck tightens. Nikolai gently pulls me in closer, his hand still wrapped around the back of my neck. There is not one inch of space between our bodies and I suck in a sharp breath when my breasts press flush against the hard plains of his chest. "I'd sooner cut off my arm than to intentionally cause you pain, Leah. Yesterday, I fucked up. I was caught off guard by my mother showing up with Katya, but that's no excuse. I take full responsibility. Had I been there when you showed up on my doorstep, I..." he doesn't finish his sentence.

A flash of pain crosses Nikolai's face, and on instinct, I reach up and palm his cheek, running my fingers through his beard.

"Fuck, baby." He shakes his head. "When Maxim told me you had been in an accident, I lost it. All I could think about was getting to you."

"Nikolai," I whisper.

"No, Leah. You don't understand. The thought of losing you. Fuck." Nikolai rests his forehead against mine. I don't realize I am holding my breath until Nikolai says, "Breathe, Malyshka."

I do as he says, my breath washing over his face. I can't help looking at his mouth as he speaks. I bite my bottom lip at the memory of our kiss. And when a growl rumbles through Nikolai's chest, my gaze abandons his full lips and travels up his face to see his nostrils flare, and his pupils dilate. Suddenly my tummy flutters as I recognize the look he has. It's the same look he gave me the night I played for him. "Fuck it," he bites out just before his mouth crashes down on mine, breathing life back into me. One second, I feel empty, and the next, his kiss is giving me back all I lost.

· · ·

AN HOUR LATER, Nikolai is sitting on the sofa in the living room with Chinese takeout on the coffee table in front of us, and I am still trying to come down from my post kiss fog. Nikolai and I spent what seemed like forever exploring each other's mouths. That kiss left no doubt on exactly how he feels about me. But that doesn't mean I still don't have questions. I stab my chopsticks into my noodles, contemplating how to broach the subject of his mother. Nikolai and I have been spending a lot of time together, but he hasn't talked much about himself. Sure, we discussed his father and, of course, Logan, but never his mom. His confession about his mother showing up has me wanting to know more about his relationship with her. Although my gut tells me, it's not a good one.

Setting my food down on the table, I turn toward Nikolai, who is sitting beside me. His eyes are already assessing me, and I realize he must have been watching my contemplation the past few minutes because he too has stopped eating like he knew what conversation was coming.

"I've never heard you talk about your mom. Earlier, you said she showed up unannounced. Was that a good thing or bad?"

Nikolai lets out a heavy sigh. "Whenever something concerns my mother, you can assume it's bad. My mother has spent my whole life lying and manipulating me. She did the same to my father for the length of their marriage. The stunt she pulled yesterday with Katya was just another one of her tactics. To be clear, before this conversation about my mother goes any further, I want you to believe me when I say Katya was never my fiancé or girlfriend."

"She was someone you were intimate with, though, right?" Nikolai's jaw clenches, and he looks like he doesn't want to answer the question but does anyway.

"Yes. It's been over a year since I last saw her, though."

At his age, I knew Nikolai was no choir boy. But having it thrown in my face stung.

Nikolai cups my cheek. "I know that hurt you, Leah. I'd probably lose my shit if I ever come face to face with an old boyfriend." He shakes his head. "Fuck, I don't like even thinking about you with someone else."

An old boyfriend? Nikolai thinks I've had boyfriends. Oh, God. How embarrassing.

"Um...I don't have any ex-boyfriends." I look down at my lap, my face heating at my confession.

"What? Surely you..."

I shake my head before the last word leaves his mouth. Nikolai places his finger under my chin, forcing me to look up. "Are you telling me there has been no one before me?"

"No one."

"In every sense?"

My breathing picks up because I know he's referring to sex. "Yes," I whisper.

Nikolai's pupils dilate. The heat coming off him is palpable as he runs the pad of his thumb over my bottom lip. I don't know what possesses me to look down, but when I do, I gasp at the sight of his very noticeable erection, resting against the inside of his thigh, tightly concealed behind the zipper of his jeans. Realizing my mouth is hanging open, I snap it shut and bring my eyes back to his. Only his focus is not on my face. No, Nikolai's attention is on my chest. And when I look down, I see why. My nipples are peeking through the front of my t-shirt. My chest begins to rise and fall with my heavy breathing. Nikolai's arm that was resting on the back of the sofa drops to around my waist. The next thing I know, I'm straddling his lap, and his mouth is on mine. The moment my center presses down on his hard length, my mouth opens on a groan, and Nikolai takes full advantage, sneaking his tongue past my lips.

Breaking our kiss, Nikolai bites his way along my jaw, and his husky tone fills my ear. "I want to make you come. Will you let me?"

Unable to speak, I nod.

"Stand up, Malyshka."

Nervously, I slide off his lap and stand between his spread legs. He doesn't take his eyes off mine as he hooks his thumbs into the band of my leggings and drags them down my legs, leaving me in my panties. I grab hold of his shoulders as I step out of them. It takes all the strength I can muster not to fidget at how exposed I am. I fail when I fist the hem of my shirt and try pulling it down to cover myself.

Nikolai knocks my hands away. "Stop. Never hide from me. Do you understand? I love your body, Leah. You have the body of a woman." He runs his palms up my calves and over my thighs until both hands cup my butt. "Straddle me," he commands, his voice gruff.

Setting over his lap, with my knees on either side, Nikolai slips his hands under my shirt, cupping my full breast. My eyes close and I let out a throaty moan when he lightly pinches my nipples. His hands then travel to my back and downward, inside my panties. My nails dig into the flesh of his shoulders when one hand slowly makes its way to the front.

"Relax for me, Leah." At the soothing tone of his voice, I allow all the tension to leave my body and focus only on the pleasure Nikolai is giving me. The world around me fades away, and the only thing I feel is his touch.

"That's it, Leah. Let go and feel what your man is doing to you," Nikolai says just as his thumb presses against my clit the same time a second finger slips inside me.

"Fuck, you're so wet and tight."

"Oh, God." I moan. I've never felt anything this good. Not even when I touch myself does it feel anything like Nikolai's.

"That's it, Malyshka. Ride my hand. Take yourself there."

At his command, I grind down on his hand. My core tightens, and my center flutters. "Nikolai," I cry when the pleasure becomes too much.

"Let go, Leah."

The second my name rolls off Nikolai's tongue, my vision fills with white flashes of light. And just as my orgasm crashes through me, Nikolai's lips are on mine.

Minutes later, I am still coming down from my post-orgasmic high, when I barely register Nikolai standing from the sofa with me in his arms and climbing the stairs to his room where he lays me down on his bed. The last thing I remember before sleep takes me is having his scent surround me as the crisp, cool sheets touch my heated skin.

THE SOUND of a murmured voice wakes me from sleep. I open my eyes to see the bedroom cased in a warm glow from the floor lamp in the corner of the room. The space in the bed beside me is empty, and the sheet crumpled, letting me know I haven't been alone long. Sitting up, I find Nikolai standing at his floor to ceiling window with his back to me, wearing nothing but a pair of black boxer briefs. I take the time to appraise his muscular thighs, tight butt, and well-defined back—a tattoo of a massive black and grey dragon, which spans the width of his shoulders.

I'm brought out of my musings when Nikolai's tone to whoever he is talking to on the phone, turns angry. He's speaking in Russian, but from the sound of things, he's not happy. A second later, he takes the phone away from his ear and turns away from the window toward me. His face is hard, but the second his gaze lands on me, his features soften, and he saunters toward the bed. Setting his phone down, he pulls back the sheet and climbs in.

Next, he snags me around the waist and hauls me up. I lay my head on his chest. "Is everything okay?"

"Nothing for you to worry about, Malyshka."

The two of us fall quiet as Nikolai begins to run his fingers through my curls. After a few short seconds, he finally speaks. "Starting tomorrow, if you're not with me, I want Maxim taking you wherever you need to go."

At his random statement, I disentangle myself from his hold and sit on my knees, facing him. Nikolai follows suit by leaning his back against the headboard.

"Why? My apartment is close enough to everything in town, I can just walk to work every day, and I'm sure Alba or Sam will give me a ride to the store when needed. At least until my car is fixed or I can save to get a new one."

"First, you won't be fucking walking to work. I plan on you sleeping in my bed every night or vice versa, so I'll be the one taking you to work. And two, there is no need to ask Alba or Sam for a ride because, as I said, if you're not with me, you'll be with Maxim. He is not to leave your side."

An ugly feeling starts to creep up my spine at how adamant Nikolai is about Maxim. Something tells me there is more going on than I know. "Nikolai, why do I suddenly need a bodyguard?" my voice quivers.

"Fuck." Nikolai runs his palm down his face.

"Nikolai," I prompt.

"I have a bad feeling about your accident. I'm cautious until I know for sure your father wasn't involved."

At the mention of my dad, my body locks up, and my heart starts beating rapidly against my chest.

Nikolai reaches for me. "Breathe, Leah."

"Nikolai," I croak. "Is he...did he...?"

"That son of a bitch won't get near you. I'll kill him if he tries."

"How?"

"I have one of my men watching him. I also visited him yesterday."

Nikolai's admission shocks me. "You what!"

"I did some digging into your father. I know the club has been keeping an eye on him, but I wanted to know more. I told my guy to find me everything he could on James Winters. Only digging up shit on James Winters uncovered other things."

I don't miss the way Nikolai's jaw ticks when I ask, "What things?"

"A broken jaw, a fractured wrist, a broken arm, three concussions, stitches."

My nails dig into Nikolai's arm as he ticks off every documented injury I received at my father's hands as tears stream down my face.

"Jesus, baby. What the hell does a seven-year-old girl do to warrant having her jaw broken? Not a Goddamn thing."

"I saw something I wasn't supposed to. Then I opened my mouth about it."

The grip Nikolai has on my hair tightens but not painfully, and his eyes flare. "Say again?"

"Dad made sure I didn't open my mouth again." I put my hand over my mouth to stifle a sob. It's the first time I had spoken about what happened when I was seven. But with Nikolai, I feel safe enough to give him my demons, the things that eat me up inside, and haunt my dreams. And when Nikolai hauls me into his lap, I do just that. I tell him everything. I tell him about the night when I was seven and what I saw outside my bedroom window. The following morning, I learned my dad was not the hero I thought he was, and he has everyone believing he is a good guy. I told him how my father preached the word of God and, to this day, sits in the front row at church every Sunday, and how he raised me to talk, dress, and act in the way that best reflected his image. I told him how my father controlled every aspect of my life right down to the food I put in my mouth when I began to gain too much weight. And although I could feel how rigid Nikolai's body got with every truth that spilled from my mouth, I kept going. I kept going because I could feel the monster inside me, breaking free with every confession. Not once did Nikolai interrupt me, and by the time I was done, I felt like new, I felt as if the weight of the past twenty years had been lifted off my shoulders.

A long stretch of silence passes between Nikolai and me. I know he's absorbing what I just laid out for him. I don't know how much time has gone by before he finally speaks.

"Never again, Malyshka. Never again."

No clarification is needed. Nikolai has made a vow, and I trust him.

AN HOUR LATER, the heaviness of mine and Nikolai's previous conversation has faded, and now the two of us are sitting in the middle of his bed, eating our previously abandoned diner. I'm still in my t-shirt and panties; my hair probably looks like a rat's nest; my eyes feel like sandpaper from crying, and no doubt, my face is red and splotchy for the same reason. So, when I catch Nikolai staring at me, I pause mid-chew and ask, "What?"

"I'm just thinking about how beautiful you are and imagining what your pussy tastes like."

Not expecting that response, I begin to choke on my food. Nikolai smirks and passes me a bottle of water. After taking a hefty swallow and getting my bearings back, I glare. "You can't say stuff like that."

"You asked, babe."

My cheeks heat. "Well, If I had known you were going to say something like that, I wouldn't have asked."

Nikolai flashes me a smile. "You're gorgeous when you blush."

I groan and cover my face. "I hate my blush. Seriously, what do you see in me? I mean, look at us. I'm awkward, shy, nerdy, and all you have to do is look at me, and my face turns red."

"Malyshka." Nikolai grips my chin, keeping me from looking away "Those are all the things that make you, you. And I happened to like awkward, shy, and nerdy. I especially like your blush. You see those traits as flaws. I only see beauty."

17

NIKOLAI

Lying in bed, I lose myself in the warmth of my woman's curves. Waking up with Leah's body draped across mine, securely in my arms is the best fucking feeling in the world.

Last night was a significant tipping point in the start of a new beginning for both of us. I've never shared so much of myself with anyone. We talked for hours.

A knock on the door stirs Leah from sleep. "Sir," Maxim speaks from the hall. "Your father has landed, and requested you meet him at The Kings' compound." Shifting, I look at the alarm clock sitting on the nightstand, noticing we've slept past 9 am, which is late for me.

"You have to go?" Leah says sleepily.

I sigh and pull her close. "Yes," I say, knowing we need to resolve the threat hanging over our heads, and my father may have answers. I kiss the top of Leah's head. "Go back to sleep if you wish." Reluctantly, I pull my arm from beneath her and roll out of bed.

After throwing some clothes on, I stride across the room, as Leah climbs out of bed. Wrapping my arm around her waist, I pull her to me. "You have free reign of the house. My home is yours. You'll notice more men hanging around than usual."

"Is everything okay?" Leah asks.

I brush the curls from her face. "They are here to protect you."

"Can I have coffee on the deck out back?"

"As long as Maxim is close by,' I tell her.

Leah sighs. "Will it always be this way. Is this what your life is like all the time, never a moment to yourself?"

"No, Malyshka. But, for now, things stay as they are." Not able to resist the urge any longer, I press my lips to hers. "I'll be home as soon as I can."

"I'll be waiting." Those three words sink deep into my soul as I walk away.

Arriving at the clubhouse, I walk through the door and look around the room, finding most of Jake's brothers hanging out, including my father. "What's bothering you, son?"

"Nothing I can't take care of." I give a vague answer. He eyes me for a moment but says nothing more.

"Well," Jake stands. "Let's get this shit show started, shall we?" Walking toward the other end of the room, he yells, "Church." I fall in behind my father and Logan.

Once everyone has filled the room and taken their seats, including Victor, who is always at my father's side, Jake slams the gavel on the surface of the table. "Alright, listen up. As you all know, we had ourselves an incident that took place out at Charley's." Jake looks at me. "Neither one of those fuckers had any identification on them, so we put the word out trying to identify who they are. Unfortunately, none of our contacts or people in town knew anything about them, and believe me, in this town, people notice new faces hanging around. I contacted Lex and asked him for a favor. I sent him images of the guys from the security feed at Charley's. If he gets any hits on the FBI database, he'll email the results. These men threatened Demetri's woman. A threat none of us are taking lightly." Jake peers around the room. "With that said, I'm givin' the floor to our brother." Jake jerks his head toward my father.

Leaning back in his seat, my father speaks. "As most of you already know, a threat was made against Glory, and those details were shared with you. Because of that, and now with what happened here in Polson, I have to assume, both threats are related, yet we have no leads."

"Well, I sure as hell was hoping for more answers than what we have. Now, we've got a bunch of dead men and zero leads on who's fuckin' with my family," Logan quips.

"Unfortunately, my son is right." My father stands. My eyes follow him as he crosses the room where a fresh pot of coffee sits and pours himself a cup. "My soldiers found nothing. No fingerprints left on the package. The surveillance video from the restaurant shows nothing but a young delivery boy arriving shortly after we did. The boy took off down the street. Nobody has seen him since. It was Victor who felt something was not right and opened the box."

"Where was Sergei during all of this?" I am irritated at the fact my father hasn't shared any of this with me until now.

His hand tightens around the mug. He sits back in his seat and glances across the table at me. "Sergei is dead."

"How?"

"I killed him." My father's eyes flick to the other side of the room where Victor sits, his arms folded across his chest. Victor looks at me, confirming my father's admission with a tight nod.

"Why?" I ask.

My father's face hardens. "He stole from me. Over two million dollars to be exact."

Logan leans back in his chair. "Do you think he was behind these threats against Glory?"

"No. None of that leads back to him or the men he was selling my inventory to. Sergei simply became blinded by his greed. In the end, it cost him his life," my father replies.

"We'll keep our ears to the ground. In the meantime, I want everyone here to keep their eyes open. Report to Demetri or me if you hear or see anything." Jake slams the gavel.

Getting up from my seat, I walk out of the room. "Nikolai," I stop after my father calls my name. I look at him, not hiding my irritation. "You are angry with me," he states.

"I should have known about Sergei's betrayal and death before the others," I'm forward with my disapproval.

"Your attention to the safety of your woman was far more important than Sergei's demise. My decision to keep this information to myself was based solely on those facts, and nothing more." Staring at my father, I try to see his point of view. "Making sure your happiness and future are secure means more to me than you realize, son."

How can I continue to be angry with him after his admission? Besides, I decided to take a step back from many of my obligations. My father could have thrown that in my face, but he hasn't. "I apologize for my anger," I tell him.

My father pulls me in for a brief hug—something he does more often than he used to. "So, how is Leah?" he asks as he pulls away.

Thoughts of her waiting for my return cause me to smile. "She's good."

"We are lucky men, you and I," my father's eyes leave my face. I look over my shoulder and notice Glory standing with a few of the other women across the room.

"I'm happy for you, father," I tell him. "She's good for you."

"I'm happy for you too, son. I have seen a change in you since Leah has entered your life," my father says, his eyes still locked on his woman.

"I was thinking of moving into the guest house," I bring up a topic that's been on my mind since he mentioned he and Glory would be spending more time in Polson. My father finally shifts his attention back to me. "I don't think two couples living under one roof is an ideal situation."

My father nods, placing his hands into the front pockets of his suit pants. "True."

"And I'm looking at another four to six weeks before the construction of my new home is complete," I add.

"I'll inform the staff," my father says and retrieves his phone.

"No need." I stop him from calling. "I'm heading back now. I'll take care of everything myself."

LATER THAT NIGHT, after leaving the party being held at the Kings' clubhouse, Leah and I are in the guest house getting settled while eating dinner. "I'm so relieved." Leah sits on the sofa. "To be honest, I like this place better, not that the main house isn't nice. It's just; the guest house feels cozier."

Grabbing a cold beer from the refrigerator, I join my woman in the living room. "You mean more intimate?" Leaning in, give her a quick kiss, then steal a bite of her pizza, making her giggle. A pounding on the front door interrupts our dinner. It seems to be becoming a pattern lately. Sitting my bottle down, I cross the room and answer it. Maxim fills the space, his chest heaving like he's been in a marathon, and I'm suddenly on high alert. "Your father needs you. Glory is in trouble. The enemy is in active pursuit of her and Sasha as we speak."

Fuck.

"You are to stay here with Leah," I order.

"Yes, sir."

Rushing inside, I grab the keys to my bike.

"What's happening?" Leah stands, worry written all over her face.

Before leaving, I press my lips to hers. "Glory is in trouble. Stay put. Do not leave this house. Understood?"

"Yes."

I kiss her one more time, then turn on my heels.

"Nikolai," Leah calls out, her voice a little shaky, and I throw a look over my shoulder. "Be careful."

GRAVEL FLIES AS I bring my bike to an abrupt stop in front of the clubhouse, and notice my father running toward his car. I jog up to him as he jerks open the door. He looks at me, his face hard with rage, but his eyes filled with worry for his woman. "Gather all my men. I want them to tear this town apart looking for those sons of bitches." My father barks his orders. While racing back to my ride, I place the call, rallying every man we have in Polson, sending them on a mission to find the bastards giving chase to Glory and one of our men. I throw my leg over the motorcycle. Gravel hits the front of my father's car as I take off ahead of everyone.

Not far behind, Victor and my father peel out of the compound parking lot, following me as I barrel down the highway toward downtown. Rounding a bend in the road, I notice an orange glow lighting up the night sky accompanied by thick grey smoke. My gut tells me I won't like what I'm about to see. My breath gets caught in my throat when I recognized the overturned and mangled car on the side of the road ahead. I slow down when police cruisers block the short bridge we need to cross to get to the other side, our only means of getting to town.

Behind me, tires squeal. Coming to a complete stop, I look behind me. The look on Victor's face as he stares forward makes my chest tighten. The passenger door swings open and my father takes off toward the accident scene as fast as his feet will carry him.

"Sir, you can't –" an officer calls out to stop him. The closer I get to the accident, I notice the tire marks scarring the asphalt and shards of broken glass crunch beneath my feet. My father disappears around the front end of the firetruck ahead. Off to the side, firefighters attempt to put out the blaze. With no thought to his safety, I watch my father run toward the fire.

"Stop!" A nearby firefighter catches him, and they exchange words I cannot hear over all the background noise. Before I reach him, my father turns his head toward where the firefighter points, and I follow. Sasha is lying motionless several yards away from the wreckage as a paramedic hovers over him.

Three more vehicles pull up close to my father's car, and our men step out of them, their eyes searching the perimeter, and taking in the chaos. Halted by the roadblock, they can do nothing but watch as everything unfolds, putting precious time between the men responsible for taking Glory and us.

Leaving my bike on the side of the road, I rush to Sasha. My gut tightens at his bloodied, burnt, and battered body. I've known Sasha and his brother, Victor, my entire life. They are my family. Death is inevitable if they don't get him to a hospital soon. Suddenly, my father is standing beside me.

One of the paramedics looks up. "Are you family?"

"Yes," Victor yells from behind us, and I look over my shoulder. "He is my brother." Victor's voice rises above the noise surrounding us.

"Lost his pulse." The EMT standing on the other side of the gurney yells, sending him and his partner into lifesaving mode. Victor drops to his knees, taking his brother's hand in his. "Fight, Sasha!" he yells at his brother. "Fight!"

My stomach sinks.

"How far out is medevac?" The paramedic questions as he begins chest compressions and the EMT bags, giving him breaths of air.

He pauses and looks down at his watch. "Five minutes." He then addresses Victor. "Sir, please step back." Victor reluctantly releases his brother. He schools his emotions as they try to save Sasha; we all do. "We've got him back. Get him on the stretcher." The paramedic announces as the helicopter touches down in the middle of the highway several yards away. As they secure Sasha to the gurney, one medic turns facing Victor and me.

"They have room for one more," he yells over the noise, and Victor turns looking to my father and me, waiting for permission.

"Go," my father tells him.

The distant rumble of motorcycles draws our attention, and I follow my father as he heads toward Jake and his men, who look to have been stopped by the police.

"Glory?" Jake asks, sitting on the back of his bike.

"She's not here," my father speaks loud enough for everyone to hear. All the men's eyes follow the helicopter as it lifts in the air. "Sasha was the only victim on the scene," he tells Jake.

Looking over his shoulder, Jake signals to his brothers sitting on their bikes behind him. "Search the roads for any possible leads that would give us direction to where Glory could be." Following orders, they make their way down the shoulder of the road, pass the ambulance and firetruck.

A short time later, we are back to the clubhouse, with no leads on which direction she was taken. I'm standing beside my brother, when my father receives a call. "Speak," he barks, grabbing the attention of every man in the room. "If she has been harmed in any way—" his hand clenches at his side. "I'm going to find you, motherfucker. When I do, I'm going to kill you," he threatens the person on the other end of the line.

My father briefly closes his eyes, like he's trying to calm himself. "Vadim has her," he declares. My face hardens. Petrov. A war between the Petrov and Volkov families can only end with death. "That was one of Petrov's men, Andrei." The mention of

Petrov's right-hand man turning his back on the family surprises me. "He has Glory on my boat," my father informs the men and me.

"The ball's in your court." Jake steps forward. "How do you see this playing out?"

My father answers Jake, "Vadim doesn't like to get his hands dirty. My boat is docked near the furthest end of the Marina. His presence not only here but on my property lets me know he wanted me to find him. We should assume he has an army of men protecting him."

"He's drawing us in?" Jake realizes, and his face darkens. "This fucker has no idea who he is dealin' with."

Damn right he doesn't. I look around the room. Like us, The Kings are no strangers to violence or bloodshed. Every man in here is willing to go to war.

"How's your supply of weapons?" I question Jake.

"Ready for war, brother," he grins.

"Good. I want to send a few men out on the roads." My father looks around the room. "Nikolai, I'd like you to join them. You know better than anyone what Petrov's men look like. Scope out the area between here and the Marina. They could be anywhere." I nod at his order.

Jake chimes in as he attaches a fully loaded clip into his pistol. "Gabriel, ride out with Nikolai, and take Blake with you."

Wasting no time, Gabriel, Blake, and I rush to our bikes to find clues that may lead us in the right direction. Several minutes pass before approaching the bridge where remnants of the crash still litter the sides of the road. Blowing past one police car and a wrecker uprighting the burnt-out car that carried Glory and Sasha, the three of us keep our eyes peeled for anything out of the ordinary. We cruise to the Marina before doubling back. Almost six miles before closing in on the accident scene from the opposite direction, my headlights reflect off something white near the ditch on the roadside. I slow my speed, causing Gabriel and Blake to do the same.

A few yards away, my headlight shines on what appears to be the body of a man. Putting my bike in neutral, I leave it parked, running on the side of the road. Navigating a fourth of the way down the shallow ditch, I peer down, taking in the shadowed eyes of a dead man.

"Recognize him?" Gabriel hovers behind me, his frame casting a shadow over a portion of the body.

I study him for a second. "Never seen him before. You?" I reply.

"He's not from around here," Blake states.

With the toe of my boot, I nudge his muddied face, pushing it to the side. That's when I notice the black inked tattoo on the side of his neck. "Fuck."

"I take it his ink means somethin'?" Gabriel asks.

"We need to get back to the clubhouse," I say with venom.

WALKING into the clubhouse a short time later, with Gabriel and Blake right behind me, I approach my father. He studies me as Blake informs everyone, "Found a body on the side of the road about six miles from the accident site." His words catch everyone's attention. "I haven't seen his face around here before. But he has a tattoo on the left side of his neck of a scorpion."

"Petrov," my father states, knowing all his men wear the mark.

"We found nothing else between here and the Marina. I would guess Vadim's army is small, and they've camped out closer to Glory's location," Gabriel informs us.

Ready for war, my father glances at the men in the room—our family. "This shit ends tonight," he declares and walks out of the small metal building. He climbs into a car, and I quickly join him.

A few minutes later, silence engulfs us. The only sound heard is the rushing of blood coursing through my veins as my adrenaline increases with the roar of six Harleys following close behind. On the east side of the lake, we come to a stop, opposite where my father docks his boat. Through my window, I watch as The Kings and the rest of our men pull off the road. I step out of the car and glance at every man's face. They've all been to war more than once. We all ready our weapons, waiting for the final words before the battle.

My father grips a revolver in his hand I haven't seen before. "Kill them all."

As we make our way through the entrance, Jake throws his fist in the air. He signals to us, pointing out three men walking the dock about thirty yards ahead. I watch Logan, Reid, and Quinn raise their rifles and aim. Simultaneously, they pull their triggers, and the three men fall. Surging forward, we stride pass the dead men, blood pooling beneath their bodies as we step over them.

Shots ring out, and bullets whiz by, hitting nearby boats. Taking shelter, we wait until the gunfire ceases. Jake quickly puts a bullet through the chest of one guy before ducking behind another boat. Aiming, my shot finds its mark, and I watch another man fall. I suddenly notice my father's boat drifting away from the pier. My father sees it mere seconds after me and takes off running. Bullets whiz by my head as I take off after him. Not stopping, I leap in the air, landing on the boat, then look back over my shoulder, noticing my father hasn't done the same. "Jump!" I yell, and he propels himself off the dock.

His feet hit the deck, hard, causing his whole body to slam into the lower deck door, landing on his back and his weapon skids across the floor, out of his reach. A single shot rings out. Overhead, a short bald bastard is standing on the flying bridge. From the rear of the boat, I raise my hand and pull the trigger. The man sways on his feet before falling over the side into the water below. My father looks back, locking eyes with me before I'm tackled. The large man wraps his hand around my wrist, trying to disarm me. The son of a bitch is massive. He throws his weight into me again, violently slamming my side against the railing. A struggle ensues as I fight to keep possession of my weapon. The instant the end of my gun presses into his gut, I pull the trigger. The man loses his footing, pulling both him and me over the railing. With one hand gripping the rail, I don't look back as I hear his body splash into the water. I pull myself back onto the boat. Looking down, blood soaks the front of my shirt. My father notices as well, and I tell him, "It's not mine." Realizing my hand is empty, I look around. "I lost my gun." Then I look over the railing, down into the water below.

"Stay close," my father tells me, knowing I am now unarmed. We turn our attention to the cabin, climb the stairs, and peer through the glass, finding no one inside. My father glances over his shoulder, shakes his head, then points to the boat's bow. Quietly, we make our way around the side.

"Show yourself. I know you're here, Volkov." The voice of Vadim stops my father in his tracks, causing me to slam into his back. "I've got a sweet looking redhead standing beside me."

"Fucking touch me again, you prick, and I'll rip your dick off then shove it down your throat." I hear Glory sass.

My father grips the revolver held at his side, and with nothing but my fist as weapons, I have his back as we walk from the shadows.

The moment I see my mother standing next to Vadim, my blood runs cold. "Mom?" I mutter beneath my breath. My eyes dart to Vadim, who has the blade of a knife to Glory's throat with one hand and a gun pressed against her ribcage with the other. "Nice of you to join us," Vadim sneers, his lips upturned in a sinister smile.

A shadow moving catches my eye, and I notice Andrei, one of Vadim's soldiers standing nearby, waiting in the shadows. My attention shifts back to Vadim, but I find it hard to focus on him alone, with my mother standing close by. Vadim jerks Glory closer to him, and she struggles with her hands bound behind her back. Finally, Vadim places Glory in front of himself, using her as a shield. The fucking coward.

"Ivanna." My father says her name with disdain.

"Demetri," her eyes cut to me, her face a mask of cold hard steel. "Son."

"You lost the right to call me your son a long time ago," I grind my teeth. The sting of my words causes my mother to cast her eyes away momentarily. She has no shame. How can she continue to be so heartless?

"This isn't a Goddamn family reunion," Vadim spits. "I don't know how you got tipped off to my whereabouts, but the outcome is still the same. You are here."

"What is your endgame, Vadim? Did you think this poorly orchestrated attempt to overthrow me would succeed? Look around you." My father raises his weapon. "All your men are dead." He then looks at my mother. "And you."

"I've moved on to better things. Once you are out of the picture, we will merge the Petrov and Solov families, becoming the most powerful crime family in Russia." The absurdity of my mother's words do nothing but add fuel to the anger and hate I have for her. She would sell out and turn against her son—her flesh and blood to seek a power that will never be hers.

"Pathetic," Glory mutters, and Vadim applies more pressure against her neck. A drop of blood slides across the silver surface of the blade, and my father lurches forward. Without warning, Vadim points his gun at me. My nostrils flare, and if it weren't for Glory's safety, I would take the bullet just to get the chance to kill him myself.

"You take another step, and I'll slash her throat, and put a bullet in your son's head. Come to think of it," Vadim cocks his head. "I think you should watch him die first." Turning, Vadim orders Andrei, "Don't just stand there. Kill him."

"Wait!" My mother throws her hands up, turns, and faces Vadim. "That was not part of the plan."

"Fuck the plan. I can't have any Volkov standing in my way." Vadim's grip tightens on his gun.

"It was I who called Volkov," Andrei confesses.

Vadim sneers. His eyes become wild with rage as he shuffles backward, pulling Glory with him. "You'll not live to see another sunrise," he warns Andrei.

I keep my eyes glued to Vadim, waiting for an opportunity to present itself where I am no longer his target. "This is no longer my fight. I am and will always remain loyal to the family, but I will not play a part in the destruction of the empire your father built," Andrei declares before I hear footsteps walking away.

"Looks like I have to take matters into my own hands." Vadim cocks his gun.

"He's my son!" My mother pleads. Her cries cause an unexpected ache in my chest. "Vadim. Please." It sounds cliché, but what happens next plays out in slow motion. My mother steps in the line of fire, between me and the bullet meant for me. I watch it rip through her chest, propelling her small body backward. I catch my mother in my arms as she falls to the deck. My knees buckle as I go down with her.

"Stupid woman!" Vadim yells, then aims his gun at my father. Both of them at a standoff.

I don't speak as I look at my mother. What the hell was she thinking? Raising a shaky hand, she palms my cheek. "I'm sorry, Nikolai." She coughs, as blood flows from her mouth and seeps from the hole in her chest. I press my hand against her wound, knowing with the amount of blood she's losing, it will do no good. I look at her, and a million things are running through my head. I hate you, and why being a couple of them. Her eyes stay fixed on my face, but I can't find any words to say. Instead, I hold her until the life in her eyes disappears, and the woman who gave me life dies in my arms.

IT'S BEEN several weeks since my mother's death, and I'm still left grasping for answers. As I watched them lower her white casket draped with pink roses into the cold ground a few weeks ago, my chest felt heavy. Why now? All these years, she left me without the love of a mother. Then she goes and dies, giving her life to save mine. Now, I'm left hating myself because I can't let go of the anger I still feel toward her last act in life because she finally showed the love I so desperately sought all my life.

It's morning here in Russia, but just around the time, Leah would be in bed back in the States. Pulling my phone from my pocket, I call her. Leah's tired voice answers the phone. "Nikolai, is everything okay?"

"Yes, Malyshka. I just needed to hear your sweet voice," I sigh, and scrub my hand down my face.

"Still can't sleep?" she asks, and I hear her moving in the bed and wish I were beside her, holding her in my arms and smelling her sweet scent. "You know you can talk to me," she whispers, but I don't reply. My eyes close. "Can I ask you something?"

"You can ask me anything," I tell her and rub my eyes that burn from lack of sleep.

"You've never really talked about your role in your family. Will you have to return to Russia full time one day?" I hear the worry in her voice.

"I am heir to the Volkov empire, and one day, when my father decides to step down, I will not hesitate to take the reins." I'm honest with her. My father has been selfless in giving me the space I asked for and honoring my wishes to step away for now, but there is no question in my mind that I will be ready when the time comes. "But, for now, my father is in full control, and I'm here to be at his side when needed. As for Russia, I can visit any time I wish, but my home and my future is in Polson." I don't miss Leah's sigh of relief at my confession.

"I miss you," I hear the smile in her voice, followed by a long yawn.

"Get some sleep. I'll talk to you again soon."

"Goodnight, Nikolai. I mean, good morning," she giggles. "I keep forgetting about the time difference."

"Goodnight, Malyshka."

Needing coffee, I dress, then navigate through the empty hallways of the house, finally venturing into the kitchen, where I find Marta. "Good morning, Nikolai. How did you sleep?" she asks, then begins to pour me a cup of coffee. She sets it down in front of me.

"I haven't slept much since I've been back," I tell her knowing she would call me a liar if I said otherwise.

"Yes, I can tell." She places a bowl of cooked oats on a tray next to a plate of eggs, toast, and bacon. "Maybe you should consider going back home. Unless there is still work left to be done here." Her eyes lift to my face, waiting for me to reply.

"Is that for Sasha?" I motion to the tray she has lifted from the table.

"Changing the subject, I see," Marta raises her brow but goes with it. "Yes, it is for Sasha."

"I'll take it to him." I drink some of my coffee before standing. Marta hands the tray over.

"You won't find what your heart needs here in Russia, Nikolai. Moving forward is all anyone can do." Marta smiles, then pats my forearm.

I let Marta's words sink in as I climb the stairs on my way to Sasha quarters. Once outside his door, I knock. "Come in," he calls out, and I push open the door. "Nikolai," he pushes himself upright, propping his back against the headboard of his bed. "I haven't seen you for several days. I thought you had left and gone back to Montana."

I set his tray of food across his lap and look him over. His burns are healing faster than expected. He winces as he reaches for his pain meds on his nightstand, but I don't interfere. "How are you doing with therapy?" I ask.

"The nurse finds me insufferable." He pops a pill in his mouth then washes it down with water.

"Then you are well on your way to getting back to your old self," I chuckle.

Sasha eyes me. "Seriously. Why are you still here?"

"To tell you the truth, I don't know."

Sasha sighs then stares out the window across the room. "You won't find answers here, Nikolai. Take it from someone who stared death in the face and lived to tell about it. Don't take the life you were given for granted by letting the past eat at your insides. Go home. Your peace is waiting for you in Polson."

Later that evening, I'm sitting alone, with a drink in my hand, stewing over Sasha and Marta's words from earlier in the day. They're right. What the hell am I waiting for? I've wasted too much time asking for answers to questions that no longer matter. My future is waiting for me in Polson, and I'm not wasting another second of my life without her at my side.

18

LEAH

It's after midnight, and still, I can't sleep. Nikolai's house feels different without him. The truth is everything feels different in his absence: work, his home, Polson. He tries to hide it when we talk on the phone, but I know he's struggling with his mother's death. Their relationship had been strained for years, but she gave her life for her son in the end. I sense that's why Nikolai is having a hard time coming to terms with her death. According to Nikolai, his mom spent his life putting herself first. She never did anything unless it benefited her. For her to place herself in front of a bullet for her son was the ultimate sacrifice. I desperately want him here with me so I can talk to him; give him comfort—the kind of support he's given me.

With a heavy sigh, I remove the tea kettle from the burner on the stove, pour the steaming liquid into my cup, then carry it down the hall and into Nikolai's office where I sit on the oversized chair in front of the window. Sitting, I sip my tea and stare out at the backyard. Nikolai insisted I stay here while he is away. If my being here and watched over by Maxim puts his mind at peace, I wasn't going to deny him that.

Hoping to get my mind off missing Nikolai, I grab the book I have been reading from the table beside me and pick up where I left off the night before.

Twenty minutes later, when I realize I have read the same page over and over, I decide to give up on reading. Slamming the book closed, I abandon it and decide on a different tactic and make my way out to the living room.

Running my fingertips along the black and white keys, I close my eyes and let my thoughts take me back to the last time I played. I smile. Sitting on the bench in front of the piano, surrounded by darkness and nothing but the moonlight filtering through the large window as thoughts of Nikolai consume me; only one song comes to mind; I play Midnight Sonata.

I'm completely lost in the music that I don't register, I am no longer alone, and the presence behind me has been watching me for the past five minutes. It's not until I play the final note a familiar scent fills my senses the same time an arm snakes around my middle. The next thing I know, I'm lifted in the air as Nikolai straddles the bench, settling me in his lap, then his mouth crashes down on mine. While holding my head between the palms of his hands, he delves his tongue inside my mouth, tasting me, owning me. He tastes like smoke and whiskey, reminding me of everything I missed.

"I missed you."

"Fuck, I missed you too, Malyshka."

"Why didn't you tell me you were coming home?"

"I didn't want you waiting up for me. Maxim told me you've been looking tired and worn down. He says you haven't been sleeping well. I wanted you to rest. If you knew I was flying back, you would have waited up for me. Why didn't you tell me you haven't been sleeping?"

I shake my head. "It's not a big deal."

Nikolai runs his hand through my hair. "It is."

I sigh. "I've been worried about you."

"I'm okay, Leah. Especially now."

"Really?" I raise a brow.

"Yeah. I gained some perspective while I was away. When shit goes down, and the evil polluting this earth gets too close for comfort, you realize the life you have can be taken away from you in a blink of an eye. I have decided I don't want to live a life full of regrets, and I don't want to live another day of my life without you. That's why I came back. I need you, Leah, and I'm ready to start our life together. No more waiting. Because not making you mine is a regret I refuse to live with."

My breath gets caught in my throat. "What are you saying?"

Nikolai softly kisses me. "I'm saying I love you, Malyshka, and I want you to be mine."

"I love you too, Nikolai," I croak as tears start to spill from my eyes. "And I am yours."

He shakes his head. "I want you to be mine completely." Reaching into his pocket, Nikolai pulls out a little black box, and I gasp when he opens it revealing an emerald cut, yellow sapphire, and diamond ring.

Nikolai takes the hand covering my mouth and slips the ring on my finger, his eyes never leaving mine. "Leah Winters, will you do the honor of becoming my wife?"

My head bobs frantically. "Yes. Yes, thousands of times, yes." I throw my arms around his neck and cry. "This doesn't seem real. It feels like a dream."

Nikolai kisses up my neck. "Not a dream, Malyshka."

I hum when he bites the space below my ear and I tip my head back, giving him better access. He takes advantage, nipping, and licking his way along my jaw toward my mouth. The heat from Nikolai's palm sends tingles between my thighs as he slips his hand inside my shirt and palms my breast. "Please, Nikolai," I beg, not knowing what I'm asking for.

"What do you need, Leah?"

"You. I need you to touch me."

In two seconds flat, the fallboard of the piano slams shut, and my backside is planted firmly on top. In one fell swoop, he tugs my shirt off over my head. Nikolai places himself between my spread legs, and without warning, his mouth covers one of my nipples. "Oh, God," I cry out, gripping the edge of the piano. When he releases one breast, he switches to the other, giving it equal attention, causing my center to ache. Too soon, I lose his mouth, and a whimper escapes my mouth.

"Lay back for me, Leah. I'm going to taste you now."

Oh, sweet Jesus.

Doing as I'm told, I lay back on the cold surface of the piano. Lifting my hips slightly, Nikolai takes his time as he slowly drags my sleep shorts over my thighs and down my legs. For the first time in my life, I am completely bare in front of a man. For the briefest moment, I wonder if Nikolai likes what he sees. But the moment doesn't last long.

"There is nothing more beautiful than the sight of you wearing nothing but my ring on your finger. You're a fucking vision, Malyshka." Nikolai's heated gaze travels over every exposed inch of my body. His hands start at my ankles, going up my calves and across my generous hips. Nikolai's fingertips leave a trail of tingles in their wake, before moving on to my belly. "This," his large inked hands span across my middle, "is a body made for pleasure."

My breaths are coming out in pants, and the ache between my thighs increases.

"Are you ready for my mouth, Leah?"

"Yes. So ready," I say, squeezing my eyes shut, my voice not sounding like my own.

"Open your eyes, Malyshka. Watch your man take his first taste."

Nikolai sits back on the bench as I peer down at him through my lashes, my body trembling with need and anticipation. There is something vulnerable about being naked while Nikolai is fully-clothed, but there is something beautiful about it too. It's because he makes me feel beautiful. With his words, his look and his touch.

Without making me wait for another second, Nikolai grabs my knees, pulls me to the edge of the piano, bringing my center inches away from his face, his beard tickling the inside of my thighs as he drapes my legs over his shoulders. His eyes capture mine, and I don't dare break our connection. Leaning into me, Nikolai's tongue licks me from bottom to top. A noise trembles from my lips.

At his first swipe, a wild noise escapes his mouth. "Sweeter than I imagined."

"Nikolai," I pant, trying to reach for something to grab hold of.

"Grab my hair, Malyshka, and hold on."

As soon as the words rumble past his lips, his mouth is back on me, and I have no choice but to do as he says. I buck my hips, searching for the release my body desperately needs. Two powerful arms capture my thighs, holding me still as his greedy mouth claims me. Soon the pleasure Nikolai's mouth delivers wracks my entire body, and I am no longer able to hold back the intense pleasure that surges through me.

"Let go, Malyshka," he growls just before sucking my clit into his mouth.

"Nikolai," I whimper.

"Now, Leah. I want you to come in my mouth. Give it to me."

Like last time, his command does me in. Releasing the grip on his hair, I brace my palms against the smooth surface of the piano, arch my back, I cry out his name as my release washes through me. "Nikolai!"

"I WANT you to call the girls today and have them come over to help you plan. There's a lot of shit to do before the weekend," Nikolai says.

I turn away from the stove where I'm making pancakes and look at him. He's sitting at the kitchen island, shirtless, hair still damp from his shower, drinking a cup of coffee. I take in his broad shoulders and his ink-covered arms. The man is a work of art. I don't think I'll ever get tired of looking at him. If a man could be described as beautiful, Nikolai would be the definition.

"Leah," Nikolai calls my name, snapping me out of my Nikolai induced haze. I tear my eyes away from his chest. He smirks knowingly. It's then I remember his question. "What's going on this weekend?"

Without missing a beat, he replies, "our wedding."

The spatula in my hand clatters to the floor, and I stare at Nikolai, trying to figure out if I heard him correctly. "I'm sorry, I could have sworn you said we are getting married this weekend."

Finally, he looks up. "You heard right."

"Nikolai!"

"What?"

"That's four days away."

"Yeah, Malyshka, I know."

"You want to get married in four days?" I suddenly sound panicked, and at that, Nikolai abandons his phone and steps around the island, taking me in his arms.

"Leah, I told you last night I was done waiting. If I had my way, we'd go down to the courthouse today, but because you deserve a real wedding, I'm willing to give you until Saturday."

"I can't plan a wedding by Saturday, Nikolai." My voice comes in a high pitch, and I'm starting to think my future husband has gone mad.

Nikolai hauls me against his chest. "Do you want to be my wife?"

"Yes. More than anything."

"I meant what I said last night. I'm done waiting, Leah. I know it feels like we are moving at warp speed, but not for me. I've been waiting over a year for you, Malyshka."

I search his eyes, and what I see is nothing but love. He's right. Our relationship went from zero to sixty in a matter of weeks, but that's just on the surface. If I dig deeper, I see what he sees. We have been working up toward this moment for a year. I'm the one who is playing catch up.

"You're not the only one who has been waiting. I've been waiting for you my whole life Nikolai Volkov."

"Are you saying you're going to take this ride with me?"

I smile. "Yes."

"Four days?"

I bite my bottom lip. "Four days."

Nikolai kisses the tip of my nose. "Now, how about that breakfast."

After breakfast, I called Alba, telling her the news of mine and Nikolai's engagement. After she was done screaming in my ear, I informed her I was getting married this weekend and required some help. She could tell I was freaking out. Once she got me to calm down, she said she'd be over in an hour with reinforcements. Alba had come through.

Forty-five minutes later, she showed up at the door with The Kings' women brigade, Bella, Mila, Grace, Emerson, and Sofia. Demetri's girlfriend, Glory, is the first to speak when I open the door to greet them. "Damn, those Volkov men don't fuck around, do they? Like father, like son." She strolls in, wearing a pair of strappy heels, a black hip-hugging pencil skirt, and a green silk blouse. Glory might be a schoolteacher, but she doesn't dress the part. She's even rocking a leopard print shoulder sling she has to wear due to her dislocated shoulder. Glory stops next to me and studies my face then looks to the group of women she came with.

"Look at her. She even has the Volkov glow." Glory turns back to me and smiles. "I had to sneak out of the house. No way was I missing this. Took your asses long enough."

"Like you're one to talk, Glory." Grace rolls her eyes, calling her best friend out.

"Whatever," Glory waves her hand.

Just then, Nikolai saunters in from the kitchen, stopping beside me and pulling me into his side. He tips his head. "Ladies."

"Hi, Nikolai," they all say in unison.

Taking his wallet from his back pocket, Nikolai produces a credit card and holds it out to me. "Have fun with the ladies today." I take the card.

"What's our budget?" Alba asks.

"No budget. Whatever Leah wants, she gets." Nikolai answers.

"We can do that,"Bella grins.

THREE HOURS LATER, I'm standing in front of the girls wearing the sixth dress I've tried on. Polson doesn't have a bridal store, so we had to drive two towns over to Caroline's Bridal. "This is the one," I tell them, smoothing down the front of the gown with my hands, unable to take my eyes off my reflection in the floor-length mirror. The satin ivory gown hugs all my curves. Spinning, I take in the fabric-covered buttons traveling the length of my spine. I run my palm down the long sleeves, which feel baby soft.

"I agree," Alba says, coming to stand next to me. "It's perfect," Bella adds.

Mila, Grace, Emerson, Sofia, and Glory all nod their heads in approval. "That dress was made for you, Leah." Glory beams.

The owner of the boutique walks over. "Do we have a verdict?"

I look over at her and smile. "Yes. This is my dress."

"Lovely," she clasps her hands together. "It appears the dress only needs a few minor alterations. Luckily, we have a seamstress in the house, and she can have your gown ready by tomorrow."

"Perfect. Thank you."

BY THE END of the day, I'm exhausted. Thankfully almost everything has been taken care of. I found my dress, Nikolai said he would take care of buying a new suit. Bella is handling the food and alcohol, Mila volunteered to oversee the flowers and decorations. Emerson informed me earlier that Quinn has insisted on officiating the ceremony, which is fine by me. And Grace is taking care of the cake. In fact, Maxim and I just left her bakery, where she whipped up six different wedding cake samples to try. By the end of the taste test, I went with a luscious lemon mousse, paired with tangy lemon curd, layered with fresh olallieberry compote.

"Would you like to stop anywhere else Miss Leah, before I take you home?" Maxim asks, peering through the rearview mirror.

Remembering I need to grab a change of clothes, I nod. "Yes, please. Can we stop by my apartment?"

"That won't be necessary. Nikolai arranged for your things to be brought to his house today."

Suddenly, I am wide awake. "What? He moved me into his house. Today?"

"Yes. It's all been taken care of."

"Well, I guess we can go home."

Maxim jerks his chin.

"Oh, wait! Can you stop at the store? I forgot I need to pick up a few things."

Maxim acts as my shadow as I shop for the stuff to make homemade waffles in the morning. Next, I move on to the frozen food aisle in search of ice cream. After the mentally draining day

I've had, I just want to go home and curl up in bed next to Nikolai with a pint of cookie dough.

"That will be twenty-three seventy-eight," the cashier relays my total as I dig some cash out of my wallet. But before I can pay, Maxim beats me to it.

"What are you doing? You don't have to pay for my things, Maxim. I have the money."

Maxim shakes his head. "Boss' orders."

The girl behind the register pops her gum. "Honey, if a man wants to pay, you let him pay."

Not in the mood to argue, I zip my mouth shut and sigh.

LATER THAT NIGHT, I'm lounging in the bed next to Nikolai eating ice-cream while he types away on his laptop. "Did you really move me in today while I was gone?"

"Yes," he replies, not looking up from what he's doing.

"And did you tell Maxim I wasn't allowed to pay for my things?"

At my second question, Nikolai tears his eyes away from his work and focuses on me. "You're mine. I take care of what's mine. It is my duty to see you have everything you want and need."

"Okay, but I can still buy my ice cream, though."

"This subject is non-negotiable, Malyshka. Part of being with me is accepting that."

"What's next, are you going to tell me I have to quit working too?" Annoyed with the conversation, I lose my appetite and set my ice cream aside.

"Leah." Nikolai's face goes soft. "I would never ask you to quit your job, not unless you wanted to."

"Good," I huff. "Because I like my job."

"I like you working for me too."

"Well, if you're not going to let me help contribute to our finances, what can I do?"

Nikolai tosses his laptop to the side, snags me around my waist, and hauls me up the bed, tucking me into his side. "You're fucking cute when you pout."

I cross my arms over my chest and jut out my chin. "I'm not pouting," I lie.

"Malyshka." Nikolai kisses the crook of my neck. "Don't be mad." He nips my earlobe, and my body starts to melt. Damn him.

Reaching behind me, I thread my fingers through his hair as he continues assaulting me with lips. "I know what you're doing."

"Yeah. And what's that?"

"You're distracting me so that I won't pick a fight with you."

I feel him smile against my skin. "You want me to stop?"

"I didn't say that."

I know Nikolai is holding back his laughter when his body begins to shake. "Like I said, cute."

I roll my eyes even though he can't see them. It's impossible to stay mad at the man, especially when his hands are on me, one of which is currently down the front of my shirt, and his thumb brushes over my nipple.

A sudden surge of bravery washes over me, and I ask, "Nikolai?"

"Hmm," he hums his face still buried in my neck.

"Will you...will you teach me how to use my mouth on you?"

Nikolai goes solid behind me, and my breath gets caught in my throat.

"Are you asking because it's something you want to do or because you think it's something I want you to do?"

Turning in his arm, I sit up on my knees and face him. "Both."

"Are you sure you're ready, Malyshka?"

"Ye...yes. Unless you don't want me..."

"Fuck yeah, I want you to," he cuts me off.

"Okay. So, pointers. Do you have any for me?"

"Do whatever feels natural. Just be careful of your teeth."

Looking down at the bulge covered by Nikolai's boxer briefs, I lick my lips. I wasn't lying when I said I wanted to try. I have been thinking about using my mouth on Nikolai for longer than I care to admit. I want to give him the kind of pleasure he's given me.

Crawling between his legs, I reach for the band of his boxers then pull them down until his erection springs free. Somehow, I knew Nikolai's cock would be just as beautiful as he is. It's long and thick, and I can't wait to run my tongue along the little veins that disappear into the neatly trimmed patch of hair at the base.

"Take your shirt off for me, Leah. I want to look at your tits while my cock is in your mouth."

Giving Nikolai what he wants, I pull my shirt off over my head and toss it to the floor. Next, I don't hesitate to take his cock in my hand. I pump my hand up and down, loving the feel of the velvety smooth skin. And when a bead of precum leaks from the tip, I lean down and run my tongue over the tip, taking my first taste.

"Fuck," Nikolai hisses, settling his head back on the headboard, his eyes closed tight. I smile, loving the effect I have on him. I wrap my lips around his length, taking as much of it in my mouth as I can. It doesn't take long for me to find my rhythm, using my mouth and my hand simultaneously. I also learn by the sounds coming from Nikolai he likes it when I pay special attention to the head.

"Fuck, fuck, fuck," Nikolai curses, followed by a string of Russian words I don't understand but sounds sexy. I love his accent. It's so thick and growly.

"Leah, I'm going to come. If you don't want it in your mouth, pull off," he warns.

I hum and keep going, letting him know I want all of him. With my go ahead, Nikolai holds my stare as he grabs a fist full of my hair. Seconds later, his jaw clenches, his abs tighten, and his pupils dilate. I know he's about to come. I feel the head of his cock swell around my lips just before Nikolai growls and fills my mouth with his release. When I'm positive I've gotten all he has to give, I release his cock from my mouth and sit back on my knees. I take in Nikolai's relaxed form, feeling happy with my performance, and I smile. "Was I okay?" I bite my bottom lip.

"Come here, Leah." Nikolai hooks his hands under my arms and swiftly maneuvers me to my back. He hovers above me.

I squeal. "What are you doing?"

"Your turn," Malyshka.

"Got them!" Alba cheers holding up a little, white plastic bag as she comes bustling into the room with her daughter hanging off her hip. I commented earlier after Bella finished doing my makeup that I wished I had contacts. I don't usually mind my glasses, but after I caught a glimpse of myself in the mirror, I realized it would be a shame to hide the perfected smokey eye Bella gave me, behind a pair of glasses.

"Oh, my God. You're the best! How were you able to get them? The doctor's office is closed on Saturdays."

"Emerson made a call," she tells me, and I make a mental note to thank her later.

After I put my contacts in, Bella spends another thirty-minute putting the final touches on my hair, pinning red roses through my curls.

The roses in my hair match the bouquet I'll be carrying, and it matches the outdoor décor. Nikolai and I decided to keep the ceremony simple by having it at the house and inviting just family. I caught a glimpse of the back yard earlier, and I was shocked at what the girls were able to throw together in such a short amount of time. The gazebo at the edge of the lake where Nikolai and I will say our vows is covered in white roses. Then closer to the main house next to the back patio is where we will serve the food during the after-party. Alba said Logan and Gabriel are in charge of that department. I figured as much when a friend to the club and local bar owner Charley pulled up in a van. Then I watched as he and some of the guys unloaded a couple of kegs of beer. It looks like we'll be partying King style later tonight.

"Are you ready to get changed?" Alba asks, tearing me away from my thoughts.

I smile, meeting her eyes in the reflection of the mirror where she stands behind me. "Yes."

Alba walks over to where my gown is hanging on a hook next to the closet. Today Alba will stand in as my maid of honor. The dress I chose for her is a champagne gold, sleeveless, knee-length chiffon. It matches her golden blonde hair perfectly.

Bella decides to take this moment to step out. "I'm going to make sure everything is ready. Are you still okay to start in thirty minutes, or do you need more time?"

I shake my head. "No. I'll be ready."

Once Bella leaves, Alba helps me with my dress by fastening the buttons on the back. "You're getting married," she says, her tone wistful.

"Can you believe it? I, Leah Winters, am marrying Nikolai Volkov."

Alba pauses what she's doing, and our eyes meet in the mirror once again. "I absolutely can believe it. Do you want to know why?"

I don't say anything, but she continues anyway.

"Because you're one of the kindest, most beautiful people I know. And because if anyone deserves a fairytale wedding and a happily ever after, it's you, Leah. So, yes, I can believe it."

Turning, I face Alba and pull her in for a hug. "Thank you. I wouldn't be here if it weren't for you and Sam."

"I knew my ears were burnin' for a reason."

I break away from Alba to see Sam standing at the door with a massive grin on his face. I take in his attire of dark wash jeans, a black button-down shirt, and his MC cut. He strides further into the room as he takes me in, stopping in front of me. "You look gorgeous, darlin'."

I beam up at him. "Thank you, Sam."

"Alba is right. You deserve your happily ever after, sweetheart." He kisses the top of my head. "I'll see you out there."

Twenty minutes later, Alba is about to call Bella and give her the word that I am ready when there is a knock on the door, followed by Demetri entering the room. He's dressed in a crisp suit, which is his standard attire, but the black and white one he has on today is more fitting of the occasion. "Am I interrupting?"

"Not at all," I smile.

Demetri steps up to me and kisses my forehead. "Tih kra-sah-vee-tsa. *You are beautiful.* My son is a lucky man."

"Thank you, Demetri."

"I come here to ask if I may have the honor of walking you down the aisle. It would bring me great joy to escort you toward your future with my son."

I release a shuddered breath. It's no secret I don't have any family to share my day with, but if I have learned anything over the past year and especially the past four days is family is not always by blood. The Volkov's and The Kings are my family.

"Thank you, Demetri. I would love for you to walk me down the aisle," my voice shakes, and I blink away the tears that threaten to spill as I look down at the floor.

Demetri places his finger under my chin, tilting my head back. "Today, I gain a daughter. And today, not only do you gain a husband, but you gain a father. Nothing will make me prouder."

19

NIKOLAI

eeding a few moments to myself, I slip out the back entrance of the guesthouse Leah, and I have occupied for a short time. I stop and glance out at the lake, making my way to the giant oak tree near the water's edge, which mirrors the bright blue sky above. In my serenity, I let everything that has led up to this day sink in.

"Thought I would find you here." My brother comes to stand beside me.

"I needed a moment of peace."

"Nervous?" Logan asks.

"Not at all," I admit.

"I'm happy for you, brother. And damn proud that you asked me to stand by your side as your best man." Logan clears his throat of emotion. I take a second to respond, schooling my own.

"You are my brother—my blood. I would have no other man stand with me on such an important day," I tell him. Soft music begins to play in the distance, and Logan takes in a long, cleansing breath before facing me.

"Ready?"

"Let no man stand in my way, brother." I smile, as an eagerness to see my woman takes over me.

On our walk to the gazebo, overlooking the lake, I take in our family. Though small, the men and women here today are the most important people in mine and Leah's lives. White flowers, along with lush greenery, cover everything from the gazebo to the chairs our guests sit on. To the side, sits a piano and a cello player. Waiting for my brother and me is Quinn, who is officiating the ceremony today. He leans in. "I now understand why you Volkov men like to wear suits so damn much," Quinn straightened his tie. "It gets you laid. My woman couldn't keep her hands off me earlier. I think I'll add this little get up to my roleplay wardrobe." Logan, who can't hold back his smirk, shakes his head, and I laugh, amused by Quinn's in your face I am who I am demeanor.

"We don't need to hear about your sexual escapades, brother," Logan jests.

"Sharing is caring, brother," Quinn quips.

Turning my attention to the crowd, my eyes find Marta, sitting beside Leah's neighbor from her hometown, Mrs. Mae. Marta waves my way, tears already pooling in her eyes, and I flash her a smile. The fact that my father flew her to Polson means more to me than he may know. The only faces missing amongst all the others today are Sasha and Victor. Though it's been more than a month, Sasha has a long road ahead of him before he's back on his feet.

The music changes and our guests rise from their seats. In the distance, French doors on the back of the house open, revealing my bride, with my father standing at her side. Suddenly, I find myself overwhelmed with emotion. Leah takes her first few steps onto the deck, into the warm glow of the setting sun. Captivated by her beauty, my heart races, and my breath catches as she floats gracefully down the steps, stopping for a moment at the end of the aisle. My woman is the most breathtakingly beautiful creature I have ever been blessed to lay eyes on. Dressed in a long satin gown, fitted to hug every curve of her body, she walks toward me, her amber eyes locked on mine. She adds to the beauty of the red roses she holds in her hands and those adorning her long, dark hair, cascading in curls down her back. Her bright smile causes a tightening of my chest from the abundance of love I feel for her.

Leah and my father stop a foot away, and before placing her hand in mine, Leah whispers, "Thank you, Demetri." Her eyes are glistening with unshed tears.

My father kisses her forehead. "It was my honor, daughter." Her tears finally fall, and I fight back my own. He then faces me, placing Leah's small hand in mine. "I've never been prouder of you than I am right now. I love you, son." My father takes his leave.

I stare at my future wife's face, memorizing every aspect of this moment, and filing away every precious memory. Her eyes sparkle as she gazes at me, and I find myself leaning down to capture her lips.

"Whoa. Hold up, Casanova. We have to get through all the mushy shit before you get to the kiss," Quinn interrupts, and bouts of laughter fill the air. Leah blushes, and it's so fucking adorable. Quinn clears his throat. "First of all, I'd like to say that I'm fuckin' honored that I was asked to hitch these two. Lord knows we've waited long enough." Again, more laughter and I laugh along with them, as my eyes never leave Leah's. "Alright, let's do this." Quinn gives me a nod, giving me the stage.

"Tih o-che-reh-Vah-tsel-na. You captured my heart the first moment I laid eyes on you. To you and others, you appeared to be broken," I shake my head, "but that was farthest from the truth. You are a woman of strength—a force of nature. You are the quiet strength in the storm you've walked through. You are the woman I wish to finish my journey through life with. You are my future. I vow to protect you, hold you, and love you for the rest of my days. I will always put you before myself—always. I give my life to you, Leah—until my last breath."

I feel Leah's hands tremble. "Nikolai, I sat down to write my vows, only to end with a blank piece of paper. So, I decided to express the depth of my love using music." Letting go of my hand, Leah walks with grace to the piano nearby. She sits on the bench. Leah has never shared her gift of music with anyone besides me. I couldn't look away if I tried. Spellbound, I watch her fingertips begin to dance atop the ivory keys, as the cello player joins her. The beautiful melody she plays—*A thousand years* grips every part of my being. She begins to sway as she plays, pouring all of herself —her love for me into every note.

When Leah finishes, there is nothing but silence. With help from Alba, who straightens her train, she makes her way back to me and takes my hand in hers. "I never had someone in my life to show me what love truly was until you came along. Nikolai, you showed me a man's hands should be gentle, and his words should be spoken with the intent to encourage and strengthen me, not used to tear me down and leave me feeling broken. You have given me a love I always thought was unattainable. You cherish me for who I am. You love everything about me when I find it hard to love myself. I feel like I've survived all the hardships in my life because we were meant to find each other. I'm finding the strong woman you see in me because of your love. I'll happily stand beside you for the rest of my life, Nikolai."

"Well, hell. I don't think there is anything else to say, except, brother, what are you waiting for? Kiss your woman," Quinn exclaims, and our family's cheers ring through the air. Wasting no time, I grab Leah's face in the palms of my hands. Leaning down, I kiss the hell out of my wife.

· · ·

A FEW HOURS LATER, the celebration of our marriage is in full swing. The sun has set, and music fills the air. "Are you happy, Mrs. Volkov?" I ask Leah after I've whisked her away from her friends, stealing a private moment with her, behind the giant oak tree.

"Say it again," she smiles at me.

"Are you happy?" bending down, I kiss her neck, inhaling her sweet perfume.

"No, the other part," Leah says breathless, as I back her up against the tree. Her fingertips graze my scalp as she plays with my hair.

I pull her body close and whisper in her ear. "Mrs. Volkov," I feel her skin prickle. "I'm ready to have you all to myself," I admit, before pulling away, and the desire in her heated gaze tells me she is ready too. With her hand in mine, we appear from our hideaway. In the distance, near the boat dock, we notice that the family has gathered. "Come. I have a surprise for you." Crossing the yard, Leah and I make our way down to the dock to my boat. Letting go of her hand, the women gather around her, sharing tears and laughter.

Holding a bottle of vodka in his hand, my brother approaches me. "I take it you're eager to take your bride and high tail it out of here?" Logan grins. Jake and the rest of the men gather around, along with my father, who stands beside me. Quinn hands each man a shot glass, and my brother fills them to the rims. They raise their shots in the air. "To Nikolai and Leah." The others repeat his words, and we down our liquor.

"Ready?" I ask Leah once she finds her way back to me.

"Wait. Where are we going," I lead her down toward the boat.

"I'm taking you home."

"We're living on a boat?" She gives me a puzzled look.

"No, Malyshka. It is our transportation."

The name of the boat is painted in bold font across the back of the boat. Leah gasps. "You named the boat after me?"

"It is a gift from my father," I lift her dress and help her aboard.

"It's beautiful," she looks around. "This is my surprise?" she looks at me.

"One of them."

Her eyes grow wide. "There's more?"

Pulling off my jacket, I hand it to my wife and roll up my shirt sleeves, then busy myself, getting the boat ready to pull away from the dock. Moments later, I'm navigating us into the open water.

"Nikolai, look!" Leah grabs my forearm, and I peer over my shoulder at what she's pointing to. Dozens of paper lanterns floating high, flickering in the night sky like stars. Beneath the beautiful display, all the women and children waving goodbye. Leah waves back, her smile so big it is infectious, and I smile myself.

I had every intention of taking my time crossing the lake to our destination, but excitement over revealing my final surprise has me increasing our speed. Before I know it, the home I've been building for over a year comes into view. Every light is on, and the backyard twinkles with hundreds of lights, I had strung throughout the trees and shrubs.

"Look at all those lights. It makes me think of Christmas." Leah leans into my side as I slow the boat down.

"You like it?" I ask

"Who wouldn't."

Bending, I kiss the top of her head, "Good. It's yours." I steer the boat bringing it to dock

"You bought us a house?"

"I built us a house," I reply. When we're close enough, I jump off and secure the boat.

"Wait," Leah rushes from the cabin. "You built this—when?" Reaching out, I wrap my hands around her waist, and she places her hands on top of my shoulders, and I help her from the boat. "How, I mean. A whole house. Who builds that fast?" Leah asks with astonishment as we make our way toward our new home.

"We broke ground last year. My crew finished the final details a few days ago." Leah's feet stop moving. Tilting her head back, she looks at me. "I told you, I knew you were the one the moment I saw you." Sweeping her off her feet, I pull her close to my chest.

Leah palms my cheek as she looks into my eyes. "How did I get so lucky?"

"I'm the fortunate one, Malyshka. I get the pleasure of kissing you whenever I want, and having babies with you."

"Babies? More than one?" Leah interrupts me with a sly grin.

"Yes, babies." I capture her lips in a brutal kiss, and she deepens it.

"I need you," Leah pants, and I am not a man to deny my wife anything. Opening the door, I carry her over the threshold.

Carrying my bride up the stairs, I don't stop until I'm in our bedroom, then let her feet find the floor. Leah looks around the room, walking over to the bed, and runs her fingertips across the smooth wood frame. My shirt comes off as I watch her turn her back to me. I kick off my shoes. Tossing her long hair to the side, Leah looks over her shoulder, finding me watching her. "You'll have to help me." She says, and I move toward her like I'm a predator, and she is my prey. My fingers make quick work of each little button on the back of her dress. Along the way, I trail kisses down her spine as her bare skin reveals itself. Leah pulls her arms free of the sleeves, which allows the dress to pool at her feet. She makes a move to spin and face me, but I stop her.

"Fuck. Let me look at you." I take in what she was hiding beneath her wedding gown—white lace lingerie. She is every man's fantasy. I tilt her head to the side, "I can't believe you are mine." My mouth is on her neck then her shoulder as my fingertips trail down her stomach. I slip my hand beneath her panties, lightly running my fingers through her folds. Leah gasps, her back arching against me as I tease her entrance. "You're perfect," I push my finger inside her.

"Nikolai," she whimpers.

"Let go, Malyshka." I pressed my palm against her bundle of nerves, intensifying her pleasure, and urging her body to give me what I want. "Come for me." Within seconds Leah's walls shutter around my finger as her orgasms rips through her body. I hold her tight against me as her legs quiver.

Spinning her to face me, I kiss her—hard. Not shying away, Leah's hands explore my body, undoing the button of my pants, lowering the zipper. Sinking to her knees, she sets my cock free. "Tonight is about your pleasure, not mine," I look down at her. Not listening, Leah locks her eyes on mine, wraps her fingers around the base of my cock, and takes me in her mouth. I hiss. I let her have her way for a few minutes, loving how her red painted lips slide down my shaft as she sucks me into her mouth. Torturing myself, I pull away, my cock cursing me for doing so.

I haul Leah off the floor. "My turn." Reaching behind her, I unclasp her bra. It falls to the floor, and I waste no time taking one of her hardened nipples in my mouth. Moaning, her fingers thread through my hair. Guiding her, I lay Leah on the bed. Ridding myself of the rest of my clothing, I press a knee to the mattress, hook my fingers in the band of her panties, and slid them down her legs.

Pushing her legs apart, I settle between her thighs, giving her a wolfish grin, before covering her sex with my mouth. Fuck, my woman tastes sweet. Gripping the comforter, Leah moans my name. Her hips buck against my face the moment I suck her clit into my mouth. Gripping her hips, I roll to my back, bring Leah to sit on top of me. She goes to move, but I hold her in place. Leah looks at me with confusion. "Sit on my face."

"What?" she shakes her head. "I can't."

I run my tongue through her folds, and her head falls back. "You can." I encourage her, and she nods. Using the headboard to hold onto, Leah straddles my face, placing her perfect pussy exactly where I want it. I nip and suck until her hips find their rhythm, and watch her heavy breasts sway above me. She rides my face until she comes undone.

Needing to be inside of her, I grip her hips, swiftly lay her back, and bring my body over hers. My cock hangs heavy between her thighs, close enough to feel the heat of her pussy. Her fingers trail down my biceps. I search her eyes. "If you're not ready—"

Leah nods. "I'm ready." Her fingernails trail down my spine.

Moving slightly, the head of my cock finds her entrance. Leaning down, I press my lips to hers, swallowing her gasp as I slowly sink into her. Damn. She is so hot and tight. Her body shudders around my cock, and it takes all my self-control to pace myself. I still my movements. "Are you okay?"

"Yeah," she breathes heavily.

Rocking my hips, I move slowly, taking my time as I gently make love to my wife. I find it impossible to take my eyes from her face; she has me spellbound as she gazes at me with a dreamy, faraway look in her eyes. I feel her pussy walls flutter around my cock.

"Nikolai. Please," she pleads.

"What do you need, Malyshka.?"

"More. I need more," she pants, her nails digging into my flesh.

Giving her what she wants, I fuck her harder. Her orgasm hits suddenly, catching me off guard. Her pussy clamps around my cock in tight waves sending me crashing over the edge with her. Collapsing beside Leah, I pull her still trembling body close to mine. We spend several minutes catching our breaths, not speaking. I hold her until her body stops shaking. Leah is quiet for a long moment before she asks, "Was I okay?"

I hear the nervous doubt in her tone.

Tilting her head back, I make her look into my eyes. "I just made love to my wife. It doesn't get better than that." Leah's body relaxes, and she smiles. I give her a soft kiss on her lips. Her kisses are always sweet, just like her.

"I love you." Those three words from her lips give me life.

"You are my world, Malyshka." I kiss her again, then make love to my woman one more time.

20

LEAH

Pulling up in front of Kings Construction, Nikolai parks his SUV. "I'm driving up the mountain today to check on the progress the resort is making. The owner is set to open this winter, and he wants to know if we're on schedule. That means I probably won't be back in time to take you to lunch."

"No worries. I can call Alba, see if she wants to swing by and grab something. She mentioned something about stopping by the garage and having lunch with Bella when I talked to her yesterday."

Nikolai cups the back of my neck. "You could just hang with me today."

I roll my eyes. "Then who will answer the phones." Since we said I do, Nikolai and I have become addicted to each other. We don't spend more than an hour apart from each other, and we can't seem to keep our hands to ourselves. I've heard some people say we are going through the honeymoon phase and that it won't last forever. I'm not sure I believe them. I can't imagine ever getting tired of being near or touching my husband every chance I get— my husband. I'll never get tired of saying that either.

"I think the two of us will survive a few hours apart." I lean across the console and kiss him. "I love you," I say against his mouth.

"Love you too, Malyshka. I'll be back in time to take you home."

Hopping down from the SUV, I make my way to the office entrance and wave at Nikolai over my shoulder before stepping through. Inside, Reid is walking out of the break room with a cup of coffee in his hand. "Mornin', sweetheart."

"Hi, Reid." I settle in behind my desk, fire up the computer, and switch the phone over from the answering machine.

"I have a guy named Lester Brickman coming in to see me at nine o'clock. When he gets here, will you send him back?"

"No problem."

"Thanks, darlin'."

As Reid makes his way back to his office, I busy myself with callbacks and emails. Once I catch up on my work, I head down the hall to the breakroom to make myself a cup of coffee when I hear the bell over the entrance door ring. Peering down at my watch, I note that it's a quarter to nine. Reid's guy is early. With my mug in hand, I make my way back toward my desk and pause mid-stride about ten feet from the man who currently has his back to me as he stares out the window beside my desk. My breath gets caught in my throat, and my palms begin to sweat. That's because I'd know that silhouette anywhere. Dressed in his state-issued uniform, is my father. The cup in my hand slips through my fingers, crashing to the floor, spilling onto the carpet. And when I finally remember to breathe, my gasp has my father spinning around to face me.

"Leah."

My name coming from his mouth causes my skin to crawl, and an ugly feeling in the pit of my stomach to form, a feeling I haven't felt in a year.

"Leave," I say barely above a whisper.

"I need to speak with you." My father keeps going.

"Leave," I repeat, voice trembling.

My dad takes a step closer then stops when something or should I say someone over my shoulder catches his attention. That's when I feel a presence at my back. I know exactly who it is because, in two second flat, Reid places himself in front of me, blocking me from my father. I peek around his shoulder to see my dad's face turning red.

"I'm here to speak to my daughter."

"That's not happenin'." Reid crosses his arm over his chest.

My dad doesn't back down. "I suggest you step aside, boy."

Oh, crap!

Reid drops his arms to his side, and his body visibly stiffens. "And I suggest you walk your ass out of here before you lose the chance, motherfucker."

"Do you know who I am?"

"Yes. You're the piece of shit sperm donor who likes to beat on women and children. The real question here is, do you know who the fuck I am?" Reid counters.

James Winters looks ready to spit nails and makes a mistake by taking a step-in mine and Reid's direction because when he does, I watch stunned as Reid reaches behind his back, beneath his cut, and produces a gun. He then proceeds to point it straight at my dad.

"Oh my, God," I gasp my heart suddenly in my throat.

Reaching around with the hand not holding a gun on my father, Reid gives my arm a reassuring squeeze.

"You've made a big mistake," my dad sneers. "I'll have you arrested."

"I'll have a bullet in your head before you do shit."

"Leah's mother is sick. She needs her daughter."

At the mention of my mom being ill, I step around Reid, but I don't get far when he holds his arm out, halting my forward momentum. "Mom is sick?"

"Yes. That's what I came here to tell you. It's bad. Doc says it's cancer."

"Oh my, God." I cover my mouth with my hand.

"Your mom wants you to come home. She's going to need you. Now is the time for family, Leah."

My stomach clenches at the thought of losing my mother. I don't have the best relationship with her, and I have spent years blaming her for not protecting me from my dad, but I still love her, and it kills me to think she might die.

"I think you're done here," Reid bites out.

I snap my head toward him. "Reid."

He ignores me, keeping his eyes and gun trained on my dad.

My father clenches his jaw and tosses one last sneer at Reid before looking back at me. "Don't make your mother die without getting to see her only child."

My father's parting words before he disappears out the door hit their intended mark, causing me to flinch. Reid must sense the shock I'm in, takes me by the arm, and guides me to the chair behind my desk. He then retrieves his phone from the inside of his cut, placing it to his ear. "Your woman's dad just paid her a visit."

Reid listens to whatever Nikolai says then hangs up. He turns to me. "Nikolai is on his way."

I nod but don't say anything. Five minutes later, Maxim shows up and stands guard outside. Ten minutes after that, Nikolai pulls up outside, the tires of his SUV squeal as he throws it into park and jumps out. By the murderous look on his face, I'd say he's not happy. Flinging the door open, Nikolai's eyes shoot straight to me. They don't waver as he eats up the distance between us. The moment he's within reach, I'm out of my chair and in his arms. It's not until I feel the warmth of his embrace, my body relaxes, and the pent-up tension disappears.

"Come on, Malyshka, I'm taking you home."

Nikolai keeps his arm around me as we pass by Reid. The two men share a look, something silent passing between them. Reid nods then stalks away toward his office. When Nikolai and I step outside, Maxim tips his head. "Boss."

Nikolai acknowledges him with a nod then says something to him in Russian.

The ride home is silent. There is an eerie vibe coming from Nikolai, so I find it best to wait until he speaks first. It's not until we are home that he leads me up the stairs to our bedroom and lets it all out. Sitting at the edge of the bed, Nikolai pulls me into his lap, burying his face into the crook of my neck. "I'm so fucking sorry he got close to you."

"It's not your fault, Nikolai. You can't always control what others do."

Nikolai jerks his head back and bites out, "I made you a promise, Leah. I promised you were free of that mother fucker."

"Nikolai," I try again, my voice soft.

"No excuses, Malyshka. I failed to protect you today." Nikolai squeezes my waist. "Now, tell me what he said to you."

My shoulders slump, and I sigh. "He said my mom is sick. He wants me to go see her."

"It's bullshit, Leah. The man is fucking with you."

"But what if he's not? What if my mom is sick? I think I should go. My dad has no reason to lie about something like that."

"You know better than anyone your father is capable of anything. You're not falling into his trap, Leah. I won't let you."

My back goes straight. "You won't let me?"

"No."

I try to wiggle off his lap, but his hold on me tightens. "Let me up, Nikolai."

"No."

"Nikolai," I snap.

"No, Leah. I know you're pissed, but you'll get over it."

"It should be my choice whether or not I go see my mom."

"Yeah. And what if that son of a bitch is lying, Leah?"

"What if he's not?" I counter.

"Don't be naïve."

"I'm not naïve, Nikolai, and I don't like you insinuating that I am. She's my mother."

"Where was your mom when your dad was beating on you? Your mother wasn't much of a mother then, Leah. So, why is it so important you be there for her when she has never been there for you?"

Nikolai's words are like a punch to the gut. His features soften when he sees hurt flashing across my face.

"You're right, but she's still my mother, and I love her."

"I know you do, Malyshka." Nikolai kisses me. "I'm still not going to take the chance on anything happening to you."

Hours later, I'm getting ready for bed when Nikolai steps out of the bathroom, his hair wet, water dripping down his chest, and a towel wrapped around his waist. Since I'm still mad, I ignore him and go about changing out of my jeans and cardigan into a pair of sweatpants and a t-shirt. Nikolai and I have had sex every night since we were married, so my choice of bedtime wardrobe does not go unnoticed by my husband.

"Leah," Nikolai calls out my name. I ignore that too.

"Leah," he tries again, sounding more pissed as I continue with my silent treatment, fully aware I'm acting childish. Once dressed, I turn toward the bed to see Nikolai already under the blanket. After cutting off the light, I go to my side, peel the cover back and climb in, turning my back to him. Two seconds later, a heavy arm snags me around my waist, and Nikolai pulls me against his hard chest. He rests his face against the shell of my ear. "You can be pissed all you want, but I don't like bringing that shit to our bed, Leah."

I don't say anything in return. I don't know how long I lay here, but the longer I do, the less mad I become, and soon I feel like a brat for the way I acted. Nikolai is right. I shouldn't have brought my crap attitude to our bed. Turning over, I face him, his eyes wide awake, shining in the moonlight filtering in through the window.

"You good now?"

"Yes," I whisper. "I'm sorry."

"I'm always going to do what's best for you. Even if it pisses you off."

"I know."

"Come here."

Nikolai moves to bring me with him, and I lay my head on his chest. It doesn't take long for the steady rhythm of his heartbeat to lull me to sleep.

THE NEXT DAY Nikolai ordered me to stay home with the doors locked and the alarm on just before he left. Now I have nothing to do but sit and stew in my thoughts, wondering how my mom is doing. What if my dad was telling the truth? Why would he risk going against Nikolai's warning? Unless my mother is genuinely sick. I have to find out.

Jumping up from the sofa, I shuffle up the stairs to the bedroom and grab my sneakers from the bottom of the closet, putting them on. Next, I snatch my phone from the charging dock and my purse. When I make my way back downstairs, I grab the keys to the black Mercedes hanging on the wall next to the garage door. I should be able to check on my mom and be back before Nikolai gets home.

It doesn't take long for me to pull up to my parent's house. The guilt of going against Nikolai and sneaking out behind his back has my stomach in knots the whole way. And as if he has some sort of connection to my thoughts, my phone rings, Nikolai's name lights up the screen. I answer. "Hello."

"You want to tell me why the fuck you're in Post Creek? Leah."

"Nikolai..."

"Home, now."

"I'm already here. I'm just going to stay a minute; see how she's doing, then I'll come home. Besides, I don't see my dad's truck, so he's not even here. I'll call you when I leave."

I hang up the phone before he can say another word. He's mad, and I'll have to deal with that when I get home. But right now, I want to make sure my mom is okay.

Climbing out of the car, I make my way up to the front door, ringing the doorbell. Several seconds pass without an answer, so I use my old key, letting myself in. I call out. "Mom!"

She doesn't answer, and the house is quiet. I cross through the living room and into the kitchen. She's not in there either. I also notice the sink full of dirty dishes. Something is not right. My father would never allow the kitchen to be a mess. Turning, I scan the living room. Several empty beer cans are littering the coffee table. Mom must be sick if the house is in such disarray.

Setting my purse down on the kitchen table, I hurry down the hallway to my parent's bedroom. I knock on the door. "Mom, are you in there?" When she doesn't answer, I push open the door. I suck in a sharp breath at what I see in front of me. "Mom!" I run over to the bed, where she lies motionless, the front of her nightgown covered in blood. I push the hair away from her face and cry out at the sight of her bloody and swollen flesh. "Oh, my god! Mom!" I nudge her a bit to see if she'll wake up.

"Leah," she groans.

"Mom, I'm here."

"Go."

"What? What are you trying to say, mom? Did dad do this to you?"

My mom wheezes out a ragged breath, "Go, Leah. Get out before he comes back."

"Hold on, mom. I'm going to call an ambulance."

Just as I turn to run out of the room, I'm knocked to the floor by a solid force striking me across my cheek, filling my vision with flashes of light. Blinking through the haze and the throbbing pain radiating through the whole left side of my face, I peer up at the shadow looming above me. "Dad," I croak. "Please."

"Shut up!" he shouts, grabbing me by the hair on my head, dragging me out of the bedroom.

"Dad! Stop! Let me go!" I kick and thrash down the hall and into the living room.

"I knew you'd come to see that bitch mother of yours. She thought she could grow a backbone and warn you. I fucking showed her, though."

"THAT'S ENOUGH, James. She's no good to me if you mark her pretty face any more than it already is." A voice says, stepping out of the shadows and further into the room, joining my father. I look at the man and am suddenly taken back to when I was seven. His face is one I will never forget. The man standing over me is older, but there is no doubt in my mind it's him. The man who was with my dad in his shed all those years ago. The one who took that girl.

The guy looks me over in a way that makes my skin crawl. "You were supposed to hand this one over to me a year ago, James. You didn't keep a tight enough leash on her. That and she's no longer pure like you said she was. My buyer has already backed out."

Bile rises in my throat when I realize what the man is talking about. My dad was going to hand me over to him; he was going to sell me—his own daughter.

I look at my father when he starts sputtering. "Novikoff."

Novikoff holds his hand up, cutting my father off. "She's of no use to my buyer, but lucky for you, she's a great deal of use to me now that she is a Volkov."

Just as the guy continues to spew his plans for me, the back door opens and in walks Maxim. Walking in behind him is another man I don't recognize, and he has a gun trained on Maxim's head. My stomach clenches.

"No! Let him go," I pick myself up off the floor and lunge for the man holding the gun. The man known as Knovikoff grabs my elbow then backhands me.

Maxim growls and says something to Novikoff in Russian. "You just started a war."

"If a war is what Volkov wants, then a war he shall have." With that Novikoff, pulls out his weapon and shoots Maxim in the chest. I scream as I watch his body crumple to the floor, blood pooling beneath him. I start fighting against the hold Novikoff has on me as I scream at my father. "What have you done? I hate you! You're all going to die! Nikolai will come for me, and when he does, he's going to kill you!" For a moment, I see a small flicker of fear pass over my father's face, like he knows what I say to be true. That fear in his eyes is also the last thing I see before I feel the prick and sting of a needle in my neck, just before everything goes black.

21

NIKOLAI

"**F**uck!" I punch the steering wheel repeatedly. What the fuck is she thinking? With the push of a button, I call Maxim.

"Sir."

"Get to Post Creek," I order.

"Already on my way, sir. I'm about twenty minutes out," Maxim tells me.

An uneasy feeling settles in my gut. Something isn't right. "Hurry," I add before disconnecting the call. Then I immediately put a call through to my brother. It rings several times before Logan finally answers.

"Hey, brother. How'd the meeting go?" he asks.

"Something terrible is about to happen to Leah," I convey to him and press the gas pedal further into the floorboard.

I hear background noise, followed by Logan shouting for Jake. "You're on speaker. Where is Leah?" Logan asks.

"In Post Creek." My grip tightens on the steering wheel. "Against my wishes, she went to see her mother."

"And where are you?" Jake asks.

"On my way to get my wife." I tell him, then, admit, "I'm not sure if you've heard, but her father showed his face at Kings Construction yesterday, claiming Leah's mother has fallen ill."

"We heard," my brothers are quick to inform me, and I'm not surprised.

"Don't ask me how I know, but Leah's in danger. I feel it deep in my bones."

Jake speaks to my brother, telling him to get a hold of the men and to send word to my father. "How close are you?" he then asks me.

"Thirty-five minutes."

"Do everything you can to get to your woman. My men and I won't be far behind." He ends the call, and I continue to barrel down the highway.

The interior of my car fills with ringing, as a call comes in from Maxim. I press the button on my steering wheel to answer. "Speak," I say in Russian, my tone harsh. "Speak," I repeat myself only to be met by silence. That's when I hear the first signs of trouble.

"Drop your weapon," I hear the muffled voice spoken in my native tongue, but not by Maxim. "Now." The command is followed by the distinct sound of a weapon hitting a hard surface. More silence hangs in the air for what feels like minutes but, in actuality, its mere seconds before hearing Leah's frightened voice.

"No. Let him go." An audible slap follows her words.

"D'yavol himself is coming for you. Ty umresh'." Maxim sneers, then adds, "You just started a war."

"If a war is what Volkov wants, then a war he shall have." A familiar voice causes my blood to run cold. Novikoff. A gunshot quickly follows his threat. I hear a loud thud before the line goes dead.

I stop fucking breathing.

"No!" I roar so loud my lungs burn.

Time slows, becoming nothing but a black empty void

attempting to swallow me whole. I have no idea how I got to my final destination because I remember nothing after the phone call ended, and my world came to a complete halt. All I know is I'm now sitting in my car outside Leah's childhood home. Throwing the car door open, I run toward the front door, as I pull my weapon from my side. I kick the door in, wood splintering at the hinges with no concern for what may greet me. From the foyer, I moved to the living room, finding nothing. After sweeping the kitchen, I push forward, toward the hallway where the bedrooms are located. The door at the end of the hall is slightly ajar, so my approach is cautious. With my gun raised, I push against the door with my shoulder but met with resistance. Putting my weight into it, I give the door a hard shove. With enough clearance, I step into the room and look down to see Maxim face down, the carpet soaked in blood beneath his body. Shit. With a glance, I clear the room, only to see Mary Winters, Leah's mother's unmoving frame lying on the bed beaten. Kneeling, I press my fingers to the side of Maxim's neck, praying I find a pulse. I find one. Rolling him over to his side causes him to groan in agony. "Hold on," I tell him.

"Novikoff has her," Maxim grunts as I search for his wound.

"Lay still." I pull my suit jacket off and press it against his seeping wound. "Keep pressure on it." I place his hand where mine was before getting to my feet.

Moving toward the bed, I look down at Leah's mother. Her face beaten, eyes swollen shut, and what seems to be a dislocated jaw. Her chest rises and falls with shallow breaths, and from the gurgling sound she makes, I'm sure she's all busted up inside as well. Not knowing she can hear me, I hover above her. "Where is Leah?" All I get from her is a ragged moan. "If you care for your daughter, you will force your body to breathe and answer me," I warn her.

Mary whimpers. "Please. They took her." She's able to push the words past her lips as a whisper. The sound of the floorboards creaking has me spinning around, the end of my gun coming face to face with Jake and my brother directly behind him in the hallway. Maxim coughs, and Jake's attention falls to the floor.

"Logan," Jake jerks his head, and my brother moves past him, kneeling beside Maxim, tending to him.

"He needs to get to the hospital," Logan says.

"My life isn't important." Maxim struggles to move.

"We don't leave our men to die." My words are stern. Suddenly, my father appears and notices his loyal soldier wounded.

"Get him to the nearest hospital," he speaks to the two men accompanying him, who then lifts Maxim to his feet and takes him from the house. My father's anger is prevalent when he looks at me. "Who?"

"Novikoff." Speaking his name leaves a foul taste in my mouth, and my father's facial expression hardens. "He wants war," I growl through clenched teeth. "Once again, someone has made it clear they are after our empire, and they are using my wife," I beat my chest, "to get it." A raging inferno inside of me threatens to break free. I'm about to snap. I feel it. That fucker has my woman, and it's taking every ounce of restraint I have to not completely lose my shit and bathe this small town in blood until I get her back.

"Look who we found hiding in the storage shed out back," Quinn sneers, and we all turn to face him as he drags a struggling James by his hair. From the looks of him, someone roughed him up. Quinn tosses him into the center of the room.

He eyes every man staring at him. "You're too late."

Aiming my gun at his head, I order, "On your knees, your worthless piece of shit." Leah's father sinks to the floor. "Where is she?" his eyes dart to the bed where his wife lays. "Your wife lies dying, and your daughter was taken from your home," I tell him, getting no response from him. "Speak!" I roar.

"Novikoff has more power than you can imagine, and no matter what you do, I won't talk." He looks to his wife, who barely breathes. "My wife will die, and I won't rot in jail for it. You may as well put a bullet in me now." His chin lifts in defiance.

"You are a coward," I sneer. "Cowards don't deserve to die so easily. You will tell me what I need to know." I step closer to him and hit him with a blow to the back of the head and watch him slump to the floor at my feet. I look back at the men behind me. "I require the use of your basement," I look at Jake, who grins.

"You got it." With no words spoken, Quinn and my brother lift James's limp body off of the floor. I toss my keys to Logan. "Throw him in the trunk of my car."

"What about the mother?" my father asks.

"Place an anonymous call to the proper authorities. From this moment on, she is not my concern." My words are cold and detached.

A SHORT TIME LATER, we've arrived at the clubhouse, and Gabriel unloads our guest of honor from the trunk of my car. My father joins me as we enter the clubhouse. "Any word on Maxim?"

"Only that he is being taken to surgery as we speak. They wouldn't release any further details." Stepping aside, my father lets me enter the basement first, where The Kings wait for us.

The air in the room is warm, humid, and smells of death. Rolling up my white shirt sleeves, I eye my prey as I circle the room. Jake and his men, along with my father, stand around the perimeter as my audience. I lock eyes with James, who is bound by his ankles and wrists to a chair in the center of the room. James watches my every move. Stepping up to him, I strike him with the back of my hand. Not allowing him to recover, I fist his hair, yanking his head back and bury my fist in his face. I feel the crunch of his teeth cracking against my knuckles. The rush I get from inflicting pain has me repeat the process a few more times until his face is a bloody mess, and his nose is at an unnatural angle. Releasing him, I roll my shoulders.

I make my way to a nearby shelf where various tools are located. Eyeing a screwdriver, I pick it up, shove it into my back pocket, and then lift another item off the shelf. "Where did Novikoff take Leah?" I ask as I walk toward him with a pair of garden shears in my hand. When I get close enough, James spits at my face. "Go to hell."

Grabbing hold of his hand, I lift his index finger, placing it between the blades. He goes from ten fingers to nine in a matter of seconds. James screams. "Fucking pussy. We've hardly started, and you're squealing like a stuck pig." Dropping the sheers, I pull the screwdriver from my pocket and drive it into the thigh, twisting and digging around in his flesh before ripping it from his body. I feed off his torturous screams as I do the same to his other leg, giving him no time to beg me to stop.

"Forgive me," James sobs like a pussy, snot running from his nose as he begins to crack. "I fucked up." Bloody spittle flies from his mouth. "I fucked up, and Leah was the price I had to pay." He hangs his head.

"You would give your only daughter to a man who sells women to the highest bidder, just to save your own worthless life."

"Forgive me," he repeats.

Bending, I grab his face in my hand and squeeze. "Where is she?" I seethe.

"She's long gone. You are too late," he struggles to look at me.

"Where?" I drive the screwdriver into his stomach, causing his eyes to bulge.

"Russia," he screams in pain. "He's taking her to Russia."

My woman is gone, taken by a skin dealer, to a country thousands of miles away due to her father's sins. Her being my wife will keep her alive for a time, but not for long. He will not sell her until he has gotten what he is after—my empire.

"Please, I told you what I know. Have mercy." James begins to beg for his life.

"Mercy? Where was your mercy for your daughter?" I press the barrel end of my gun between his eyes. "You'll find no mercy in this room." I put a bullet in his head.

22

LEAH

Thump, thump, thump. What is that noise? Thump, thump, thump. Is that my heart? Am I dreaming? Can a person dream about dreaming?

"We take off in five, boss."

Wait. Who is that talking? What does he mean by take-off in five?

I struggle to open my eyes as the voices that surround me continue to speak. One was in English, the others in Russian. It doesn't take long for my memories to come flooding back. My mother's near lifeless, beaten body lying on the bed, and my enraged father dragging me away from her by the hair on my head just before handing me over to that monster, the one whose voice I recognize now. Listening to the sounds around me has my heart rate increasing, the pounding of each beat knocking against my ribcage.

Finally, my eyes open, and I blink several times as my vision fights against the blinding white light.

"Nice of you to join us, Mrs. Volkov."

I jerk my head in the direction of the man speaking. My limbs are heavy, but I manage to lift my hand to my face and rub my palm against my eyes, clearing away the fog. It takes a minute for my eyesight to clear, and when it does, I focus on the man sitting six feet away to my left. Novikoff.

A million thoughts start running through my head as my senses come rushing back with a vengeance. My once numb legs begin to prickle as the tingling sensation in them fades. The whooshing sound in my ears intensifies with every breath I take as I realize that I'm in a terrible situation. My eyes dart around what I can only guess is the interior of an airplane. My nails dig into the armrest of the seat I'm sitting in as several armed men flit about the cabin as if kidnapping a woman is an everyday occurrence.

I bring my attention back to Novikoff. "Please let me go."

"I'm sorry. I can't do that, Mrs. Volkov," he says, not looking sorry at all.

"You can't just kidnap me. Whatever deal you had with my father has nothing to do with me."

"Unfortunately for you, that's where you are wrong. Your father and I made a deal. And though he did not live up to his end of the bargain and it cost me a client, I was still able to come out on top. You are married to a Volkov."

I grow increasingly angrier with each passing second. "What does that have to do with anything?"

Novikoff studies me for a moment then shakes his head. "So young and beautiful, yet so naïve. Women are a weakness in my world; in the world the Volkov's live in. This is a lesson your husband will, unfortunately, learn the hard way. You are but a pawn, Mrs. Volkov. One I plan to use to my advantage."

I swallow past the lump in my throat. It doesn't take a genius to figure out the odds are stacked against me. Though Nikolai has not shared details about this side of his life, I knew some parts include danger. Only it wasn't Nikolai placing me in the path of uncertainty. It was my father.

Just as Novikoff finishes his spiel, a woman walks in from the front of the plane, pushing a cart filled with glasses and liquor bottles. To the left of her, a man climbs the steps from outside, entering the cabin. I make a split-second decision to make a run for the exit, hoping my legs have enough strength to carry me. With Novikoff's attention on the woman, I bolt from my seat, making a mad dash for the open door. Fresh air hits my face, teasing me into thinking, escaping is possible. Then out of nowhere, something hard strikes the back of my head, making me stumble and lose my footing. I scream as my body gives way and I tumble down the stairs to the tarmac below, landing on the hard surface with a bone-jarring thud. A groan escapes my mouth, and my vision begins to fade once again. The last thing I see before I'm thrusted into darkness is the star-filled Montana sky. Then my thoughts drift to Nikolai. I hope he can forgive me for how stupid I was and for not listening to him.

I JOLT awake when a hand slaps me across my face.

I take in my surroundings to find I am no longer on the plane but in a room with metal walls. The only noise heard is the sound of my heavy breathing. Panic takes hold of my chest and squeezes when I realize I am tied to a chair, my wrists bound to the arms, and my ankles strapped to the legs. I try to wiggle free, but the bindings don't budge.

"Shall we begin," Novikoff says, stepping forward into the light. I watch as he jerks his chin toward another man who walks over to where a camera is set up on a pod, aimed directly at me. With a flick of a switch, a red light appears next to the lens.

"What are you doing," I ask, my trembling voice fills with panic as I continue to pull at my wrists, causing the rope to dig further into my flesh. My skin breaks open and starts to bleed, but still, I struggle.

"Please!" I try again. "Let me go!" My cries for help go ignored.

Finished with his tirade, Novikoff nods to a large beefy man who has been standing in the corner. My breathing picks up, and my eyes dart back and forth between the two. "What are you doing?" My chest heaves. Neither of the men answers me. The bigger man steps up to me, his face blank, and his eyes empty. There is no warning when the first blow strikes, hitting me in my stomach. I cough and wheeze as all the air is forced from my lungs by his fist. There is no time to recover when I am wrenched back by the hair on my head, and a second later, a fist comes flying at my face, my body seizes up as I prepare myself for the pain that follows. And though I am no stranger to having a man raise their hand to me, nothing can prepare you for such brutality. I cry out in pain when the man hits my face with such force my head snaps back.

"Such a shame it had to come to this," Novikoff says through the sounds of my panting echoing off the walls as he comes to stand behind me. I shiver when he runs a finger up my bare arm, over my shoulder, then fists the hair at the back of my neck, forcing my head up and the one eye not swollen shut gazes into the camera where I know Nikolai is watching, and I can't stop the tears from running down my face.

"Let's see, does your new bride have any last words, shall we?" The grip on my hair tightens. "Anything you'd like to say, Mrs. Volkov?"

23

NIKOLAI

Several hours later, I'm sitting on our plane, heading to Russia, accompanied by my father, and three of our men. It's been almost twenty-four hours since my wife was taken. There is nothing more to do but wait. My hands are tied, and it's killing my insides, knowing how terrified she must be. My thoughts consume me as I stare out the cabin window into the vast darkness as night has fallen. My imagination tortures me—conjuring up all the things Novikoff could be doing to Leah now, and I'm not there to protect her.

The ringing of my father's phone jerks me from my growing turmoil. "Victor," he speaks into the phone. My father's expression changes, putting me on the edge of my seat. "Send it through." Are his final words before ending the call. He brings his eyes to my face, and I know whatever follows will not be pleasant to hear. "A flash drive containing Novikoff's demands was delivered to our home moments ago." My gut turns, fearing the worst. "Victor is uploading the file and sending as we speak." My father reaches for the laptop nearby and accesses the file via email. I hold my breath as he clicks.

The cabin falls silent as the video plays. A dim spotlight flickers. My wife comes into focus, tied to a chair. Fresh blood trickles from her nose, her face reddened, making me aware someone struck her. The rage I've been stewing in intensifies, and my hand's fist at my sides.

"What are you doing?" Leah's voice trembles as she tugs at her restraints. The fear in her eyes guts me. "Please," my wife pleads, "let me go," her cries like a knife to my heart. This is my fault.

Novikoff steps out of the shadows, showing his face to the camera before coming to stand behind Leah. "Seems I have something which belongs to you." Novikoff runs his finger down the side of my woman's tear-stained face. "May I extend my congratulations on your marriage? It's a shame really, someone so young, beautiful, and innocent must pay for your sins."

As difficult as it is to watch the scene play out, I will myself to not look away.

"Your grandfather," he pauses. "He was a good businessman, saw value in all prospective endeavors. My business flourished with his iron fist in control." He stares directly into the camera, his eyes narrowing. "Now, I must steal, taking what I want from those who have turned their backs on me because you severed the ties your grandfather created." Novikoff's filthy aged hand touches my woman once more. He runs his palm down her arm until he reaches her hand, slips her wedding band from her finger, and whispers in her ear, but loud enough, the camera catches his words. "Do you love him?" Tears flow down Leah's face as she stares into the camera lens. She doesn't answer him. "You fell in love with the wrong man. What happens next is your husband's doing. You see, he took something from me—killed my son when he torched one of my warehouses." Novikoff eyes the rings he holds between his fingers. "For that, he will watch you suffer." Novikoff lifts his eyes, speaking directly to me. He cocks his head. "Your wife will pay the price for the death of my son. Her pain will be your pain." He steps to the side, and I notice two large figures step into view. "Don't worry. I will not kill her right away. With luck, she will last long enough to watch her husband take his final breath." Leah's eyes dart frantically between the two large men flanking both sides of her. I know what is about to happen, and I can do nothing to stop it. His last words turn my blood cold. "Consider this my wedding gift."

The beating that follows causes my stomach to recoil, and bile to rise in my throat. Each blow my woman endures feels like a knife to my heart. I release a guttural roar, screaming at the computer screen. "Motherfucker. I will kill you."

Not long after my outburst, the video ends. "We land in thirty minutes, sir," one of our men informs, and my father's nods.

I pull a ragged breath in through my nose, trying to bring my emotions under control. "Do we have a time stamp on when this video was recorded?" I pace the floor.

My father stares at his computer. "Six hours ago." Closing his laptop, he approaches me. "Control the rage. Right now, Leah needs you to be level headed and thinking clearly. Don't let your emotions cloud your judgment." His hand clamps down on my shoulder, and he looks me in the eyes. "Leah is a strong woman. She will fight for her life. We will get her back."

Thirty minutes later, the plane touches down on the tarmac. When we deboard the flight, an army of our men are waiting for us. Victor steps out in front of them. "We just got word Novikoff, and at least two dozen of his men are held up down at the shipping yard. I've sent two soldiers to keep watch. They will report back with more information when it becomes available."

"We need weapons," I tell him. Victor grins. My father and I follow him to the back of an SUV. Opening the hatch, he pulls out a hidden compartment, loaded with extra guns and magazines, then opens a nearby trunk. "You need more?" he raises his brow, and I begin to arm myself.

"This will do." I reach for a semi-automatic with a night scope and laser point accuracy, load it, then sling it over my shoulder. "For now," I add.

With every man armed, we load into the vehicles. Victor takes a call as he drives down the road, and I listen to his conversation from the backseat. He looks in the rearview mirror as he ends the call. "They know we are coming," I state, checking my gun.

Victor keeps eye contact with me. "Yes."

"And?" I ask, sensing there is more.

"Novikoff was last spotted in building C near the loading dock. There hasn't been any sign of Mrs. Volkov."

As we approach the shipyard's east gate, an explosion rocks the SUV we're in, and Victor slams the brakes bringing us to a dead stop. In front of us, three vehicles ahead, I can see one of the SUVs carrying a few of our men in flames. A spray of bullets peppers our windshield, only cracking the bulletproof glass. Men are shouting as they step out of their armored cars, returning fire on the unseen gunmen. I need to get to Leah. "Go—go—go," I yell, and Victor floors it, surging ahead. "Get us through the gate."

"Hold on," Victor yells, just before busting through the metal gate. The SUV crashes against the side of an empty shipping container. The windows shatter, sending shards of glass flying. Through the window, I catch the approach of an armed man.

Lifting my gun, the laser point finds its mark, placing the red dot center of his forehead, and I pull the trigger. Flinging the doors open, we exit the battered vehicle. Gunfire erupts around us, and bullets bounce off the pavement as the three of us climb from the wrecked vehicle. My father and Victor ready themselves. At the gate, I notice the rest of our men in a battle of their own.

My father looks at me. "Go."

Keeping to the shadows, I weave my way past containers until I have Novikoff's location in my sights. Scanning the area, I spot three men standing guard outside the building. I'm a fair distance away, so I ready my rifle. Kneeling, I look through the scope, lining up my first target. *Pop.* In quick recession, I squeeze the trigger two more times, dropping all three men in a matter of seconds. With my gun raised, ready to fire again, I approach the building. Out of nowhere, a car appears, barreling toward me. Blinded by the headlights, I fire, emptying the magazine before feeling the impact.

Propelled backward, the side of my body slams against the pavement, knocking the air from my lungs. Shaking the daze from my head, I look for my weapon, which lies several yards away. I get to my knees, feeling a burning pain in my side. The hairs on the back of my neck stand on end at a shuffling noise from behind. I fight through it, quickly getting to my feet. A fist to the side of my head causes me to stumble. My eyes lose focus. Just before the asshole lands another blow, I block it. Bringing my fist up, my knuckles crack against his chin, knocking him back a few steps. My attacker steps into the path of the headlights. Novikoff's other son, Yuri, advances on me, pulling a long-serrated blade from a sheath on the side of his thigh.

"You killed my brother." He lunges, and a searing hot pain hits my shoulder as the blade cuts into my flesh. I take hold of his wrist, contorting it in an unnatural angle until the knife falls from his hand. Stepping behind him, I wrap my arm around his neck in a chokehold. Stumbling backward, he slams my body up against the building. The back of my head smacks against the brick wall. He does this repeatedly, before throwing his weight forward, rolling us both to the ground. He elbows my ribs, and I struggle to maintain the hold I have on him. Within arm's reach, I spot his blade. In a risky attempt that may give him the upper hand, I release him, grab the handle of the knife in my hand, swing my arm back around and impale the blade into his chest, then rip it out. Doubling over, Yuri clutches his chest, blood dripping between his fingers, pooling on the ground beneath him.

Breathing heavy, and wincing from pain, I stand. Walking a few yards away to where my weapon lays, I bend, picking it up off of the ground, but spin on my heels when I hear the sound of heavy footfalls coming up behind me. The barrel end of my gun comes face to face with my father. "Shit," I do my best to take deep breaths as the pain in my side intensifies. My father looks at the body on the ground.

"Our men—Victor?" I ask, heading for the stairs leading into the building.

"Cleaning up the mess," my father states.

With precious time wasted, I jog up the stairs, flinging the door open. A bullet whizzes past my head, leaving a hole in the door behind me. Before I can raise my weapon, my father kills the man who fired the shot. His body falls over the second level railing. Ascending the second set of stairs, we cautiously approach the only room on the second level, overlooking the ship dock. With the door already open, I enter the room, finding it empty—our heads jerk at the ringing of a phone lying on the desktop, a cell phone. Walking over, I swipe the screen, putting the phone to my ear.

"Nikolai?" Leah's weak voice comes through the other end.

"Leah. Baby, where are you?" I ask, desperately waiting for her to answer.

"Come now. You didn't think it would be that simple, did you?" Novikoff's sinister voice is what I hear instead. "The clock is ticking, Volkov." An explosion rattles the glass window panes. "In twenty minutes, a bomb, similar to what you just heard, strapped beneath your wife's chair will detonate. I wonder if you will find her in time before all that's left of her is tiny pieces."

"I'm going to kill you with my bare hands," I seethe, my hand tightening around the phone.

He laughs. "It's your wife or me. The choice is yours." The line goes dead, and I throw the phone against the wall.

Rushing from the room, I say to my father, "Tell the men to search every container, and block all exits. Find Victor. He's the only man we have who knows explosives." Stepping outside, a dark figure steps away from a fifteen-foot container across the yard. Raising my arm, I look through the scope, trying to get a look to see if it's one of my men: the motherfucker himself, Novikoff. I put a bullet in his leg and watched him fall to his knees as I stride toward him. He reaches into his jacket, pulling a small pistol from his pocket, and aims it at me. I fire again. This time, I put a bullet through his forearm, causing him to drop the gun in his hand. My steps never falter.

"You son of a bitch. You can kill me, but rest assured, my other son will avenge me." Novikoff spits at my feet.

"You mean the one lying in a pool of his own blood after I drove a knife through his heart?" Fear strikes his face knowing his bloodline dies with him. I walk up behind him as he sits on his knees before me. Bending, I whisper in his ear, "You didn't think it would be that simple, did you?" I use his words against him before gripping his chin and the back of his head, snapping his neck.

"Nikolai," I hear my name called out from the nearby container. *Leah.*

Sprinting, I fumble with the hinges, before pulling the heavy metal doors open. On a chair inside sits my wife, her head rolling from side to side. I fall to my knees in front of her. Her face is swollen, and her lips split open. She's in bad shape. I suddenly remember the bomb. I have no time to assess her injuries. "I'm here," I press my lips to hers.

"Nikolai?" she whimpers as I look beneath her chair, finding the device fixed to the seat with tape, and a small, red flashing light coming from it. Lifting my head, I make quick work of the restraints on her wrist then her ankles.

"Wait," Victor's voice stops me from making another move. Kneeling, he looks beneath the seat. "It's not attached to any type of trigger device, so it's on a timer." He looks at me. "Get her out of here." He jerks his head.

Lifting Leah in my arms, I cradle her against my chest and carry her away from danger. An SUV pulls up, and one of our men opens the back door. Not letting her go, I climb into the back seat with her in my arms. Looking over my shoulder, Victor closes the container doors and makes a run for it. The bomb detonates, rocking the container from side to side, but the thick steel keeps it contained.

"Nikolai," Leah's palm finds my cheek, and I lean into her touch.

"I've got you."

Through the night, I watch Leah lay in my bed, sleeping. No bones were broken from the beating she endured, but bruises cover her face and most of her torso. The doctor gave her pain meds to help her rest and said within a few weeks, Leah would be able to resume normal activities and fly home. As for me, I suffered two fractured ribs during the ordeal.

Leah whimpers, reaching to the empty spot beside her. "Nikolai?"

Getting up from my chair beside the bed, I walk around, and slide in beside her, careful not to jostle her too much, as I ignore my own pain. "I'm right here, Malyshka." I take her hand.

"Hold me," she mumbles, trying to tug me closer.

"I don't want to hurt you."

"I would feel better in your arms," she states, and I can't deny her what she wants. Leah slowly turns to her side, and I snuggle in behind her, resting my hand on her hip. I bury my face in the crook of her neck. Her body relaxes against me, and she begins to fall back to sleep. "Don't let go," she whispers.

"Never."

EPILOGUE

Leah

I knew Nikolai was worried about how I was going to take visiting my mother's grave for the first time, and if I'm honest, so was I. Knowing she is dead is one thing, but staring at the headstone with her name scrolled across it, is another. In a way, it makes it more real. I'm not sure why I waited so long to come here because it turns out, I don't feel anything but closure. The first couple of months after I was kidnapped, I felt nothing but anger. I was angry at her because had she put me first all those years ago, I would not have had to endure the years of abuse at the hands of that man, and she'd still be alive. I'm angry because she chose him over me. I was mad because she waited until it was too late to pick her daughter over the monster she'd married. I'll admit I felt guilty about it because that's what got her killed, but Nikolai quickly set me straight. He said she did what a parent was supposed to do. He's right. The guilt I was carrying around after I heard of her death, no longer eats me up inside. I spent my whole life longing for the kind of mother-daughter relationship the kids who grew up around me had. I longed for a real family until I met Alba and Sam, then later The Kings. First, Alba and Sam became my family, and soon after, The Kings adopted me as one of their own. It was they who showed me the true meaning of family. Then came Nikolai. My husband taught me the meaning of patience, true love, and loyalty. And one of the most important things he taught me was self-worth. He showed me I was somebody worth waiting for. After all, he waited a whole year before making me his. He now spends his days loving me and making sure I love myself. I've even become close to Demetri in recent months. Nikolai's father has shown me what it's like to have a dad. I genuinely feel like I'm a daughter to him and not just the woman who married his son. I no longer refer to James Winters as my father. Growing up, he was a monster, and now he is nothing more than an afterthought. He no longer controls my life or haunts my dreams.

"You okay, Malyshka?" Nikolai keeps his arm planted firmly around my waist.

I lean further in, drawing in his warmth. "Yeah, I'm good.

He squeezes my hip. "You sure?"

I nod. "I'm sure. I'm glad I came. It was time. I'm ready to leave the past where it belongs and move forward."

I loved my mother. She wasn't perfect, and she, despite everything, loved me in her own way. I know this because, in the end, she proved it. In life, we must learn to accept and let go of the things we can't change. We also must learn when to let go of the anger caused by others. As long as you hold on to anger, the person who hurt you, keeps that hold, even in death. I spent months being angry, and today, I'm letting go. I have a beautiful future ahead of me—a future that has no room for the negative energy I've been battling. As I stand in front of my mom's grave, I can feel the last bit of it leaving my soul.

"Are you ready to go?"

I stare down at the headstone a second longer, silently saying my final goodbye, then turn to Nikolai. "Yeah. Let's go."

As we make our way to the car, Nikolai asks, "What do you want to do today?"

I smile. "Do you think the family would be up for a cookout?"

Nikolai grins. "Hell, yes, since when are the boys not up for food and booze?"

Two hours later, the sound of laughter fills mine and Nikolai's yard. After Nikolai put a call into Logan, the whole club and their women didn't waste time showing up.

Sitting in Nikolai's lap on the back deck, I giggle at Quinn and Reid's banter. They are arguing over whose BBQ sauce is better. Logan shakes his head. "Some things never change."

"Whose turn is it to win this time?" Bella asks.

Alba once told me Quinn and Reid have the same argument over and over. Then everyone is forced to vote on whose BBQ is better. She says the guys take turns on picking a winner. She also says Quinn and Reid know the votes are done that way but still play along because it's standing tradition.

"Quinn's," Gabriel answers, stepping up to our group with his daughter in his arms. Valentina is so adorable with her little princess swimsuit and floaties.

I peer over his shoulder to see Alba wading in the swimming pool, watching her son splash around. Climbing off Nikolai's lap, I tell him, "I'm going to go change and get in the pool for a bit."

Nikolai tugs on my hand, and I lean down, kissing him. "I'll be back."

Once upstairs in the bedroom, I quickly change out of my dress into my swimsuit. A few weeks ago, I was shopping with the girls, and they convinced me to buy a two-piece. It's red, with high-waisted bottoms, giving me that vintage fifties look. The way the top plunges, makes my breasts look fantastic. Nikolai stands in the doorway of our room, and with his heated gaze glued to my chest, I'd say he agrees.

"Hey," I giggle, jarring his attention away from my breasts to my face. He steps away from where he was leaning against the doorframe and prowls toward me wearing a look I know all too well, causing a familiar tingle between my thighs.

"Malyshka," Nikolai's endearment for me rolls off his tongue as he steps up behind me, placing his face in the crook of my neck. My skin prickles the moment his hands grip my hips, pulling me back into his erection. I hum my appreciation as I reach behind me and thread my fingers through his hair. "Nikolai."

"Can you take fast?" he rasps into the shell of my ear as he pulls at my swimsuit's ties, letting the top fall to the floor at our feet. My breasts feel heavy with need. Knowing what my body craves, Nikolai palms them in the cups of his hands.

"I can take any way my husband wants to give it."

My words are all the encouragement he needs. Nikolai folds me over with a growl until my hands are planted firmly on the bed in front of me. My swimsuit bottoms are ripped down my legs, and in the next second, Nikolai is inside of me. I scream. "Oh, God!"

My husband then proceeds to show me how fast it can be, and I show him I can indeed take it any way he gives it.

WHEN NIKOLAI and I return to the party, I get a knowing look from Alba and Bella. My face heats. "What?" I look back and forth between the sisters.

Bella grins. "You forgot to close your bedroom window.

Alba cackles at my mortified expression.

"Oh my, God." I bury my face in my hands. "Please tell me no one else heard us."

Alba bites her lip. "Umm, I'm pretty sure Gabriel heard. Because soon after, he cranked the music up."

"Great. I'm never going to be able to look him in the face again."

At my confession, Alba burst out laughing.

"Shut up," I laugh as I sit at the edge of the pool and splash her with water. Soon our commotion draws the attention of Mila, Sofia, Emerson, Grace, and Glory.

"What's so funny?" Mila asks, wading over toward us.

"Nothing," I lie, turning redder.

Glory who is on a monster size pink flamingo float, sipping on a Margarita, lowers her shades and eyes me up and down. And with a straight face, she says, "Our sweet Leah just got herself a good Volkov dicking. I'd know that look anywhere."

My eyes nearly bug out of my head.

"Jesus, Glory. Slap a filter on that mouth of yours every once in a while, will you," Grace chastises her best friend.

"Where's the fun in that," she counters. "If you can't be real with your girls, who can you be real with?" Then she adds, "Besides, it's not like the men aren't over there doing the same shit. Scratching their balls and congratulating each other on getting some."

Eight sets of eyes turn and look to where the men have assembled. As if they can sense that we are talking about them, the men turn their heads. We burst out in a fit of laughter.

HOURS LATER, as the sun begins to set, I stand by the lake and take a moment to reflect on how perfect today has been when a hand brushes my hair away from my neck and Nikolai's warm lips settle on the spot below my ear. "What are you doing over here by yourself, Malyshka?"

I settle back into Nikolai's embrace and stare out at the sun setting over the water. "Just thinking."

"About what?"

"About how happy I am."

"You know I'd give you anything, right? That I'd do everything in my power to give you what you deserve."

"I know you will, and you have."

"I don't want you ever to feel like you are missing out on anything."

"I don't feel like I'm missing out on anything. I know some women strive to finish college and for a career, but that's not my dream, Nikolai. My dream has always been to have a real family, and to love and be loved."

Wrapping his arms around me, Nikolai cradles my growing bump in the palms of his hands. I smile as our daughter makes her presence known by doing summersaults, something she does whenever she hears Nikolai's voice. Still in the womb and already a daddy's girl.

"Thank you," Nikolai says.

Tilting my head back, I peer up at him. "For what?"

"For loving me, becoming my wife, and giving me a child. You and the baby are my world. You've given me everything I've ever hoped to achieve in my life." Then he kisses me.

Lightning Source UK Ltd.
Milton Keynes UK
UKHW021108110722
405683UK00009B/2078